Tests of Fate

ASHLEY WILLOW

This book is for anyone who has ever felt too broken to try again. Sometimes, the people you need show up when you stop looking.

· Never give up.

Chapter 1

MALLORY

"Dan?" she called out from the doorway. "I'm here! You better have my coffee. And you better be wearing pants."

Mallory stepped just far enough into the apartment downstairs to close the door behind herself. Every morning before work, she stopped in to have coffee and bullshit with her neighbor. Her mornings started early, and so did his. They had become an accidental family to each other, so they always made time, somehow.

Dan emerged from the kitchen, wearing only a pair of sweatpants and had his shoulder-length dreads pulled up into a sad excuse for a bun. "Why do you insist on stopping in the doorway if you're only going to make a racket anyway?"

"Well, I don't want to interrupt if you have company," Mallory answered with a grin.

"With all that noise? You'd definitely be interrupting." Dan rolled his eyes and chuckled under his breath. "Get in here, girl, before you make me late for work."

She made her way to the kitchen and sat at the small table. They lived in a newly constructed two-family home that looked like every other house on the street. A single car garage and shared laundry room took up the ground level, while the second and third levels boasted nearly identical apartments. Mallory's had an island in the kitchen instead of space for a table.

"If you're late for work, I'm late too. We work together, remember?" she joked.

"Yes, but the lab is on the first floor. I have to take the elevator furthest from the parking garage in order to get to pediatrics," he pointed out. "Anyway, have you gotten back with Aiden yet?"

Mallory accepted the coffee cup Dan offered and took a careful sip. "No. Why are you so worried about him? It's been over for a few months now, so you need to let go of all that hope. I'm fine."

He grinned. "I know you're fine, but so was he."

Mallory nearly spit out her coffee. She swallowed down the hot liquid just in time to avoid dribbling it down the front of her blue scrubs. It was no surprise that Dan had been checking out her ex-boyfriend, but she wasn't expecting the conversation to go that direction. Not before they'd finished their coffee, anyway.

Dan crossed his arms and sat back with a satisfied smirk on his face. With his arms crossed, his muscles were clearly visible. She wondered how he stayed in such good shape when she knew he didn't spend much time working out. It was especially impressive at his age. He was far too vain to tell her his exact age, but she figured he was in his early fifties.

"Is that why you're walking around here half dressed? Hoping I'd have Aiden with me?"

His shoulders shook with laughter before he took a drink from his coffee cup. "You know I don't need to take my shirt off if I want to steal your man. My winning personality gets them every time."

"Okay, Mr. Personality, what time are you getting off today?"

Her relationship with Aiden hadn't been serious. That's why they broke up. He wanted more, but she didn't. After the nasty breakup that had been the last puzzle piece needed to throw her into a depression, she was determined to avoid finding herself in a situation where someone else was the cause of her happiness. Without giving the topic of Aiden much thought, she easily shifted gears back to real life.

"I work until 3:30. Want to ride in together? I'll drive; my car is nicer," Dan responded.

"It should be, with all the money you make. Hurry up and get dressed, before we really are late. I'll put your coffee in a travel cup," she suggested.

She made a fresh travel mug of coffee for herself and for Dan even as she continued to sip on her original cup of coffee. Mornings would always be a struggle. Even with the routine of having coffee with Dan before work, she needed several cups before she felt human; and at forty-two, it wasn't likely to change.

Dan came from his bedroom fully dressed in less time than it took Mallory to finish her coffee. She thought she would have time to run up to her apartment to grab a few things, but she was wrong.

"That was fast. Do you have a hair tie I can borrow? I was going to grab that and a few snacks while you were getting ready."

She had barely finished her request before he brandished one from his pocket. "I always travel prepared."

She knew he did. There was a time he wouldn't have been allowed to wear his hair in dreadlocks and work at the hospital, so he had to be careful to make sure he kept his hair tied up. It was stupid, since child life specialists weren't directly involved with any medical procedures, but Dan never complained. Mallory put her light brown hair into a messy bun and followed him out the door.

She was sure people tried to figure their relationship out, but she never had been one to care about appearances. Dan was a gay black man in his fifties, Mallory was a white woman in her forties, and they were completely inseparable, riding to work whenever their schedules matched, and meeting for coffee even when they didn't.

By the time they pulled into the parking garage, her coffee was beginning to kick in. It wouldn't be long before she felt human. They walked through the parking garage in comfortable silence, knowing it would be the end of the road for their little commute.

"I'll text you. Maybe our lunch breaks will match up," Mallory said before making a left down the hallway toward the lab.

She hadn't worked at the hospital for very long, but she was able to get to her department from any entrance with her eyes closed. Phlebotomy was supposed to be a steppingstone. The course was short, and she could earn a living wage. When she straightened her life out, a stable job and place to live was her first priority, but she ended up loving the job. Dan helped her to get a job at the hospital he worked at which was a step up from the lab she'd started at right after school, and the rest was history.

"Good morning," she greeted as she walked through the doors to the lab.

Doris and Jenna were huddled together looking at a computer screen. The outpatient lab was due to open in a few minutes, so they were likely looking to see what was already scheduled for the day. Even without many prescheduled appointments, the day could become busy without warning.

"Hey, honey," Doris replied once she looked up from the screen. "So far, we don't have much scheduled before noon. The system hasn't updated yet, so I'm not sure if there are any walk-ins already waiting."

Doris was one of Mallory's favorite coworkers. She was kind to a fault. Her favorite way to greet people or say goodbye was with a hug. She wore her hair in shoulder-length waves and would never be caught walking around without makeup, which was the complete opposite of Mallory who was the definition of low maintenance. With an endless supply of energy, Doris preferred to know how her day was going to go, so she could prepare.

"The busier the better," Mallory commented as she unzipped her sweatshirt and draped it over the chair by her computer. "Makes the day go faster."

"Speak for yourself," Jenna chimed in. "The days always drag. You're just new and excited."

Mallory sat down at her computer and logged in. "I'm not new anymore. And I'm definitely not excited."

"Well, you better get excited because you get the first stick. Me and Doris both said, 'Not it,' before you got here."

Mallory laughed to herself. Jenna was always trying to get her riled up. The three had become close in the few months they'd been working together. She hadn't been sure about Jenna at first, but once they got used to each other, they found out they had a lot in common, aside from their living situations. Jenna was Mallory's age but was at a different stage in her life. She was on her second marriage; finally living her happily ever after. Mallory wasn't envious. She preferred to have the least amount of complications possible, and marriage was the biggest complication anyone could have.

"You say that as if you don't always give me the first patient," Mallory said lightly.

She didn't mind getting the first person as long as her coffee had kicked in. She didn't really mind either way, but the patients might not agree after dealing with her grumpy ass. She clicked into the name of the first patient and printed off the order form and the labels before walking out to the waiting room to call the patient back.

"Christian Ramirez?" she read off the sheet before scanning the waiting room.

Across the waiting room, a man met her gaze as he got to his feet. He was tall, wearing navy blue uniform pants and a form fitting white t-shirt as if he had recently gotten off shift. She tried not to notice how snug the shirt fit across his chest. But she did notice.

After plastering on a professional smile, she greeted him. "Christian?"

"Yep," he answered with a grin, showing off a pair of dimples and nearly perfect teeth. Not to mention those full lips. She silently thanked Jenna for her routine of giving the first patient to her.

"My name is Mallory, and I'll be drawing your blood. Follow me back."

Once they arrived at her station, she gestured for Christian to take a seat while she gathered what she needed to draw his blood. He appeared relaxed while he watched her and answered the questions confirming he was the correct patient.

"I take it you've done this before," she commented as she placed the labels on the tubes and one onto the top of his lab order.

"Yeah. This is my last set of labs since the exposure three months ago."

She had suspected something along the lines of bloodborne pathogen exposure based on the order and his uniform, but she wasn't allowed to outright ask such questions if he didn't bring it up. "Oh no. Needle stick?"

"I wish," he said with a low chuckle. "A patient bit me."

Taken by surprise, she swallowed hard before moving the conversation forward. "I was trying to decide if you worked Fire or EMS."

His green eyes met her blue ones. "I'm an EMT."

She reached for his arm and ignored the jolt of electricity she felt when she touched him. "I'm just going to tie the tourniquet."

He watched in silence as she tied the orange piece of rubber a few inches above his elbow. Once it was tied, she put gloves on and cleaned the area on the inside of his elbow with an alcohol pad.

"How bad was the bite?" she asked casually.

"It hurt like hell," he admitted. "But the worst part was worrying if I'd picked up anything from it. You hold my fate in your hands."

Goosebumps spread across her body as she gripped his muscular forearm. She looked at the words tattooed in script stretching from his wrist to just shy of the underside of his elbow. The words were in Spanish, so she couldn't read them.

"Only positive vibes. Manifest the negative test results you hope for," she murmured. "Big pinch."

He didn't flinch when the needle penetrated his flesh and made its way into the vein. She glanced up to find his gaze on her face. She swallowed and looked back to the task at hand. She filled the tubes one at a time until they were all full, untying the tourniquet as the last one filled. Once the last tube was full, and she had set it with the others, she picked up a gauze four by four and folded it before pressing down while she removed the needle from his arm.

"All done," she breathed as she placed a band-aid over the gauze. Her cheeks felt hot and all she could do was hope her face wasn't extremely red.

He smiled at her, once again showing off his dimples. "You're really good at that. I barely felt it."

"Thanks," she mumbled as her face grew even warmer.

"So, all that good vibes and manifesting stuff … does that work for you?" he asked.

She tossed her gloves into the trash before she finally looked up to meet his gaze once more. His eyes seemed to look through her. It was as if he already knew her thoughts.

"I try to make it work. When I was starting over after a rough patch, manifesting and thinking good thoughts really did help," she answered honestly.

His eyes never left her face. A small twitch of his lips had her preparing for another blinding smile, but it didn't come. He narrowed his eyes briefly before standing to leave. "It was great meeting you. If I get bit by another patient, I'll make sure to manifest a positive outcome."

Before she could respond, he was exiting through the door he came in. Yes, she watched the way his uniform pants clung tight in all the right places. As soon as the door shut, she turned to see both Jenna and Doris watching her with unmistakable smiles plastered across their faces.

"You're welcome," Jenna said before turning back to her computer.

Mallory saw Jenna take in a patient shortly after her, but she was far too distracted to pay attention. A glance at the computer told her there wouldn't be much time to chitchat. She quickly completed the chart for Christian and did her best to put him out of her mind. There would be plenty of patients with sea green eyes she could get lost in. And dimples that made her forget what she was doing.

It didn't feel like much time had passed when she looked at the old analog clock hanging on the wall and realized the day was more than half over. Once she had seen the number of patients waiting, she sent a quick text letting Dan know she would see him when the shift was over. Legally, she was guaranteed a thirty-minute break, but when it was busy, they were creative with lunch breaks. No one wanted to disappear for half an hour while the others were struggling to keep up. Doing so, would only ensure they had to stay over. Any patient with an appointment who arrived on time couldn't be turned away.

"That was the last one," Doris announced after her last patient walked back out the double doors.

Mallory quickly started restocking and sanitizing her area. One busy day and it looked like a bomb had gone off. Shelves were bare, things were in the wrong place, and it was in need of cleaning. Mallory knew better than to save anything for the following day.

"Today was crazy," Jenna commented as she restocked her area.

"Crazy isn't a strong enough word," Mallory replied.

Doris snorted in agreement from her station. "But don't think we forgot about your first patient."

Mallory's heart skipped a beat. She had done a good job of putting him out of her mind, once they had gotten busy. His green eyes were nearly forgotten. "Nearly" being the key word.

"Yeah, did you get his number?" Jenna chimed in.

"No, I didn't get his number," Mallory said in exasperation. "He's a patient. That's not how it works."

"We all saw him and would have been more than happy to turn a blind eye," Doris continued.

"Of course, you would," Mallory muttered. She quickly finished up so she could get out of there before being forced to acknowledge the way she was affected by that man. It didn't matter anyway, since she'd never see him again. She stuffed her sweatshirt into her canvas tote and made her way to the coffee stand to meet Dan.

CHRISTIAN

Chris walked into quarters to find his partner, James, already waiting with the bags and radios. James had been his new partner since Alyssa finished school, leaving him without a partner. He'd lucked out. When he found out his new partner was going to be a transplant from Chicago, he'd nearly quit on the spot. Fortunately, they had started off on the right foot, because Chris rarely formed a new opinion of someone after a first impression.

"Hero. Anxious to save lives, I see," Chris joked after opening the door to quarters and taking a seat at the table across from his partner.

"Listen, asshole, some people like to be early, so they don't have to rush," James retorted.

"I'm always on time, and never in a rush. Where's our truck?"

"Day shift killed theirs, so they threw them into ours. They were arriving at the hospital when I got here, so they shouldn't be too long," James explained.

James stood and stretched. He was even taller than Chris, and broader across the shoulders. His skin was dark, and he kept his hair in a well-maintained fade. He was born and raised in a less than desirable section of Chicago, so he was rarely caught off guard by anything they encountered on the job.

"I hate when another crew uses our truck. I like being able to quickly check it then go for coffee without worrying we missed something," Chris complained. "I really need coffee."

"Maybe you should sleep between shifts."

Chris flipped him off. "I had to get labs after work and then take my mom to the store. I did sleep eventually, though."

Before they could continue the conversation, the day crew walked in and tossed the truck keys onto the table in front of Chris. "We fueled up. You're welcome."

"You better have stocked up, too," Chris mumbled.

They went out and started their truck check. The vehicle was exactly the way Chris expected to find it. A mess. He took inventory as he cleaned up and reorganized. He hated when things weren't where they belonged. It wasn't hard to put something back where you found it. He left James still checking things over and went to the stock room to fill a bag with supplies.

"Find anything else missing?" Chris asked as he began refilling the compartments.

"Nope. How were your labs, anyway? Get the all clear?"

Chris was instantly reminded of the woman who drew his blood. She was gorgeous without even trying. Her skin had a bronze glow as if she spent time outside, even though it was only late spring. Her blue eyes were cool beneath her dark lashes. She'd gently chewed her full bottom lip when she was concentrating, making him unable to look away. She was not his type at all.

"Haven't heard anything yet. I'm sure I'll hear something by tomorrow. The phlebotomist was hot, though," Chris answered.

"Did you get her number?"

Chris laughed and finished restocking the last cabinet. "No. You know I'm waiting to make sure I didn't catch anything from that patient you let bite me."

James ducked down as he stood, making his way to the side door. "Let's get you coffee, because clearly, you're delusional. I didn't let that lady do shit. That was all you."

Chris got in the driver's seat and waited for his partner to get situated before he pulled out of the lot and drove toward the coffee shop. He wasn't delusional, but James was right; he did need coffee. Even after he had gotten his mom home earlier and made sure her groceries were put away, he had a hard time winding down. His mom, for once, hadn't hassled him about staying to visit, so he couldn't blame her. It was Mallory. Mallory and her damn eyes and positive affirmations.

Chris looked at his partner once he put the truck in park in front of the nearest coffee shop. He looked over to find James watching him with the most annoying grin across his face. Ignoring his best judgement, he acknowledged the look with a raised eyebrow and a shrug.

"It's true love, isn't it?" James commented.

"*Pendejo*," Chris muttered. "Just get out so I can lock the doors."

Coffee shop was an over statement for the small corner store he chose to go to for coffee. The linoleum floors were worn out, but clean. There were a few aisles of non-perishable foods and necessities like toilet paper and feminine products. The back wall offered a selection of different fresh brewed coffees and a station to add cream and sugar.

As they approached the register to pay for their coffee, Chris felt his pager vibrate followed by the crackling of a voice coming over his radio. *"Unit 706, for the assignment, 706."*

"Go ahead," he answered the radio after placing a five-dollar bill on the counter to cover both large coffees.

"706, respond to 101 North Briar Street. That's going to be Briar Manor skilled nursing facility. Room 225 for the unresponsive patient."

"Received and responding," Chris said over his portable radio as they climbed back into the truck.

Chris was thankful they at least made it for coffee. He took a cautious sip as he flipped on the emergency lights and put the truck in drive. The coffee was hot, but even the small sip seemed to touch his soul as he navigated traffic. He could get to Briar Manor nursing home in his sleep. He couldn't remember going more than one shift without a call there. They were understaffed, as most skilled nursing facilities seemed to be, and a person never knew what they'd be walking into.

They had responded from the other side of town, but still made it within a few minutes. They pulled up behind the paramedic unit and called on scene. Without speaking, Chris and James exited the cab of the truck and went around back to gather what they needed. Chris pulled out the stretcher which already had the bag on top, and James met him around the back and tossed the AED and suction unit on top. He felt around his neck to make sure he had his stethoscope before closing and locking the doors.

They walked into the building to find a security guard standing in front of the open elevator doors. Inside, Alyssa and Michael stood waiting.

"We saw you pull up as we were walking in the door, so we figured we'd wait," Alyssa explained.

Chris nodded at his old partner. He'd stopped giving her shit about abandoning him once he started getting close to his new partner. She looked happy. The diamond on her left ring finger caught the light as she absently placed her hand on her slightly rounded abdomen.

"I thought married couples weren't allowed to work together anymore," James said.

"We can't be permanent partners," Michael spoke up while he placed the monitor and med bag on the stretcher. "If one of us takes an open shift they won't rearrange everything. The whole thing is stupid. Everyone knows we work well together."

"Yeah, we can tell," Chris said through a laugh while looking pointedly at her baby bump.

Alyssa rolled her eyes and shook her head, her eyes gleaming. "You're such a child. Anyway, I'll bet you a coffee this ends in a pronouncement."

"We already have our coffee. But I'll bet you dinner the patient is wide awake," Chris countered just as the doors were opening.

The smell of bleach and bodily fluids hit them as soon as they stepped out of the elevator. When Chris was a new EMT, it had been the smells that got to him the most. Now, he was used to it. It wasn't pleasant, but he was able to ignore it.

"What do we have?" Michael asked as they approached the nurses' station.

The nurse looked up at Michael and smiled briefly before her gaze lingered on the white gold wedding band around his finger. "She's over there."

Chris made an obvious point of looking from Michael to Alyssa before he looked in the direction the nurse indicated. Down the hall seated at a table in the dining area was an elderly woman. She wore a plain black dress that fell to the center of her bronze shins. Chris and Alyssa made eye contact with each other as both James and Michael turned toward the nurse.

"Unconscious?" Michael asked.

"Yeah," the nurse answered deliberately, as if speaking to a child. "She won't take her medicine and is being belligerent to the staff."

At this point Chris snapped his head in the direction of the nurse. He briefly glanced at Michael, whose face was reddening in anger, and couldn't hold back his laughter.

"You mean uncooperative?" Chris asked.

The nurse's eyes widened briefly before she covered her mouth and laughed. "Yeah, that's what I meant. Uncooperative."

"Oh, my god," Michael muttered as he rubbed his temples before directing his next question to Chris. "Do you want us to stick around for vitals?"

"Nope. But, instead of dinner, you can buy breakfast after our shift. I have a feeling it's going to be one of those nights."

Ordinarily, the situation would have pissed Chris right off, but while annoyed, he was too busy trying not to actively laugh at Michael's reaction when he realized there was no need for advanced life support, whatsoever. He was already making his way over to the patient when he'd requested breakfast.

"Fine. Meet you at the diner at a little after seven," Michael said before grabbing their bags from the stretcher and leading Alyssa to the elevator.

Chris and James walked the rest of the way over to their patient. Her legs were crossed, and she smiled pleasantly at them. She took her time looking each of them up and down before her smile spread wider.

"Hi ma'am. What's going on?" Chris asked.

"I was out of control," she said simply, using the palm of her hand to smooth her hair back.

"You were? Tell us what happened, mama," James encouraged, seamlessly using an over-familiar pet name, and getting away with it as usual.

"Well," the woman began before letting out a heavy sigh. "I told that bitch I wasn't ready to get into my night clothes just yet. She started talking to me crazy, so I told her I was gonna whoop her ass."

Chris felt his jaw drop. He was not expecting that response to come out of the old woman. She had to have been at least in her eighties. He decided at that moment she was his favorite patient. She sat with her arms folded as she waited for their response.

"Well, why don't you come with us?" Chris suggested. "That way you can get out of here and everyone will be happy by the time you get back here."

The woman nodded and moved to stand. Chris put his hand out and stopped her. He'd noticed her walker sitting near the table and didn't want to risk her falling. After moving the bags, AED, and suction unit off the stretcher, he helped her up. She crossed one foot across the other, clasped her hands, and appeared to be perfectly content.

Once they got to the truck, and away from her stressful situation, he took a set of vital signs. As expected, she was completely stable. She sat quietly while Chris copied the information from the printout the staff passed along into the chart. They were nearly at the hospital when she finally spoke.

"Are you married?" she asked.

Chris hesitated for a moment before deciding she was harmless and answering her question. "No, Mrs. Horne, I'm not married. Why?"

"Well, I caught my special friend looking at that bitch of a nurse, so I think I might be in the market."

Chris looked back down and laughed while he finished up the chart. He could feel her watching him, so he looked up once he finished entering everything into his tablet.

"Something funny?" she asked.

"Nope," he answered quickly. "Nothing is funny, but I think you might be my favorite patient ever. Don't tell anyone, though."

"I think they'll figure it out at our wedding."

This time, Chris couldn't hold back his laughter. Wiping the tears from his eyes, he stood and opened the back doors as soon as they were parked in the ambulance bay. He really hoped that was a sign of how the rest of their night would go.

Chapter 2

MALLORY

Fridays would always be Mallory's favorite day of the week. It was date night with Dan. Dan had been there for her when she broke up with her boyfriend of ten years. For the most part, they had only seen each other in passing, but one day Dan went up to check on her. He hadn't seen her in several days and wanted to make sure she was okay.

She had been struggling with depression before the breakup. With no one there to remind her to take care of herself, even if the reminders were to avoid having to actually deal with her mental health concerns, finally feeling the weight of all the emotional trauma she'd suffered, she quickly spiraled into a very dark place. She went from missing a few days of work here and there, to calling out sick once a week, to not showing up at all. It didn't take long for the school she worked for to send a letter that she was no longer needed. It didn't matter that she didn't like the job. That job had been her last reason to even consider getting out of bed. Until Dan became her reason. And so began their morning coffee routine.

She moved around the kitchen wearing her favorite comfy jeans and cropped t-shirt. The best part about having date nights with Dan was that she didn't have to dress up. Healthy eating was another thing she started doing when she pulled herself from the black hole of depression. It wasn't a cure, but it was something she could control, and sharing it with a friend made it even better.

"What's on the menu?" Dan asked from behind her, causing her to jump.

"Vegetable lasagna. I just took it out of the oven, so we have a few minutes while it sits. What's new?"

"Since this morning?" Dan asked with a laugh. "Not a whole lot. I finished reading that book I started."

Dan took a seat at the island, while Mallory cut up fruits for dessert. He no longer offered to help. Mallory hated anyone near her while she cooked, so he was lucky to be allowed to sit in the kitchen at all.

"Just feels like I haven't seen you in forever. It's always like that when we don't ride in to work together," Mallory said.

"Oh, I did get engaged."

Mallory nearly dropped the bowl of fruit. "What?"

He started laughing immediately. "You are way too easy. No, I did not get engaged. But I do need to introduce you to Ian. I won't call things serious, but ..."

Mallory only partially recovered from his betrothment joke and was equally caught off balance by the thought of him being in a serious relationship. His relationship with Ian wasn't secret, but she hadn't met him. As close as they were to each other, they respected each other's privacy. Aside from their regular scheduled coffee and dinner dates, there was to be no barging in. That was the reason they'd scheduled morning coffee. A way for him to make sure she was doing okay without crossing her boundaries.

"I would absolutely love to meet him. I'm excited for you!"

Dan waved her off. "I said things aren't serious, but I think I'll keep him around for a while. The two of you would probably get along."

"If you like him, I'll love him."

Dan took two plates and two bowls down from the cabinet and silverware from the drawer, while Mallory finished cutting up the fruit and made place settings for them. She didn't mind that sort of help because he didn't get in the way. She served up two hearty portions of lasagna and took a seat next to him.

"Have you seen your sexy mystery patient lately?" he asked.

She shook her head as she finished chewing her food. "I should have never told you about him."

"I think what you meant to say was that you should have gotten his number," Dan teased. "This is delicious, by the way. Thank you."

"You should really come with me to that new gym tomorrow. They have Pilates and hot yoga," Mallory suggested.

It was Dan's turn to shake his head as he ate. She was always inviting him to take Pilates and yoga with her, and he always turned her down. Going to the gym at the hospital with her a couple times a week was the most she could get out of him.

"You already know my answer," he said eventually.

"This one is walking distance, so I thought maybe I could talk you into it."

"I love your new outlook on life and your focus on health and wellness, especially the food, but those classes are not for me. I'm not about that woo-woo stuff."

"Manifestation affirmations are not woo-woo!" she argued. "And Pilates builds strength and flexibility."

Dan just looked at her with one raised eyebrow. They'd had this conversation over and over. She would never say it out loud, be he may have been right about yoga. She often mentally recited her positive affirmations while doing the breathing exercises.

"I'm plenty strong and flexible, just ask Ian."

Mallory nearly choked. He had a bad habit of saying things for shock value while she was eating or drinking.

"I'll take your word for it," she said once she recovered enough to swallow her food.

"Now back to Mystery Patient ... It shouldn't be hard to find him. If he was an employee health referral, he probably works for the hospital," Dan pressed.

"Yes. I'm sure I could find him. But I'm not looking for him. I'll see him again if I'm meant to."

He rolled his eyes as he helped himself to a serving of fruit. She knew what he was thinking. He wanted to tell her she was afraid to put herself out there, but the last time he pushed the point, it ended in an argument. She wasn't afraid to put herself out there, but whatever was meant to be, would be.

CHRISTIAN

Chris was wide awake. It was a rare morning when he could sleep in, but of course his body didn't cooperate. He worked a lot of overtime and sometimes only allowed himself one or two days off each week. His regular schedule gave him three or four days off out of seven, but he could always use the money. Most of his coworkers worked a second job, but that idea never appealed to him.

After throwing his blankets to the side, he got up to look out the window. The cloudless blue sky greeted him as soon as he pulled back the heavy blackout curtains. He had plans to eat dinner at his mom's house and wanted to get a few things done beforehand, but until then his day was free.

He usually went to the gym with James after work, but there was a new gym that had opened up just a few minutes from his house that he'd been wanting to check out. If it was nicer, he'd talk James into checking it out. Their usual one kept raising the fees and didn't even have a lot of the amenities that the other ones had.

He took a quick shower, brushed his teeth, and dug through his drawers in search of gym clothes. Without much thought, he put on a pair of blue basketball shorts, a white muscle shirt, and a gray hoodie. He wasn't even sure if he would work out. The main purpose of his trip to the gym would be to check it out and ask about the fees.

There were several cars in the parking lot, but it didn't seem too packed for a Saturday. The gym was in a large building that shared a parking lot with a shopping center. Red and yellow flags surrounded a white Grand Opening sign. The doors opened to a large front desk staffed by several employees.

The young blonde closest to him greeted him with a smile. "Welcome to Iron Fitness. Do you have your membership card for me to scan?"

Chris stepped forward and leaned against the counter. "Actually, I'm not a member here. Is it okay if I just check it out?"

"Well, I'm Katie and I'll be happy to show you around if that's okay. And afterwards, feel free to stay and do your work out."

Sounded like a good idea to him. He followed Katie as she gave him a tour. The lower level was mostly strength training equipment and free weights. He glanced at everything as she brought him upstairs to point out all the cardio machines. There were plenty of ellipticals, stationary bicycles, and treadmills. TVs hung from the ceiling throughout the area for anyone who wasn't listening to music.

They made their way downstairs and Chris was able to get a better look at the weights. All of the equipment was top of the line and spaced out so people could work out without feeling like they were on top of each other.

"Along the back, there, is where we offer classes," Katie explained as they moved closer. "That far corner is where they do hot yoga. The middle room is for spin classes. This right here is where they do Pilates, as well as aerobics and step classes. Right now, it's Pilates."

Chris watched through the glass while women dressed in fitted clothing held various poses while using resistance bands. He felt like a voyeur and was about to look away when someone caught his eye. In the back row, closest to him, he spotted a woman with light brown hair wearing a stunning messy bun. Her yoga pants showed off every curve, and the cropped tank top revealed a toned upper body. She moved gracefully on to the next pose, and he couldn't take his eyes off her, even though she hadn't turned enough for him to see her face. The grace in which she moved had him completely captivated.

"How long are the classes, Katie?" he asked, his eyes never moving from the woman on the other side of the glass.

She seemed slightly surprised by the question. "Forty-five minutes. This one should be over in about ten minutes and then the next Pilates class should start in twenty, if you're interested. Feel free to join. The full schedule is up at the desk."

"Thank you," he said, forcing himself to drag his eyes away from the woman in the Pilates class.

The rest of the tour was a blur. There was a juice bar, swimming pool, and hot tub. Something about a trainer. They were only closed from midnight until six in the morning. He didn't care. He was already planning on joining anyway. He kept looking at his watch, determined to get the tour and spiel over with in time to catch the Pilates class leaving. Creepy or not, he had to talk to the woman from the back row.

"If you decide you want to join, just stop at the desk on your way out. It only takes five minutes. Have a great workout!"

She had barely finished the word "workout" before he turned and made his way back to the Pilates class. Class must have been over because everyone appeared to be packing up to leave. It was fine by him.

As he stood waiting, the woman finally turned around and looked right at him. It felt like his heart stopped beating when he realized who he was looking at. It was the woman from the lab. Mallory, with the manifestations. Once his heart resumed to its normal function, it was at a much faster pace. He watched as recognition crossed over her features and a small smile formed on her sculpted lips.

She broke his gaze in order to finish packing up her things. The way her cheeks flushed as she packed told him she felt him watching her. He'd only met her one time, but when she stilled and took a deep breath before standing with her bag, he could practically hear her reciting something in order to calm her nerves.

"Hey," he greeted once she made her way over to him.

"Hey yourself."

She looked up at him through her lashes, and his mind immediately flashed to another visual of her looking up at him. He cleared his throat after giving his head a slight shake and tried to think of what to say next. This was a new development. He never had any trouble talking to women.

"Are you following me?" she asked when he failed to come up with anything to say.

For whatever reason, her teasing put him at ease. "No. I just came in to check this place out and maybe join after getting a workout in. Running into you was just a bonus."

"Well? Did you get a workout in?"

"Nope. I was just finishing up the tour when I saw you." She didn't need to know he was checking her out before he realized who she was. "Care to join me?"

She cocked her head to the side and studied him a moment before answering. "I only do cardio on Pilates days, no weight training."

"Perfect," he said before turning toward the stairs.

He knew she'd follow him, just like he knew she'd be intimidated if he put her on the spot for a response. Once again, he reminded himself that he had only met her once. He found a treadmill with an empty one on either side, and quickly wiped down the surface. Just as he expected, Mallory joined him.

"So," she began once they started their warmup. "Do you work for the same hospital?"

"Yes and no."

Her laugh went straight through him. "How very cryptic."

"Been looking for me, huh?" he teased.

"No! I was just making conversation," she explained before turning up the speed on her treadmill.

He enjoyed making her blush entirely too much. Just the little bit he knew about her told him she rarely allowed herself to get flustered. All of her positive thinking and manifesting kept her feeling grounded. He was willing to bet she went out of her way to feel cool, calm, and collected.

She jogged next to him for twenty minutes before slowing back down to a walk. The silence felt comfortable, as if she had jogged through her nerves. He couldn't keep his eyes from wandering in her direction. Her tanned skin was shiny from the thin layer of sweat that covered her body. Her hair was damp and beginning to curl around the edges. She wore no makeup which, as reasonable as it would seem, was unusual for a lot of the women at the gym. She carried an air of confidence, even though it didn't take much for him to throw her off balance.

While he was busy trying not to watch her, she had somehow stopped the treadmill and picked up her bag. "I'll see you around."

She was already walking away before he could come up with a response. That was twice he'd seen her and parted ways without a way to contact her. She had the nerve to look over her shoulder and smile at him before walking down the stairs and out of his life. He continued his workout and tried to convince himself he didn't care.

Chapter 3

MALLORY

Mallory walked into Dan's apartment for Sunday coffee. Unless Dan had to work, their weekend coffee time was a bit later in the morning. Sundays were dedicated to rest, as far as she was concerned. Unless she couldn't help it, the only place she went on a Sunday was downstairs to have coffee with Dan.

"Dan!" she called out in order to annoy him. "I hope you aren't naked, because here I am!"

Dan appeared in the doorway of the kitchen and crossed his arms. Before she could make a smart remark, another man appeared in the doorway behind him. Dan started laughing as Mallory worked hard to keep her jaw from dropping. When he mentioned introducing her to Ian, she had no idea he would be sleeping over any time soon.

"Good morning," she said once she recovered her ability to speak. "I'm Mallory."

The other man stepped forward with a smile that matched hers. He was the definition of tall dark and handsome. His brown skin was flawless, his hair was neatly cut in a short fade, and he had the most perfect mouth she'd ever seen ... aside from Christian's.

"I'm Ian. I've heard a lot about you." Even his voice was perfect.

"Oh really?" she said, giving Dan a look. "I've heard about you as well."

Dan hadn't told her much about Ian, but she decided not to rat him out. They understood each other. She liked to keep some things to herself as well. She was annoyed at herself for wanting to dissect her latest interaction with Mystery Patient.

"Mallory, what is on your mind? Come on. Let's have coffee," Dan said as if reading her mind. "Ian, are you staying for coffee?"

Ian looked from one to the other before answering. "Do you mind if I skip this one? I don't want to be rude, but I have a few things to do this morning."

Mallory didn't miss the extra-long look exchanged between the two men before Dan spoke up. "Nope. Of course, we don't mind. I'm just glad you got to meet my girl Mallory."

"Mallory, it's been a pleasure," Ian said before moving in for a quick hug and to give her a kiss on the cheek. "Dan, I'll call you later."

Dan walked Ian to the door, kissed him goodbye, then quickly made his way back to the kitchen. He filled two mugs with coffee and joined Mallory at the table, looking at her expectantly.

"What?" she finally asked after being held under his gaze for several moments.

"You have something on your mind, I can sense it. And you're going to deny it. And I'm eventually going to get it out of you, so let's skip to that part."

"I saw Mystery Patient yesterday," she blurted.

Dan stood and raised his arms in triumph. "I knew it! I knew there was something. Okay, tell me all about it."

Mallory laughed and then took a sip of her coffee to stall. She wasn't even sure what to say. Just thinking about the encounter gave her butterflies, like some pubescent teenager. The way she reacted to him was ridiculous.

"I ran into him at the gym. Apparently, we joined the same day. I was doing my first class as he was finishing up his tour. Dan, he looked even better than I remembered. His eyes ... those dimples ... those lips!"

Dan was back in his seat, leaning forward as he listened intently. He drank his coffee and nodded for her to continue. There was nothing he loved more than some gossip or girl talk, and she loved him for it.

"There's not really anything to tell. I was finishing class, looked up as I was packing up, and locked eyes with him. He has a name, by the way. It's Christian."

"Okay, but did you talk to Christian?"

"Yes," she answered with a sigh. "We even worked out a bit together. He's really easy to be around."

Dan got up to pour himself a refill, then leaned against the counter. "So, when are you seeing him again?"

Mallory's stomach dropped at the thought. She still wasn't sure what had gotten into her. She'd had no reason to suddenly leave, but the thought of him thinking she was interested in him was too much, even if he wasn't wrong.

"I'm not."

Dan patiently waited for her to go on. "We didn't exchange numbers or anything," she explained.

"Let me get this straight," Dan finally interjected. "The man was watching you in your Pilates class, you worked out together, but you didn't exchange phone numbers?"

It sounded even worse when he said it out loud. "I didn't exactly give him a chance. I asked where he worked, and he made a comment about me looking for him. So, I panicked and left a bit abruptly."

"Why are you so upset at the idea of him knowing you're interested?"

He hit the nail on the head. She was upset at the thought of him knowing. She wasn't sure why, but she went straight into panic mode the second he made the comment about her looking for him. Okay, maybe she did know why. Ever since her big messy breakup, she was determined to avoid getting involved with anyone she felt real feelings toward. A therapist would point to her mother's death and her father's remarriage as the reason behind her behavior, but she chose not to worry herself with the details ... It was one thing to have a good time and go out on dates, but to feel a pull toward someone wasn't something she planned to repeat.

"It's not that," she protested.

"Are you interested?" he asked her directly.

"I'm not sure. I don't even know him."

"Then why not just tell him that?"

"Because he hasn't asked," Mallory said, pointing out the obvious.

"Exactly!"

She stared at her friend. She was quite certain he made a point, but she refused to admit to seeing it. He hadn't asked her anything. He hadn't even asked her out. As usual, her reaction had been way over the top. She always had such a visceral response to emotions. When most people described being in fight or flight mode, they meant figuratively. When Mallory experienced it, it was very literal. She was prepared to physically fight or immediately leave a situation. There was no such thing as working through that emotion for her.

"Well, none of that matters anyway," she said with a sigh. "It's not like I'll be seeing him again."

"You don't know that. But even if you don't, it was good practice. Maybe next time you'll realize that it's okay to just live in the moment. It doesn't have to be scary."

"You're right," she agreed. "I think I'll add that into my affirmations. Now tell me about Ian!"

Dan pulled out his chair and rejoined her at the table. The smile he shared with her was contagious. "He's not bad, right?"

"He's gorgeous!" she agreed. "But tell me about him. You've told him all about me, and I know almost nothing about him."

"Well," he began before hesitating a moment. "The way we met was a bit unorthodox."

It was Mallory's turn to pry. "And? You know how I met Christian. I'm not one to judge."

"But you and Christian aren't dating," he pointed out.

"But you're encouraging me to. So, spill."

Dan's eyes briefly narrowed before he let out a short laugh. "Fine. I met him at work. I was working with a new admit, and he was the patient's uncle. I was professional the entire time, don't worry."

"So, he gave you his number right there in front of his niece?" she asked.

"God, no! I ran into him at the hospital's coffee shop a couple days later. And I may have mentioned my favorite happy hour location."

"I can't believe I'm just now hearing about this," Mallory complained.

"Anyway," he continued, "we happened to see each other at the bar and decided to share a table."

Mallory listened to his entire story. It sounded so normal; so matter of fact. She needed to take that approach with things. When people said she takes things too seriously, they weren't wrong.

"Come to find out he's a physician's assistant," Dan continued. "He knows the medical field, which is nice. He also knows how taboo it is, the way we met. That also makes it nice. Plus, I feel like I've known him forever. I know I've never really introduced you to anyone before, so I hope that wasn't weird. I just want you to know it's possible. Give Mystery Patient a chance."

"I'll think about it." That was as close as she planned to get to giving in.

Chapter 4

CHRISTIAN

Chris waited by the doors just outside of the lab. Once again, he felt like a total creep, but he convinced himself it was worth it. He had watched her like a creep outside of the Pilates class and it hadn't scared her off, so hopefully she'd be okay. By calling to get the hours of the outpatient lab, he was able to figure out about what time Mallory would get off work. And that wasn't creepy at all ...

After he ran into her at the gym, he tried to put her out of his mind. He tried to forget her. But every time he closed his eyes, her blue eyes met his. He wasn't sure of the reason behind her fast getaway at the gym, but he intended to find out.

The double doors opened, and out walked Mallory and the two other women who were working with her the morning he went in for his labs. She was wearing her blue scrubs with a gray zippered hoodie. She hadn't spotted him yet, so he took a moment to watch her. She laughed freely with her coworkers as they started down the hallway.

"Hey," he said after a moment.

She looked up from her conversation and stopped in her tracks. The look on her face leaned more toward surprise than hostility, so he took a step closer. Both of the other women looked from Mallory to him, before the younger woman broke into a grin.

"We'll see you tomorrow," the younger woman spoke up before taking the other one's arm and pulling her away.

"Hey, yourself," Mallory finally replied. "What are you doing here?"

Chris struggled to come up with an explanation. Clearly, he hadn't come up with a plan beyond showing up at her job like a stalker, so he went with the truth. "You left so fast the other day I didn't get to ask you to lunch ... or get your number."

Mallory resumed her walk toward the parking garage. He knew he'd better keep up or it was going to be a repeat of the day at the gym. Falling into step behind her, he tried to think of what to say. He reached out and placed his hand on the back of her arm. She immediately turned around and looked from him to the hand on her arm.

"I'm sorry," he said, holding his hands up in surrender. "I didn't mean to grab you. Just—" He paused, trying his best not to fumble over his words. "Can you give me a minute? Please?"

She closed her eyes and took a slow breath before opening them again. She seemed a little more relaxed as she folded her arms and looked at him expectantly. He had to put his hands in his pockets to keep from reaching out to touch her again. There was nothing left to do but lay everything on the table. Something he never did.

"Okay, listen. I know how ridiculous I sound, but I've wanted to spend more time with you from the moment I met you. I want to know you. I didn't ask you out, because it's not a good look for a patient to ask out anyone who is part of patient care. I know you just drew my blood, but still. When I happened to run into you at the gym, I took it as a sign. Yes. I know that also sounds ridiculous."

Mallory looked down toward the floor and laughed. "You don't sound ridiculous."

"Then will you have dinner with me? Please?"

The panicked expression was returning to her features. "I better not."

"It's just dinner. Don't even give me your number first. If you don't have a good time, then you never have to see me again. I won't be able to call you, and I promise not to show up here again. I just want a chance to know you."

He could see her resolve beginning to crumble. After another slow breath, she answered him. "Okay. But just dinner."

"Tonight?" he asked before she could change her mind. "There's an Italian place right next to the gym. Meet me in an hour?"

She finally let a smile break free. He knew he probably sounded over-eager, but he didn't care. As long as she said yes. The feelings he had when he was around her were unfamiliar. Wanting to know her was the best way to explain it. All he could do was go home, get ready, and hope she didn't stand him up.

MALLORY

Mallory walked in the door and went straight for her closet. Why she agreed to the date was beyond her. She thought about standing him up, but she'd never stop feeling guilty if she did something like that. After opening her closet, she selected a simple yellow wrap dress with a long black cardigan. She didn't have much to wear as far as dates went, so that would have to do. After taking a final look in the mirror, she picked up her purse and walked back out the door before she changed her mind.

The restaurant wasn't busy. It was early enough in the evening that they had beat the rush. She immediately spotted Christian sitting at a table. He stood and pulled out her chair as she approached. He had changed into black slacks and a black button-down shirt. He'd been attractive before, but her mouth went dry when she saw him dressed up.

"Mallory," he greeted before placing a quick kiss on her cheek.

She nearly forgot how to speak. Heat spread across her face, starting with where he kissed her and moving its way over. "Christian."

"I'm glad you showed up," he said, his face displaying genuine relief.

She smiled at him, even though she felt slightly insulted by his words. Did he think she was the kind of person to stand him up? Sure, she considered it, but only for a brief moment.

"I wouldn't do that. I said I'd come so here I am."

His smile felt too familiar, and his eyes seemed to see deeper than the surface as he studied her. The familiarity was slightly unnerving, but she basked in the warmth of it. She didn't need all the fingers of one hand to count how many times she'd laid eyes on him, but she felt as though she knew him.

"Tell me about yourself," he requested.

She laughed. "That's quite the open-ended question. For a second there I thought I was on a job interview."

"I told you I wanted to know you." He shrugged.

"Well, if we're doing this, let's do this. What do you want to know?" Mallory asked.

"I want to know everything."

"Smart ass." She forced herself into her outgoing persona. She wasn't usually an outgoing person, but she was able to fake it for a while, when necessary. "Ask me a question and I'll answer it. But you have to answer my questions too."

"Okay. How did you get into phlebotomy? That should be an easy enough question."

Mallory sat back and folded her arms. The question sounded simple enough. He had no idea about the circumstances surrounding her career change. The server showed up to take their drink order, allowing her some extra time consider her response. Christian ordered them a bottle of red wine before sending the man on his way, his eyes narrowed in obvious annoyance at the interruption.

"Well, after my live-in boyfriend of several years left, I needed to figure something out fast. Everyone knows the medical field is always growing. It was either CNA, EMT, or phlebotomy, and I don't have the patience or bedside manner to be a CNA," she explained.

"And EMS?"

She froze for a moment before she was able to shake it off. He wasn't trying to make her feel uncomfortable. He just happened to stumble into two landmines in a row. She knew he hadn't done it intentionally.

"You're really bad at this," she tried to joke.

He sat forward, his eyebrows drawn together in concern. "Did I ask something off limits?"

"Not on purpose, I'm sure. But finding a new career was during a traumatic time, and I have personal reasons for avoiding getting into EMS. The short version? My family is dysfunctional."

Christian tilted his head back and laughed. The first time she saw him laugh freely was at her expense. Instead of being offended, she felt more at ease. She got the feeling he was a what you see is what you get kind of person, which was refreshing. Her own laughter bubbled out along with his.

"Really? I'm glad my fucked-up family is amusing," she said with a laugh.

Christian composed himself just in time for the server to show up with their bottle of wine. He poured a small amount into Christian's glass and waited for him to taste it. Christian gave him a nod and he filled both wine glasses before taking their order. Mallory was still feeling slightly off-kilter, so she was grateful when Christian ordered for them both.

"Everything is served family style. The baked ziti is really good. I hope you don't mind that I ordered for us, but I wanted to get rid of that guy. He is really starting to piss me off the way he keeps showing up when we're in the middle of talking."

Mallory chuckled. Christian apparently had a bit of a short fuse. The fact that he didn't hide it, and that it wasn't directed at her in any way made her relax again still. She couldn't explain her response to him. Her ex wasn't good to her. His controlling behavior was the main reason she had been in such a bad situation when they broke up. He didn't want her to have a demanding job or to be gone whenever he was home. Working at a school was the best way to ensure she would always be available to him.

"It's literally his job, you know," Mallory pointed out.

"Yes. I know. But he knew we were trying to talk. He could have waited for us to stop talking," he said quickly. "Anyway, everyone's family is fucked-up in some way. I'm just glad you're like the rest of us. Do you want to talk about it? You don't have to."

"I'd rather not. So, what about you? How did you get into your job?"

He leaned forward and took a drink of his wine before answering. "I guess that's a bit of a loaded question for me as well. My mom raised us on her own. I hated seeing her struggle, so I needed something fast and inexpensive. I also always liked helping people and my uncle was a retired paramedic. So, it just made sense at the time."

His honesty was disarming. She was suddenly in less of a hurry to get the date over with. "What about now? Do you still like helping people?"

Christian tilted his head to the side and studied her before he answered. She felt his gaze every place he looked. Right as he opened his mouth to respond to her question, the server placed their meal in front of them.

Chris's anger was palpable, and it took everything for Mallory not to laugh out loud.

"What's funny?" Christian asked as soon as they were alone.

"You are," she answered as she picked up the serving spoon and filled both bowls with pasta. "Now, back to my question. Do you still like helping people?"

Christian grinned; his dimples plainly visible. Mallory swallowed hard and begged her body to remain in control of itself. Refusing to label her response with a name, she instead enjoyed the way it made her feel.

"The simple answer would be yes," he answered after a long moment.

"And the not so simple answer?"

Christian leaned forward and surprised Mallory by covering her hand with his, the warmth taking up her entire focus. His fingers lightly stroked her wrist and she nearly forgot how to think.

"Well ... I enjoy helping people, but it's hard. I really do want to help people. If you have family in the field, then I'm sure you've heard it before. People treat us like shit. We get attacked. All those things ruin it for people who need help. You already know what recently happened to me. My old partner was attacked a while back. She was nearly killed, and the people responsible barely got a slap on the wrist. Stuff like that makes the job harder than it needs to be. I'm probably known for having a bad attitude, but it's not because I don't like my job. It's just so hard going into work knowing anything can happen and we don't have the protection that the police have. If that makes sense," he tried to explain. "I'm sorry. I don't mean to drag you down. You know how it is when you're dealing with people. But all it takes is one patient to remind you why you do the job."

It was hard for her to not immediately think of him as that patient, but for other reasons. She was being silly. Just the other day an elderly woman had made her entire day. She was so sweet, and her smile could light up the room. When Mallory had asked the standard questions, the woman's eyes lit up and she smiled as she answered. Mallory had wanted to adopt her as a grandma.

"I know what you mean. We're just people. The job can get to us the same way any job gets to anyone. And just because we may get annoyed, it doesn't mean we don't give every patient our all," Mallory said quietly. "Even the ones who don't deserve it."

"Even the ones who don't deserve it," Christian repeated.

They ate their meal in silence. Mallory really did feel a connection to him. He was brusque, but she understood him. He had a short fuse, but she knew he would never direct it at her. She couldn't explain how she knew, but she did. Without a word, she wrote her number on a cocktail napkin and slid it across the table.

"So ..." Christian said as he filled their glasses with the last of the wine. "Can I see you again?"

Mallory had already decided she wanted to see more of him. She'd been single for some time, and this was the first time she found herself wanting more than a first date or a one-night stand since she'd stopped seeing Aiden.

"Yes. Why else do you think I gave you my number?"

"Tomorrow?" he asked, nearly talking over her.

She laughed at his enthusiasm. "Whoa, what's the rush? I have yoga tomorrow night. We can do something this weekend, though."

He leaned even closer and flipped her hand over. She shivered when he began tracing designs along her palm. "It's my weekend to work ..."

It was tempting, but she didn't want to be that person. Fridays were for her best friend. She wouldn't ditch him for the first man who came along and asked her out. Never mind that Dan would probably approve. He hadn't pushed her aside even though things were getting serious with Ian.

"Come to the gym with me tomorrow. Have you ever tried yoga? You might like it," she suggested, assuming he'd say no.

It was his turn to laugh. "I am not taking a yoga class, but I'll go to the gym with you. I'll do a workout while you do your yoga. Sound good?"

Going to the gym together sounded strangely intimate even though they'd already done part of a workout together before. She liked the idea. "Meet me there tomorrow at around four?"

Christian stood and tossed a few bills on the table. When Mallory joined him, he reached for her hand and gave it a gentle squeeze. "It's a date."

The butterflies were back. She wasn't sure what the hell was wrong with her. She was behaving like a teenager who'd never been on a date before. Everything he said and did made her heart flutter. They had come to a stop beside her car, and she realized he was watching her with an amused smile. Her thoughts were always displayed on her face when she wasn't paying attention.

"Okay, then. I'll see you tomorrow," she said as she turned to open her car door.

Christian stepped forward and placed his hand on her car door, both closing her in and preventing her from opening the door. It was excitement, and not fear that coursed through her. She sucked in a breath and searched his face. He had the same amused smile as before when he stepped closer and used his free hand to tilt her chin. His scent overwhelmed her senses as he closed the distance between them. He smelled of soap, and either cologne or after shave. Whatever it was had her closing her eyes and breathing it in.

His lips grazed her cheek where he lingered for several seconds before stepping back. She opened her eyes in surprise, almost certain he was about to kiss her. She had imagined the way his mouth would feel on hers since the day they met. Using the back of his fingers, he gently stroked the place he'd kissed.

"I'll see you tomorrow," he said before he opened her door and waited for her to step in.

Completely off balance, it took everything for her to not fall into the car. Her face burned, and she could feel his lips as if they were still there. Once she was inside the car, he closed her door then walked away.

Chapter 5

CHRISTIAN

Chris knocked on Alyssa's door the following evening. He wasn't able to convince Mallory to cancel her dinner plans while they were at the gym, so he accepted Alyssa's invitation to hang out. Michael, Alyssa, and Chris all picked up extra shifts when they could, so it wasn't easy to find time to get together, and Alyssa had made it her mission to make sure they spent time together since they weren't partners anymore.

"Hey!" Alyssa greeted after she yanked the door open. "I'm so glad you could come over. I feel like I haven't seen you in forever."

Chris rolled his eyes. "I just saw you on a call the other night."

She pulled him into the house and then into a hug. "You know what I mean. Whenever I see you at work we're working. I miss just being around you and hanging out."

"Pregnancy has made you soft," Chris teased. "Speaking of ... where's your baby's daddy?"

"My *husband*," she enunciated then paused for emphasis, "had to go help his dad with something. He'll be back at some point. I hope you don't mind Chinese food. I didn't feel like cooking."

Chris looked her up and down, unsure of how to react. Cooking was her favorite hobby. He could count on one hand how many times she'd invited him over and didn't provide a home cooked meal. He didn't mind takeout since he was there to spend time with her, not just eat her food. But still.

"Are you sure you're okay?" he asked after following her into the kitchen.

"Just fix your plate. Growing a baby is exhausting."

He piled his plate high with fried rice, lo mein, sesame chicken, and two eggrolls, before making his way to the dining room table. He laughed when Alyssa sat across from him with her plate piled just as high as his own. She always had been a big eater.

"So, tell me how I managed to catch you free on a Friday night. I figured you'd be out sticking your thing in every single woman in New Jersey since you got your test results back."

He almost choked on his food. "God, you haven't even popped that kid out yet and you already sound like an old mom."

Her eyes sparkled and he could tell he gave her the reaction she had been hoping for. "Seriously, though. It's Friday night."

"I think something happened to me while I was busy not getting any. I'm reformed."

It was Alyssa's turn to nearly choke on her food. "You can't *not* flirt with women. You mean to tell me you haven't created a waiting list for when you got the all clear? Personally, I'm surprised you didn't just wrap it up and get back to it after your first negative test."

He had considered it, but as much as he enjoyed sleeping around, he was always careful. The idea that he could have something and accidentally pass it on made him rethink his choices. He knew the real reason behind the change. He was no longer interested in sleeping around indiscriminately.

"A waiting list? I'm not that bad, am I?"

Alyssa just stared at him as she continued eating.

"There's no waiting list. But I have been talking to someone," he admitted.

"I knew it. I knew you wouldn't have gone all this time."

Chris shook his head and laughed. He knew his next admission would get the biggest reaction, yet. He took a few bites of food and braced himself. All the years they'd been partners, he'd never had more than casual flings; and those flings always started off as a one-night stand. No promises, and no pretenses.

"I'm not sleeping with her."

Alyssa's eyes grew wide, and she swallowed quickly. It was the exact reaction he had been expecting. She picked up her napkin and wiped her mouth.

"I'm sorry, I think I heard you wrong. It sounded like you said you aren't sleeping with her."

"*Dios mio,*" he groaned. "Am I seriously that bad? I haven't corrected her from calling me Christian, so hopefully it'll be a while before she finds out about my reputation."

"What do you mean? She's not another ER nurse, is she? Because that'll never work. No one wants to date someone when everywhere she turns is someone who's slept with him," she warned.

Chris wasn't an idiot. He knew that. One of his biggest fears was that she would find out the way he used to be and assume he couldn't change. In reality, he already had changed. It was just too soon to be able to prove it.

"She works in the lab, not the emergency room," he answered.

"Oh, thank god," Alyssa said just as Michael walked in the door.

"Sounds like I'm missing out," Michael said as he walked in the room and kissed his wife.

"He was just telling me about a girl he started talking to," Alyssa told Michael.

"Talking? Isn't that unusual?"

"You guys are both assholes," Chris said lightly. "Anyway, when do you find out what you're having?"

"Two weeks," Michael answered. "Tell him about it, honey. I'm going to take a shower because I'm disgusting from helping Dad redo their bathroom."

Chris watched as Alyssa's eyes followed Michael until he disappeared from view. The old him would have rolled his eyes and made some smartass comment about hearts in her eyes. Two dates with Mallory had him wanting the same thing.

"We want to torture ourselves and wait for at least the twenty-week ultrasound. There's something about seeing them point out the anatomy on the screen and going home with that black and white ultrasound picture … but I kind of want to be surprised and wait until the delivery room. We'll see."

"Any names picked out?" he asked, mostly to distract her from his lack of a smart remark.

"We do, actually. I insisted on Michael Junior if it's a boy. I've always liked the tradition of naming the firstborn after the father if it's a boy. And Marissa if it's a girl. I wanted Mallory, but I didn't realize that's his sister's name, and they don't get along. I always knew of her as Sammy, and I wish he would just go along with it."

Chris choked on air and felt his stomach bottom out as if he was on a roller coaster. "Mallory?"

"Yeah. You probably think it would be confusing, but I don't think so. Her family has always called her Sammy after her middle name," she began to explain. "What? Why do you look like you've seen a ghost?"

"It's just that the girl I was telling you about is named Mallory. It's not a common name, so it threw me off."

"Her name is Mallory?" This time Alyssa looked as though she'd seen a ghost. "But she works in our lab, right?"

Chris was beginning to panic a bit even though he knew it had to be a coincidence. The world wasn't that small. "No. She works at our hospital up north. I had to go help my mom, so I went to that hospital to get my last set of labs. Why?"

"Oh my god," Alyssa whispered.

Chris locked eyes with her. Her eyes were wide and reflected the panic he was feeling. His heart was racing, and a cold sweat was beginning to form above his brow and down his back. There was no way. There was no way the first woman to make him want more since ... since he last wanted more, was Michael's estranged sister.

"Alyssa?"

"What's her last name?" Alyssa demanded. "Tell me you know her last name."

Chris's panic was increasing. "I don't know her last name. I didn't even know her phone number until last night."

"Michael's sister works in the lab up north. You're right. It's not a common name. It has to be her. Don't tell Michael. We need to figure this out."

"We?" he whispered. "This is the first woman I've considered wanting more with since Vivian. I can't keep something like this from her. She already doesn't know about—I just can't keep this from her."

"Okay," Alyssa breathed. "Okay. Here's what we do. We'll invite her over. The sooner the better. We'll be in Vegas in two weeks for Kerry's wedding," she began. Kerry was her best friend, and the wedding was a long time coming. "Do it before then. That way she won't assume you knew the entire time, and Michael will have some time away to work it out in his mind. Don't find out her last name. That way we aren't lying if anyone asks if we knew. Is your long week coming up?"

Chris quickly went over his schedule in his head. "No. Last week was. After this weekend, I'm off until Thursday."

"Okay. Invite her over here next Thursday. I think that's the last time both me and Michael have off before vacation. Are you sure she's different for you? Not just another good time?"

"I wouldn't have said anything if she wasn't, so don't say that about her," Chris explained in exasperation. "She's not my type at all. She's wholesome. She's into wellness and positive thinking. But she's mentioned family issues. Are you sure this is a good idea? Keeping it a secret?"

"It's the only way. Okay, drop it. Michael will be out here any minute," Alyssa pleaded as she cleared their plates.

Chris didn't like it, but what choice did he have? Of all the people who could have drawn his blood, Michael's sister. Of all the people he could have instantly fallen for, Michael's sister? What were the chances?

"Okay. I'm here. Now, what did I miss?" Michael asked as he walked into the kitchen to join them.

Chris was just standing there watching Alyssa clean up after them. He wished he was busy doing something so he could get away with avoiding Michael. But he was the only one not doing anything, so it was on him to act like everything was fine.

"You didn't miss anything," Chris answered.

"Okay then go back and tell me about this person you're talking to. Seemed like I was walking in on a good story," Michael requested.

"Oh, you weren't missing much." He wanted to go back to the baby name subject, but there was no way he could leave out the fact that he was seeing a Mallory ... and that there was a good chance his Mallory was Michael's Mallory. "Your wife just can't get over the fact that I've gone out with someone a few times but I'm not sleeping with her."

Michael took a beer from the fridge and cracked it open. "Honestly, I can't really believe it either."

"Seriously?" Chris asked incredulously. "I know I joke around a lot, and have some crazy stories, but I'm really not that bad."

Michael handed Chris a beer. "I know you aren't. If I thought you were that bad there's no way I'd leave you alone with my wife."

"Listen, dickhead," Chris said, beginning to get annoyed. "She was my partner long before she was your wife."

"Don't get yourself all worked up," Michael said with a chuckle. "When do we get to meet her?"

Alyssa piped up from the other side of the kitchen. "I was thinking next Thursday. That's the last day we're all off before Vegas."

Chris felt the immediate need to get out of there. Somehow thirteen days was both too close and way too far away and he began to question that decision. He had to figure out a way to warn Mallory. It was his weekend to work, so he'd made tentative plans to meet her during her lunch break on Tuesday.

"Okay, Alyssa. You get some rest," Chris began his departure announcement. "You were saying how tired you were, so I don't want to keep you up. I know how hard it is to get caught up when you work nights. Thanks for dinner."

Chris could feel Michael burning a hole into the side of his face with his gaze. When he couldn't ignore it any longer, he turned and made eye contact. Chris wasn't afraid of Michael, but he wasn't someone he'd mess with if given the choice. They had only recently become more than friendly acquaintances to each other, and he really didn't want to do anything to ruin that. And this lie would definitely ruin that.

Once Alyssa turned around and watched the interaction between the two men, Chris could see her resolve begin to crumble. He tilted his head, silently pleading with Alyssa to bring Michael into their conversation.

"Um …" Alyssa began. "You should probably sit down for this."

"I'd rather stand," Michael countered.

"Okay … well …" she hesitated some more.

"Am I going to be pissed?"

"Probably," Chris answered. He knew he would be if the tables were turned.

Michael folded his arms across his chest and alternated his gaze between Alyssa and Chris. Chris could nearly hear his thoughts.

"Whoa, hold on," Chris jumped in with his hands up. "It's not anything to do with me and your wife. It's about the woman I've been seeing."

"What about her?" he demanded.

Chris looked to Alyssa for help, but all she did was shrug. Headfirst was the only way he could dive off that cliff. "We think she might be your sister Sammy."

Michael staggered before leaning against the countertop. "You, what? Explain. And explain quickly."

Chris and Alyssa went through all the details and what led them to believe Mallory was his sister Sammy. His expression became more and more grim as they spoke. By the time they'd finished, he was leaning with his back to the counter, his head back, and his eyes closed.

"You aren't dating my sister," he finally said.

"No, seriously, I'm pretty sure I am."

Michael opened his eyes and lowered his head to look straight at Chris. "What I meant was you may not date my sister. Is that clearer for you?"

Chris closed his eyes briefly as he reigned in his temper. He loved Alyssa like a sister and didn't want to fight with her husband. Michael had a few inches on him as far as height was concerned, but Chris spent more time at the gym. If a physical fight were to break out, it wouldn't be pretty.

"I'm going to head out," Chris said as he made his way to the door. "I really don't want to argue, because it won't stop there."

Chris pulled Alyssa into a brief hug before turning to leave. When he'd met Mallory, he had no idea who she was. Her blue eyes seemed familiar, but he didn't realize it was because they were nearly identical to those of his best friend's husband. He had to get the hell out of there. He made his way to the door and then to his car before Michael could stop him.

Chapter 6

MALLORY

"Why are you in such a rush to get out of here?" Doris asked as Mallory was rushing around to get everything finished on time.

"I'm just ready to go," Mallory answered.

By the time Mallory had everything cleaned up, both Jenna and Doris were standing in front of her. She tried to be as nonchalant as possible, but she had a hard time hiding how excited she was to spend time with Christian. They had set up a lunch date, but it was so busy, she didn't end up taking her entire half hour. After a quick cup of coffee, they made plans for dinner.

Just seeing him for those few minutes had melted her resolve. She would more than likely regret it at some point, but she was tired of fighting her feelings for him. All the time she'd spent in therapy was so she could stop to avoiding life. Her focus on wellness meant nothing if she couldn't even consider that happiness was a part of it.

"You're seeing him again, aren't you?" Jenna said with a pleased grin.

There was no use denying it. "Yes. We were supposed to have lunch together, but it turned into coffee because we were swamped."

Jenna and Doris high fived each other. "We knew it!" Doris said triumphantly. "You were in a rush to go on break and you're in a rush now. We've never seen you move so fast."

"You guys are the worst," Mallory said, unable to suppress her smile.

"Since your secret is out, why don't you give us the details? There's no use holding out on us now," Jenna said.

They headed out, leaving the hospital-wide lab techs to take over. Mallory didn't know how to explain her connection to Christian. They'd only been on one actual date, and they hadn't even kissed ... yet she felt like there was more to it.

"There isn't much to tell," she finally settled on. "We've seen each other a few times, but there's only been one actual date. But I think I like him ... gosh, I sound like a freaking teenager."

Jenna pulled her close once they reached the parking garage. "You don't sound like a teenager. You sound like someone who might have finally met her person. Have fun tonight!"

Jenna and Doris both walked off before Mallory could respond. She didn't think it was possible to know if a person was meant to be after seeing them just a few times. She also didn't believe in coincidences. She always took the first patient, but it could have been a sign that he wandered into her hospital on a whim.

As she was parallel parking in front of her house, her music was interrupted when her phone started ringing. Her heart sank when she saw Christian's name appear across the screen when she glanced at her phone, assuming he was calling to cancel. She maneuvered into the parking space before accepting the call.

"Hello?"

"Hey," he replied. His voice was even sexier over the phone. "Are you on your way to the restaurant?"

She knew it. He was calling to cancel. "Not yet. Traffic was a nightmare. I was just about to change clothes real quick. Do you need to cancel?"

"No," he answered quickly. "It's just that I forgot I was supposed to have dinner at my mom's house tonight."

Mallory was having a hard time guessing where he was going with the conversation. "Did you want to meet up after? I have work in the morning ..."

"No, I uh ..." he hesitated. "I actually wanted to see if you'd join me."

"What?"

"It's not as crazy as it sounds," he rushed on. "Mom cooks enough to feed an army of people. Me and my brother always had friends show up for dinner when we were teenagers and she never got out of the habit of cooking way more than we could eat. Her food is better than anything we'd get at the restaurant."

Mallory's mind raced as she tried to think of a response. The idea of a family dinner threw her into a panic. She had distanced herself from her own family for the sake of her mental health. After losing the family member she cherished most, she was determined to never repeat that experience. And when her dad was so quick to replace her mother and her brother didn't seem to care, she knew she'd be better off without them. As soon as she was old enough to go her own way, she did.

"Please?" Christian breathed. "I really want to see you. Those few minutes earlier today weren't enough. I picked up overtime, so I'm off tonight, tomorrow night, and then I work every night until next Thursday. It won't be awkward, I promise."

"Okay," she answered before her brain could catch up.

"Perfect. I'll text you the address. I'm here now, so whenever you're ready," he said before hanging up.

Mallory stared at her phone, the reality of the situation hitting her like a bucket of cold water. She didn't do family. She certainly didn't do family dinners. Eyes closed, she thought back to the things both her therapist and Dan had told her. She had to work through her past on her own schedule, but she shouldn't let it determine her present.

She took a deep breath and recited a couple of her favorite affirmations. "I inhale peace and exhale worry." Deep breath. "I am safe and in control." Another deep breath.

She repeated the sequence a few more times and was in a much better state of mind when she finally got out of her car and went inside. She could do it. Christian's family was not her family. Christian was not her abusive ex. If she wanted to leave the situation, she had no doubt Christian would let her.

Mallory double checked the address before parking the car and stepping out. The weather was that weird in between stage where one minute it felt warm, then it was cold the very next. She had decided on some loose-fitting black linen pants, a white fitted tee, and her favorite long black cardigan. The outfit would fit in for a casual dinner or a fancy one. It was really important to her that she make a good first impression. She told herself to relax before making her way up the walkway and to the front stoop.

The door opened before she even had a chance to knock. Christian grinned as he stepped outside to join her, closing the door behind himself. Dressed in a plain black tee and faded blue jeans, he looked sexier than ever. She'd seen him partially in uniform, in gym clothes, dressed up, and now casual. The dressed down casual look was her new favorite.

"Hey," he said as he pulled her into a quick embrace. "I'm so glad you came. You look amazing."

"Thank you ... are you sure this isn't weird? We barely even know each other and here I am meeting your mother."

"It's fine. Don't overthink this. My mom would feed the entire neighborhood if they let her," he reassured her.

He pulled her into another embrace. This time he didn't let go until she began to relax in his hold. The strong hug was exactly what she needed. She smiled up at him when he stepped back to look at her.

"Okay. Let's do this," Mallory said before grabbing hold of his elbow.

When they walked through the door, she was immediately greeted by the mouthwatering aroma of garlic, onions, and—she didn't recognize all of the scents that hit her, but her mouth really was watering.

"Come in! Come in!" An old woman stepped into the doorway of the kitchen and waved them inside. Her silver hair was pulled into a bun, and she was slightly hunched over in her simple green dress. "I hope you're hungry."

As they made their way to the kitchen, Mallory was shocked when the woman pulled her into a hug. "*Hermosa,*" the woman breathed as she looked Mallory up and down. "I'm so glad you could join us. Christian said he had dinner plans with you, and I insisted you join us. I've had the *pernil* cooking since early this morning. There's rice and peas, green beans, *platanos...* I can't eat all this food."

"Mom, this is Mallory. Mallory, this is my mom, Gloria Ramirez," Christian introduced.

Mallory immediately felt at ease. Christian's mother was older than she anticipated, but she was a dream. Her warmth was genuine. "It's so nice to meet you, Mrs. Ramirez. I'm glad Christian talked me into it."

"Mom, do you need any help with anything?" he asked as he pulled Mallory to his side.

"Don't pretend to be helpful now. You've been here for two hours but suddenly you're interested in helping me in the kitchen?"

Mallory looked up at Christian and started laughing at the incredulous expression on his face. "Really, Mom?"

Mrs. Ramirez started laughing and shooed them away from the kitchen. "The food will be ready in fifteen minutes. Why don't you two relax in the living room, and I'll call you when it's time to eat."

Christian took Mallory's hand and led her to the living room. The house was small. A large couch, a recliner, and television took up the entire space of the room. He took her to the couch where they both sat down.

"Thanks for coming. You definitely made my mom's day," Christian said has he entwined his fingers with hers.

The electric charge didn't go away just because they were in his mother's house. She did what she could to ignore it and suppress the shiver his touch caused. She turned her attention to the tattoo on his forearm. She'd been curious since she met him. Carefully, she ran the fingers of her free hand over it, ignoring his sharp intake of breath.

"What's this say?" she finally asked.

He looked over at her and she could see conflict cross his features. He let go of her other hand and covered the one gently tracing his tattoo. "It loses something in translation."

She watched his reaction. His usual confidence had begun to slip as soon as she asked him the question. Surely, she couldn't be the first person to ask about his tattoo. He looked down at his arm before looking back up and maintaining eye contact.

"Roughly translated, it says 'a lily never pretends, its beauty is that it is what it is.'"

Unexpectedly, her eyes brimmed with tears. She didn't know the significance of the quote, but she could feel how important it was to him. She wouldn't ask. He'd tell her when he was ready.

"That's beautiful," she murmured as she continued to look at the writing.

Christian placed a hand on her cheek and used his thumb to trace the path her unshed tears would have traveled. She felt his touch everywhere, causing her breath to hitch, despite her efforts to maintain control. When she looked up at him through her lashes, she found him watching her intently.

"You're beautiful," he breathed.

Christian's gaze moved from her eyes to her mouth. Her body stilled as he moved closer, the distance between them slowly disappearing. With her eyes closed, she only knew he was close when she felt his body heat surrounding her. She struggled to remember how to breathe. He repositioned his hand and held her in place as his mouth grazed hers. The kiss was gentle, and she wasn't sure if he was holding back because of her or because his mother was in the other room.

"Christian," she breathed against his mouth.

He tightened his grip and claimed her mouth. Her lips parted as she gasped in surprise, and he used the opportunity to slide his tongue into her mouth. Her sigh turned into a whimper as she eagerly kissed him back, her tongue twining with his. She wanted to feel his hands on her body, but she remembered his mother was right in the other room as he eased back, breaking the kiss.

"I'm sorry," he said softly. "I've been wanting to do that since day one."

Before she could return the sentiment, she heard his mother call them from the other room. "Dinner is ready! Come eat, before it gets cold!"

Christian stood and gripped Mallory's hand to help her up. Once she was standing, he maintained the grip on her hand and led her into the kitchen. His mother glanced at their joined hands, but she didn't say anything. She simply smiled and gave Christian a long look before inviting them to take a seat at the table.

Mrs. Ramirez rushed around the kitchen, placing mismatched serving dishes filled with food onto the table. The meal wasn't something Mallory would usually eat, but it looked and smelled amazing. Everything was so relaxed she nearly forgot about her nerves.

He gave her thigh a quick squeeze under the table before he picked up her plate and served up small amounts of everything. She glanced up in time to catch his mom smiling warmly at them from across the table.

"Everything looks amazing, thank you, Mrs. Ramirez," Mallory said when Christian set her plate down in front of her.

"I hope you like it. These are all of Christian's favorites."

"Mom," he groaned.

"What?" Mrs. Ramirez asked. "They are."

"Is today a special occasion?"

Mrs. Ramirez's smile widened. "No. But even though I see my Christian all the time, it's rare I get to have him over for dinner. He's so busy, you know. So, when I know he's coming I try to make it worth it. I always make plenty anyway, so I try to send him home with leftovers when I see him during the week."

Mallory felt a pang of sadness at their interaction. She wished she had a mother to make a fuss over her. The sadness of not having a mom was always there in the background, but watching Christian and his mother brought it up to the forefront.

"Do you have a big family, dear?"

And there it was. The question she'd been dreading. Aside from Dan, she usually kept people at just enough distance to not have to discuss her life story. When people did bring it up, she was pretty good at avoiding the details or telling a half truth. But she felt guilty even thinking about lying to Christian's mom.

"Oh, Mrs. Ramirez, you're about as bad as your son at picking questions," she said with a nervous laugh.

When Mrs. Ramirez creased her eyebrows in concern, Mallory rushed to explain. "It's nothing you said. When I was at dinner with Christian, he kept accidentally making the wrong small talk. It's okay. My mom died when I was in first grade. Dad remarried right away, so I have a brother and two stepsisters, but we aren't close."

"Oh, I'm so sorry about your mom. That must have been hard. You're always welcome here. Christian and his brother do a lot to help this old woman out. Mostly Christian," she said before pausing to look at her son. "But I love having a full house, so come visit anytime."

Mallory believed her. She usually struggled with feeling welcome, but she had no problem accepting everything Mrs. Ramirez said at face value. Even though it did make her feel better, she still missed having that connection of her own. Christian firmly squeezed her thigh as she was regaining control of her emotions. A sane person wouldn't cry over an open invitation to "come back any time". The firm touch on her thigh brought her back to the present, and after blinking several times she was able to return Mrs. Ramirez's smile with a fake one of her own.

"Are you okay?" she asked. "I didn't mean to upset you."

"I'm fine. Don't worry about me. I'm just glad I let Christian talk me into coming over. I needed this."

Mallory laid her hand on top of Christian's which was resting easily on her thigh. Everything she'd told his mom was the truth. If Christian hadn't talked her into coming over, then she would be up to her usual routine of spending time alone doing things to convince herself she was fine. Affirmations and manifestations had their place, but if she was honest with herself, she needed more.

"Are you ready for dessert?" Mrs. Ramirez asked, already clearing their plates away.

"Oh, I shouldn't," Mallory answered, patting her stomach. "I already ate more than I normally would because everything was so delicious."

"I made *arroz con leche*. At least try it. I'll fix Christian a bowl and give you a spoon, how about that? It's his favorite."

Mallory found herself giggling. Everything was Christian's favorite. If she didn't know any better, she'd think he was a bit of a mama's boy. Without much prompting she accepted the offer of an extra spoon. One taste of the rice pudding quickly turned into half of Christian's bowl. There was no question why it was his favorite. If he ever invited her over to his mom's for a meal again, it would be an automatic yes.

Christian turned to her with a playful grin as he watched her scrape the last bit from the bottom of the bowl. "Good?"

She put her spoon down after licking it clean. "Sorry. I guess that was a little more than a bite. That was so good I think I might move in."

Mrs. Ramirez laughed from behind her. "I told you; you are welcome anytime."

"Thank you. I might take you up on that. And not just for the food. I had an amazing time. Thank you so much."

"Do you need to get going?" Christian asked.

"I better. I have work in the morning."

Christian stood, and Mallory accepted his outstretched hand. Before they made it to the door, Mallory stopped to give his mom a hug. She'd already thanked her, so after the quick embrace she continued on to the door hand-in-hand with Christian. He walked her all the way to her car the same as he did at the restaurant.

"Thanks for coming," he said quietly.

"I'm glad you talked me into it. Thank you. I really did need this."

"Have breakfast with me Saturday morning? It'll be after I get off work, but I want to see you and that's the next time I'm free," he asked, watching her carefully.

Mallory tried not to let her disappointment show. She wanted to see him before Saturday. As unusual as it was, she was already getting used to him. Saturday seemed extremely far away. She had to remind herself that things were new, and Saturday was only four days away. Her feelings were ridiculous, and she knew it.

"Okay," she agreed. "Saturday morning."

When he brought his mouth to hers, she closed her eyes and surrendered her precious sense of control. His tongue teased at the seam of her lips which she willingly opened for him, sliding her tongue along his. His soft groan vibrated through her chest as he pulled her closer before breaking the kiss to rest his forehead against hers. She relaxed against him as they stood in silence.

"Saturday ..." he whispered, before pulling back to look at her.

"Saturday," she repeated, trying to read the emotion in his green eyes.

He opened the car door and waited for her to climb in, before carefully closing it. Same as he did at the restaurant.

Chapter 7

CHRISTIAN

"So, are we going to the gym Saturday?" James asked.

Christian and his partner were sitting down at a coffee shop between calls. It was a slow night, and they were both tired of sitting in the truck. Fortunately, there was a coffee shop near their post. Chris wished it was busier so the time would go quicker. There was nothing worse than sitting around watching the clock.

"Actually, I have plans," he answered.

"Plans?" James questioned. "Since when do you make plans on Saturday mornings?"

Chris knew James would give him shit. They almost always went to the gym on Saturdays after work. His mom never had doctor's appointments on Saturdays and if she needed to go to the store, it could always wait until later in the day. Especially since he could stay up when he didn't have work that night.

"I'm having breakfast with Mallory."

"I thought we decided that wasn't going to be a thing," Chris heard Michael say from behind him.

"We didn't," Chris said before quickly changing the subject. "You guys having a night like ours?"

Kathy walked in and pulled two chairs over while Michael made his way to the counter. "I refuse to answer that. I don't care if we don't use the Q word, I'm still not willing to risk it."

James was watching the interaction intently. He and his partner were close, but he wasn't exactly wanting to have that discussion in front of him. It felt wrong enough without someone else taking Michael's side. Besides, they weren't even certain there needed to be a discussion yet.

"Anyway," James continued, "I was hoping to finally make it over to join that new gym. You're seriously not going because of a breakfast date?"

Chris shrugged in response. There was nothing he could say that wouldn't encourage James to harass him. There wasn't much to say, period. He was skipping out on their gym day to have breakfast. No point in denying it.

"Damn," James said with a smirk. "She must be amazing in bed. This is certainly a first."

Kathy raised her brows and fixed her gaze behind Chris, and he knew without even turning around that Michael was standing behind him. It was a done deal. They were having the discussion.

Michael passed a cup over to Kathy before pulling a chair out and taking a seat. He set his cup down and folded his arms across his chest, looking at Chris expectantly. Michael didn't need to say a word. His rigid posture and furrowed brow said it all. While people who didn't know him often confused his usual demeanor as pissed off, Chris knew him well enough to know when he was actually angry; and he was angry.

"We talking about this here and now?" Chris asked.

Michael said nothing. He continued to stare Chris down.

"Guess we are ..." Chris said with a sigh. "First of all, I'm not sleeping with her, James. And Michael, what's the big deal? You and your sister don't even get along, so what do you care? If it's a problem, I don't have to bring her around."

"Sister?" James asked as soon as Chris stopped speaking. "You're dating his sister? I didn't even know he had a sister, but still. You're dating your old partner's sister-in-law. That's messy as hell."

Messy didn't even begin to cover it. He felt like he was being torn in half. Not coming clean to Mallory after she spent the evening with him at his mom's house made him feel like a complete asshole. He came close to telling her when he kissed her goodnight, but he'd chickened out. He had wondered for a bit if she could tell something was bothering him, but she hadn't said anything.

"You and my wife are practically siblings. Not bringing Sammy around would be basically impossible. Anyway, that's not the point. She's my sister."

"Sammy?" James asked, clearly confused. "I thought the girl you were seeing was Mallory."

"It's a long story," both Chris and Michael said at the same time.

Before the conversation could go any further, both Chris's and Michael's pagers beeped, followed by the scratchy sound of two different dispatchers speaking over the radios. Chris stepped outside to answer his radio where he could hear, and felt immediate relief upon walking outside.

"706 receiving, go ahead," he said into the radio.

"*706: respond to Kennedy Boulevard and North Main Street for the motor vehicle collision with entrapment. ALS was notified.*"

The others joined him as he keyed up the radio. "Received and responding."

"We'll finish this later," Michael said as he walked past.

"Let me guess," Chris said once they climbed into their truck to head to the call. "They are our ALS?"

James chuckled and pointed at the side mirror where they could clearly see Michael and Kathy following behind in their ambulance. Chris wasn't known to avoid confrontation, but getting into it with his best friend's husband was not at the top of his list of fun things to do.

They pulled on scene to find the police and fire department already there. It appeared to be a two-vehicle accident. The driver's side of one car was up against the Jersey barrier while the front end of the other car was smashed into the passenger side, making it impossible to get to the patient.

"Is there a second patient somewhere?" Chris asked as they approached a police officer. "I see the woman entrapped, but what about the other car?"

"Stolen car. It was empty when we got here," the officer answered, shaking his head.

They made their way over to where the fire department was busy working to get the woman out. They had somehow managed to place a collar on her, but the way her body was wedged against the door, it would be tough to get any vital signs before they got her out.

"What do we have?" Michael asked a firefighter from over Chris's shoulder.

Chris rolled his eyes, knowing for certain Michael was being petty after their discussion had been cut short. It wasn't like him to jump in and take over for no reason. Chris just kept his mouth shut and waited to hear the response from the firefighter.

"Thirty-five-year-old female. She's conscious and alert. She keeps complaining about her leg and her back. They're working on cutting the top of the car off, so if we must, we can pull her up, out, and over the Jersey barrier. If the wrecker gets here soon, we'll move it to cut the door off."

Michael turned to Chris and smirked at him. "You better grab your K.E.D., it's not looking good for a rapid extrication."

"I'll grab it," James spoke up before Chris had a chance to walk away.

"I'll grab our med bag, just in case," Kathy announced before leaving Michael and Chris alone.

"As I was saying," Michael began once again, "I don't want you dating my sister and me and her not getting along has nothing to do with it. Even though we don't talk, I don't want her getting hurt."

Chris turned to face him, surprised that he wanted to continue the conversation as if they weren't on a scene. "I'm not going to hurt her."

"You sleep with everyone. She's had enough heartbreak in her life. Last thing she needs is to fall for you and then you get bored and move on."

Chris was about maxed out on patience. His temper was being contained by one last thread of control. Going off on Michael wouldn't help anything, so he walked away to check on the patient.

"Ma'am, you doing okay?" he asked through the missing back passenger window.

"Yeah. Just my back and my leg really hurt. Get me out of here."

Chris hated that Michael was right. It was sounding like they were going to need to clean the dust off the Kendrick Extrication Device that James had just tossed on top of the backboard on top of the stretcher. That was one of those things they had to do training on every year, but almost never used it. It was a pain in the ass, took forever, and rarely caused a better outcome than rapid extrication which was easier and much quicker in most cases. Unfortunately, it was looking like they'd be lifting her from the roof of her car.

"Alyssa told me you claim my sister is different," Michael said as he carried the K.E.D. over and handed it to Chris. "How? And I think you're going to have to climb the barrier to get to her."

Chris's irritation quickly turned to amusement. Michael had always been a man of few words. He was obviously flustered by everything going on. Chris never knew him to pursue a conversation that the other person wasn't interested in having. Regret began to creep in as he put himself into Michael's shoes. Chris only had a brother, but if he did have a sister it would probably throw him for a loop if someone he was friends with wanted to date her. Especially if that friend was known for sleeping around.

Chris set the K.E.D. on the trunk of the car in order to free up his hands to climb over the barrier without ruining his uniform. Once on the other side, he leaned on it and faced Michael. He couldn't do anything until the roof was off of the car anyway, so might as well finish what they started.

"She's different. Just trust me on this, please. Everything so far has been different. I was telling the truth when I said we aren't sleeping together, and she's been to my mom's house for dinner. I've only ever brought one other person over to meet my mom. She's different," Chris patiently explained.

Before Michael could respond, one of the firefighters got their attention. "You guys are up. Watch the edges."

James joined Chris on the other side of the Jersey barrier so they could secure the patient and get her out of the car. Even with both of them being tall, they ended up having to kneel on the concrete barrier and lean against what was left of the car in order to slip the K.E.D. behind her and strap her in. The device was made to slide behind a seated patient with part of it wrapping around the torso and several straps that would immobilize their spine while they remained in a seated position. It wasn't an easy task.

Together, Chris and James secured the woman to the device. After re-checking for movement and sensation of her extremities, they called a few firefighters over to give them a hand. Even with the top half of the car removed, they still had to lift her up and over in order to clear the barrier. Kathy and Michael stood waiting at the stretcher which was right on the other side of the barrier. Two of the firefighters climbed into the car to lift from the inside.

"On your count, James," Chris directed.

At the count of three, they lifted the woman up and out as smoothly as possible and placed her onto the stretcher. After unhooking the leg straps, they went on to straighten her out on the board.

"My leg!" she shouted as soon as they moved to straighten her legs.

Without wasting any time, they moved her to the ambulance where they could cut her clothes off to examine her injuries. Chris did a quick head to toe assessment while James started cutting her clothes. She yelled out again when he got to her right thigh, and he noted slight deformity beneath the swelling.

"Looks like a femur fracture," Chris said to Michael with a nod toward the patient's leg.

"Kathy, get an order for pain management. We need to set that leg," Michael said.

"Set my leg?" the woman asked. "That's going to hurt. Just take me to the hospital."

Chris glanced at the monitor and knew they were going to have to set her leg no matter what. Her blood pressure hadn't fallen drastically, but it was slightly lower than when they first took it. Chris continued his assessment and didn't find anything else major.

"They're going to have to, ma'am. But don't worry, they'll give you the good stuff," Chris joked in reference to the narcotics the paramedics were getting an order for. "And I wouldn't suggest the bumpy ride to the hospital without us stabilizing that leg."

Chris felt his phone vibrating in his pocket, but it would have to wait. "I need to get under that bench if you want to use the Hare traction splint," he said to Michael.

After rearranging everything to get to the also rarely used Hare traction splint, Chris measured it against her good leg and got everything prepared while Michael started an IV and ran fluids. Kathy stepped back into the truck as she was ending the phone call, and James stepped out to make space.

"Okay we've got the order," Kathy announced as Michael was opening the med box. "I'll push the narcs if you want to help Chris."

Chris's phone vibrated again as soon as they started setting her leg. Of all times for someone to call him instead of sending a text. He was pretty sure he knew who would be calling him, and it could wait until he finished up with his patient. She whimpered a bit but didn't cry out the way she did when they first moved her. Between the pain meds and the relief felt once the leg was properly positioned, he expected her to be feeling better before they started transporting her to the hospital.

It didn't take long to transfer the patient over to the staff since they had transported to the hospital up north which was never as busy as the other trauma center. It was rare that they used that hospital, but the accident had been at the very north end of their coverage area. His thoughts went to Mallory, and how it was too bad they worked opposite shifts, since it would be nice to be able to stop over to the lab for a quick hello.

He felt like he was losing his mind when every other thought brought him back to Mallory. He finished up his chart before making his way back to the truck. As he was pulling the stretcher through the automatic doors, he pulled his phone out to see who'd been calling him. Instead of seeing "Liliana" appear in his missed calls, he saw his brother's name. His brother rarely called him. Before he could call him back, he stepped aside for a crew bringing in a patient. One glance at the stretcher and his blood went cold.

Chapter 8

MALLORY

Mallory was so glad it was finally Friday. She still had one more day before she would see Christian, but at least she was closer. And Friday nights always went fast because of her standing dinner date with Dan. She adjusted the passenger seat and turned on her heated seat inside Dan's car.

"Seriously? You know winter is over, right?" Dan commented, giving her major side eye.

"Yeah, I know what today's date is. But it's chilly out and these scrubs are thin. Not everyone gets to go to work wearing jeans and designer sweaters every day."

"Hey, it's not my fault they don't want me looking too formal or doctor-y. Sounds to me like you should have opted for a program that takes a bit longer than phlebotomy, then maybe you'd get to pick out your own clothes."

"First of all, 'doctor-y' isn't a word," Mallory pointed out. "And second: you're a dick."

"Why am I a dick for pointing out things you already knew?"

Dan pulled into a parking space and stepped out of the car before quickly making his way to the other side to open the door for Mallory. She accepted his offered hand and stepped out. Their short commute was drawing to a close. Mallory waved and Dan did a tilt of his head as a response.

Once again, she hadn't grabbed anything to snack on from home, so she decided to pick up a bran muffin from the coffee stand. She always woke up with enough time to do a few deep breathing exercises and say her morning affirmations, but never enough time to get herself organized. She was a walking contradiction, riddled with anxiety despite all of her calming rituals. She was both independent and insecure, craving validation but needing no one. She contemplated her quirks as she stepped up to order her muffin.

She turned with her small paper bag in hand and walked face first into a solid mass of muscle. Startled, she looked up to meet a pair of haunted green eyes, rimmed with red and surrounded by dark circles. Familiar eyes. She bent down to pick up the bag she dropped before standing to get a better look at Christian.

"Christian?" she whispered. "Are you okay? What are you doing here?"

He blinked much longer than was necessary, and when he opened his eyes, the redness was more noticeable. "My mom is here."

Her heart sank. She stuffed the muffin bag into her tote and took both of his hands in hers. "I'm so sorry. Is she okay?"

His large hands squeezed hers as he shook his head no. She pulled him over to a nearby bench and indicated for him to sit down beside her. Sensing he needed comfort, she pulled him into her arms and squeezed him as tight as she was able. Her own breath hitched when she felt him take several deep uneven breaths.

"She fractured her hip. She didn't want to leave the bag of trash on the porch until I could take it out for her, so she tried to do it on her own. She missed the first step and fell."

Mallory didn't think her heart could sink any lower, but there it was. She immediately pictured the sweet old woman lying on the ground in pain. "I'm so sorry."

"But Life Alert is for old people," Christian scoffed. "She stayed on the sidewalk until a neighbor heard her cries for help."

"My god," Mallory breathed, fighting back her own tears. "Is your brother here with you?"

Christian swiped away the wetness under his eyes and shook his head. "He's over the road. He can't just drop everything to get here. I'm with her so she isn't alone. He's going to finish his current trip and as long as Mom doesn't have any complications, he'll be back next weekend, which is still a week early."

"I meant for you. You shouldn't be alone. I'm going to tell them I'm not working today."

Christian straightened in his seat, obviously surprised. "You don't have to do that."

"I know. Give me five minutes; I'll be right back," she said and rushed toward the lab without waiting for an argument.

She'd made it from the coffee shop to the lab in record time. It was now only a few minutes before her shift began, which was unusual for her. Doris was setting up her section and her facial expression quickly changed from surprise to concern as Mallory approached.

"Are you okay?" she asked.

"No," she answered before correcting herself. "I mean yes, but I need the day off."

Doris raised an eyebrow and waited for her to continue. Before she could explain, Jenna had joined them, never one to miss any action. Mallory closed her eyes and braced herself for the barrage of questions that would be headed her way.

"The other night I had dinner at Christian's mom's house," she started to explain, holding up a hand when Jenna tried to interrupt. "She's the sweetest old lady on the planet. Anyway, I literally ran into Christian at the coffee shop a few minutes ago. She had a bad fall and broke her hip. His brother is an over the road truck driver, so he's here alone. Someone should be with him."

"And that someone needs to be you," Jenna said as soon as Mallory had finished. "You didn't tell us you met his mom. That's huge!"

"I'll put you in for PTO. I can pull one of the other lab techs and dedicate them to the outpatient lab. Let me know if you need Monday off," Doris said, practically shoving her out of the lab and allowing the doors to close behind her.

Mallory stood in the hallway slightly stunned. She didn't expect it to be so easy to get the day off. She didn't even get a chance to say anything else about it once they knew why she needed off. After taking a moment to regain her bearings, she rushed back to the coffee stand.

Christian was where she'd left him, only now he held a cup of coffee. His eyes widened slightly as he looked up at her.

"That was fast."

"As soon as I told them why I needed the day off without notice, Doris literally shoved me out the door after telling me I could have Monday off too, if I needed it. I thought it would be a problem since we're supposed to give at least two hours' notice when we call out."

"Well, thank you. You didn't have to do that," Christian said.

Mallory took note of how tired he looked. It wasn't long after his shift would have ended, but he looked as if he'd been up for days. His hair, slightly longer on top, was rumpled instead of the carefully styled waves she had become used to seeing.

"Do you need to get back to your mom?"

"She's in surgery. Should be another hour or so, but I guess we should get back in case something goes wrong, and the doctors come looking for me."

Christian stood and took the hand she offered as they made their way to the other side of the hospital. They rode the elevator in silence before Christian led the way to a small room. The words "family room" caused her to stop in her tracks. She didn't have many memories surrounding her mother's death, but the family room would forever be engraved into her mind. She'd stared at that sign while her dad held her brother with one arm and held her hand with the other while the doctor explained things using words she didn't understand before ushering them into the room.

"Are you alright?"

Mallory looked away from the sign to find Christian watching her closely. She wasn't alright, but she couldn't fall apart. Not when the whole reason she was there was to support Christian. Even though she already knew that at some point she would have to face the things she'd been avoiding, it didn't make it any easier. She took a slow breath.

"Don't worry about me. Are you okay?"

Christian brought them to the far corner of the small room. Wooden chairs with blue vinyl cushions were situated in groups spaced throughout the room. Mallory knew all too well that the spacing was for the illusion of privacy. No one wanted to be surrounded by strangers when receiving the worst news of their life.

"I'm doing okay. Are you ready to answer my question, now?" he asked as they got situated on one of the larger bench style seats.

"Yes. I'm doing alright. This room just reminded me of when my mom died. I wasn't expecting the memory to hit me the way it did. I don't think of that day very often. But your mom is going to be okay," she quickly added.

She looked up to find Christian watching her with a small smile. She always had been good at putting her foot in her mouth. What was she thinking, telling him this room was associated with death. She silently berated herself and tried to think of a way to change the subject.

"Don't beat yourself up," Christian said, as if reading her mind. "I expected this to be hard for you. That's why I said you don't have to do this. To be here with me."

Mallory looked over at the man sitting next to her. He was thinking of her when he clearly had more important things to worry about. She had never had that before. It was time she got over herself and actually let him past some of her walls.

"My mom was the best. She was the room mom in school. She volunteered at every opportunity and made sure all the special class activities went on without a hitch. She told me a bedtime story every night and woke me up saying something inspirational," Mallory said with a wistful smile.

"And that's where you get your affirmations and manifestations." Christian leaned over to bump her shoulder with his.

"I never really thought about it until now, but yeah. I guess I did get that from her. One night she was gone, and everything changed. My dad's a cop and not very good at warm and fuzzy. Fast forward thirty something years. I finally saw a therapist because my life was falling apart. She suggested, among other things, that I try meditation and reciting some affirmations. I was hooked. Next came manifestations and a general path of mindfulness," she continued. "I'm sorry. I didn't mean to make this about me."

"What happened to your mom? If you don't mind me asking," Christian asked, completely ignoring her apology.

"Pulmonary embolism. She was young and healthy. This was before doctors associated PE with certain birth control. By the time they caught it, it was too late. I remember standing in front of this room with my dad as the doctor explained that she was extremely sick, and they'd be back soon with an update."

Christian squeezed her hand. She was surprised by the words that spilled out. She usually clammed up anytime someone asked her about her mom. As the queen of avoidance, she was an expert at saying just enough before changing the subject. Christian appeared to be fighting an internal battle as his eyes searched her face, and she began to worry she'd said too much.

"Thanks for being here. You have any of those affirmations handy? She's been in there a while and ... well ... I'm struggling," Christian admitted.

Mallory's chest felt tight as she imagined what he was going through. "Okay. Close your eyes. I'll say one of my favorites, and you can join me if you want."

Christian took a deep breath and licked his lips before he closed his eyes, giving her a small nod. She reached for his hand and took a few cleansing breaths of her own. It was one thing to say her affirmations when she was alone, and something totally different to say them aloud in public. Christian was sure to think she was crazy, but she forced herself out of her comfort zone. It was worth it if it helped him.

"I will get through today," she said softly. "I open my soul to peace."

She squeezed his hand and paused before repeating the phrase. Before she repeated it for a third time, she felt Christian squeeze her hand. His voice was so soft she nearly missed it. He recited the words along with her three more times. On the last one, his voice cracked with emotion. She opened her eyes to find his eyes, now a mixture of dark green and blue, glistening with moisture as he watched her carefully.

"Thank you," he breathed before closing his eyes and leaning closer to her.

She repositioned herself so he could rest his head on her shoulder. He must have been exhausted. Warmth spread throughout her chest as he relaxed against her, his breathing growing more even. She ran her fingers through his already mussed hair, and before long she could tell he was asleep.

CHRISTIAN

Chris opened his eyes when he felt Mallory giving his shoulder a gentle shake. He wasn't sure how long he'd been asleep, but his neck was stiff. He stretched his neck from side to side before coming fully awake to notice the doctor sitting in a chair across from them. She still had on her surgical cap and her mask was hanging down by her chest. She smiled warmly once he finally met her eye.

"Mr. Ramirez, I'm Dr. Smith. I'm part of the surgical team working on your mom. They are finishing up, but everything went well. Because of where the breaks were, we decided to do a replacement. She'll have a better outcome than if we were to have to go back in and do it. The recovery will be slower, but I'm confident she'll return to her previous level of mobility with proper care and physical therapy."

He felt Mallory give his thigh a supportive squeeze which reminded him it was his turn to speak. "When can she come home?"

"Well," the doctor hesitated. "I'm not the physician in charge, but I would suggest she go to a rehab facility for a while."

"I'm not putting my mom in a nursing home."

"Not a nursing home. A facility that will offer her the care as well as the physical therapy she needs. Once she's situated in her room, you'll be able to see her, and a social worker can come up and explain your options once she's awake."

With that, the doctor gave him a quick pat on the shoulder and then turned to leave. He was supposed to make a major decision about his mother all on his own. He ran his hands through his hair as he tried to figure out what to do. The thought of his mom in a nursing home gave him a cold chill he couldn't seem to shake.

"Call your brother," Mallory suggested. "You'll feel better if you run it by him. You don't need to carry this by yourself."

"I'd rather call him after I see her. He's not going to want to know what the doctor's said as much as he'll want to know how she's feeling."

Mallory put her arm around him and rubbed his back. Her warm touch was the soothing contact he needed. She had managed to become more important to him than any woman had in years, and yet he was keeping things from her that she may never forgive him for. He needed to tell her, and soon. If he continued to wait, he knew the line between not saying anything and purposely withholding information would be crossed.

"I need to call more than just my brother," he said after a long sigh.

Mallory watched him warily, as if she could tell whatever was about to come next wasn't going to be easy to hear. Her brow was creased with worry, and her blue eyes watched him carefully. Her arm went still behind his back, but she rubbed his thigh with her other hand.

"What is it?" she asked when the silence grew longer than was comfortable.

"I have to call my daughter and tell her about her *abuela*."

Mallory flinched. She removed her hands from his body and squinted as a mixture of hurt and confusion crossed her features. "You have a daughter?"

"She's thirteen and the reason behind my tattoo. Her name is Liliana. Lily for short."

Chris sat still as Mallory stood and began pacing the room. He felt like shit dropping the news on her the way he did, but if things were serious enough that she was sitting with him in the hospital waiting room, he couldn't keep things from her.

"She lives in Florida with her mom. My ex-wife." He closed his eyes for the last part, unable to watch her reaction.

"Jesus, Christian," she said, releasing her hair from her ponytail. "I know we've only seen each other a few times, but I would think an ex-wife and a daughter would be something you mention in the beginning."

Chris stood and closed the distance between them. With both hands on her shoulders, he turned her to face him. "I wasn't keeping it from you, I swear. I wanted to tell you when you asked about the tattoo, but it I didn't want to have that conversation with my mom right there."

"But you were okay kissing me with your mom right there."

He ran a hand through his hair as he tried to come up with a way to explain things. "I've never had to have this conversation before, I'm sorry."

"What do you mean? Oh my God, you aren't still married, are you?" She twirled the ponytail holder around her fingers as she waited for him to explain.

"No. Of course not. We've been divorced for nearly ten years. I just haven't been serious with anyone since. You probably would have met her at my mom's house if Vivian hadn't moved her to Florida."

He stopped talking and attempted to gauge her reaction. She hadn't left, so that was a good sign. Chris imagined her mentally reciting something about accepting peace as he watched her take several slow breaths. She opened her eyes and folded her arms, obviously waiting for him to go on.

"I'm not some dead-beat-dad. We shared custody until she moved. Now I get her a few weeks over the summer and every other holiday. Like I said, I've never needed to have this conversation before. I'm sorry I'm screwing this up. I'm worried about my mom and I'm going to have to break the news to my daughter that she won't be able to come here this summer because my mom can't watch her while I work," he said with an exasperated sigh. "And I have to tell her that Mom had surgery. Everything is fucked up."

Mallory put her arms around him and held him tight. Once again, her firm hold instantly calmed him down. He assumed she knew from experience how to calm someone down who felt like everything was falling apart, because she knew what to do without him saying a word. She did things that he wouldn't even know to ask for. As a person who seemed to crave closeness, he wondered how she managed to be without her family.

"Mr. Ramirez?" a nurse called from the doorway. "I'll take you to your mother's room."

They followed the nurse down the long corridor and around the corner past a nurses' station before stopping in front of a room. "She's sleeping, but we got her to wake up and respond to us before bringing her to her room. She should be waking up again soon. Are you both family?"

"Yes," Chris answered without hesitation. He knew the truth would keep Mallory from being able to stay with him.

"Well, you are welcome to sit with her. Visiting hours end at nine. Feel free to talk. Hearing your voice might help her to come the rest of the way out of the anesthesia quicker."

He took Mallory's hand, and they sat in the only two chairs in the room. His mom looked comfortable despite the oxygen going to her nose and everything she was connected to that monitored her vital signs. He was relieved to see her breathing on her own. He released Mallory's hand and moved his chair close enough to hold his mom's fragile hand in both of his.

"Family, huh?" Mallory asked once the nurse left them alone in the room.

"I didn't want her to kick you out."

Her lips curved into a small smile. "I used to think of family as a bad word ... but now I kind of like the sound of it. I have your mom to thank. One dinner at her house and I wanted to be a part of it."

"She does have that way about her, doesn't she? That's probably why my friends spent more time at my house than they did their own. I'm sorry you didn't have that growing up."

Mallory leaned back in the chair and chewed her bottom lip. "Actually, I kind of did. I was just too angry to appreciate it. They acted like Mom never existed."

"Tell them."

Chris and Mallory both looked up at the sound of his mom's soft voice. She had managed a weak smile and was looking back and forth between the two of them.

"Mom. You're awake. Tell who what?"

"Mallory. Tell your family how you feel," his mom said. She was so quiet they had to strain to hear her.

"It's too late now," Mallory answered quietly. "Enough about me. How are you feeling?"

"It's never too late," she said before closing her eyes and drifting off to sleep.

Chapter 9

MALLORY

"Well, that's it," Mallory said after giving Christian a tour of her apartment.

She had convinced him not to go home alone, and there was no way she was inviting herself over to his place. When his mom woke up, she had all but kicked them out. She insisted they get out of there to get some rest. Looking over at Christian, he did look exhausted. He would be, having worked most of a night shift and then staying at the hospital only taking an occasional cat nap.

"I like it. It's very you."

Mallory tried to look at her place from his point of view. Everything was light and airy. White curtains hung in the windows, neutral tan and cream throws were draped across the furniture. Plants lined every windowsill.

"I hope that's a good thing. Once my ex left and I got back on my feet, the first thing I did was make this place feel more like home."

Christian leaned against the kitchen counter and studied her for a moment before he spoke. "Well, I like it and I'm glad you talked me out of going home. I really wouldn't have been in a good place."

"Just like your mom opened her house up to me, you are always welcome here. I'm sure you're tired. I'll cook something. Feel free to relax or get some sleep. I don't have anywhere to be. There's a full bath connected to my bedroom if you want to take a shower."

"You don't mind?"

She stepped closer to him and placed both hands on his shoulders. When he looked down at her, she was able to see the exhaustion written all over his face. His eyes drooped and the dark circles were pronounced.

"How could I possibly mind anything about you being in my apartment? I hope you don't mind using my bedroom since I don't keep the spare room made up. Take a shower. I'll fix you something to eat," she said before standing on her toes to give him a quick kiss.

As soon as their lips met, he wrapped his arms around her and held her in place as he deepened the kiss. She had intended on giving him a chaste kiss before sending him on his way, but her body betrayed her. Her nipples hardened when he eased his tongue into her mouth, making gentle swipes along hers, causing a groan to vibrate through her.

He pulled back just enough to break the kiss. "Shower. I should take a shower."

"Right," she whispered. "Shower."

She missed his touch as soon as he unwrapped himself from her arms and made the slow walk to her bedroom. It took everything in her to keep from following him. After clearing her head with a quick shake, she opened her pantry and took out a box of organic spaghetti and a jar of organic sauce. It was cheating, but she always kept quick items on hand so she could still eat relatively clean even when she was short on time. Hopefully Christian wouldn't mind ground turkey in place of ground beef.

She had just finished adding diced tomatoes and onions to the sizzling pan of ground turkey when she heard her door open. It wasn't until she whipped around to find Dan walking in with a bottle of red wine that she remembered it was Friday night.

"It's Friday," she squeaked out.

He had texted her that he would be getting off work late and she told him she had a ride home. She hadn't even told him everything that had happened that day. As far as he knew, she'd worked her normal shift.

"You forgot. I should be hurt." He put his hand over his heart for added effect, but his smile gave him away.

"Today has been a day. I didn't even go to work."

"What are you talking about? I drove you there," Dan asked as he placed the wine on the counter and reached for two glasses.

Before she could explain, she heard her bedroom door open. They both turned to find Christian walking out wearing nothing but a pair of black boxer briefs and a fitted white t-shirt, towel drying his wet hair. Mallory's mouth went dry, and she nearly forgot Dan was standing next to her. Christian froze when he looked up, obviously surprised to see they were not alone.

"Why, hello there," Dan greeted, breaking the silence.

"I forgot it was Friday," Mallory said in an attempt at explaining why Dan was there.

"I'm Dan. I live downstairs," Dan continued since words had failed Mallory. "We have dinner every Friday night. But since you guys clearly have other plans, I had better get back to my own apartment."

"No, it's not what it looks like. I needed a shower and the only clothes I had with me are the emergency items I keep in my bag that go along with the spare uniform always hanging in my car." Hurt flashed across his eyes. "I can throw on the clothes I took off and get out of your way."

Mallory was still stuck in her freeze response. Inviting him over on a whim was out of her comfort zone. Having Dan see him half naked as their first introduction was a whole different level. As much as she teased Dan about walking in on something, she should have been able to take it in stride, but she wasn't. Her heart was racing for a completely different reason than it had just a few minutes earlier, and her skin prickled as she broke out into a sweat just imagining how angry Christian might be over the entire situation.

"No. Stay. Don't mind her, she's not great with surprises, and me catching you like this is definitely a surprise," Dan, a true godsend, continued to explain. "I probably shouldn't go into detail, but when she was going through a rough time, we started having dinner every Friday night as a way to check in. And it became our thing. I wish I knew you were going to be here. I would have invited Ian, and it could have been a double date."

Mallory finally broke free of her panic and found her voice. "Please stay. Both of you. It's my fault for forgetting it was Friday. I'm so sorry."

Christian, apparently sensing her panic, made his way over to her and put his arms around her. "It's okay, I was just surprised. You don't have to apologize. It's been a crazy day."

"I'll grab you something to throw on. I'll be right back," Dan said before disappearing from her apartment.

Mallory returned to the stove to stir the food before it burned. Her cleansing breaths did nothing, so she closed her eyes and recited a few of her trusty affirmations. It was a struggle to keep the memories at bay. Her ex would have been furious if he was caught in any situation that could be embarrassing. Not Aiden. Aiden was just a place holder who couldn't hurt her since she didn't have any deep feelings for him. The ex who put her in such a dark place? He would have made sure she paid for her error. Christian came up behind her and wrapped his arms around her, placing a kiss on the back of her neck. It was his touch that began to bring her out of her thoughts.

"You're shaking," Christian whispered.

She didn't realize her reaction had been as strong as it was. It had been a long time since she was hit with the bad memories. "I just can't believe I let that happen. I should have told Dan not to come. I'm so sorry you were put in that situation."

Christian held her tighter and kissed her shoulder. "You think no one has seen me in my underwear before? It's not a big deal. I'm fine. We're fine. I'm not upset about it."

"Even if he was checking you out?" Mallory asked, her voice rising as she began to panic all over again.

Christian laughed. "Stop getting yourself worked up. In case you haven't noticed, I'm very comfortable with myself. As long as I don't have to worry about him checking *you* out, we're good."

Her muscles finally began to relax. He massaged her neck as if he could sense her tension, which helped to further relieve her stress. She closed her eyes and leaned into his touch just before her door swung open.

"Here you go," Dan said, walking a direct path to Christian. "Some sweatpants."

They weren't just any sweatpants. They were gray sweatpants. Dan gave her a wink as soon as Christian turned his back to go change. Mallory waited until her bedroom door closed before she spoke to Dan.

"Really? Gray sweatpants? You might as well have let him walk around in his underwear," Mallory whisper shouted.

Dan shrugged, then took a third wine glass from the cabinet and filled each of them. "It's all I could find that might fit him."

Mallory, already feeling better about the entire situation, pointed her finger at Dan. "You are a liar, and you know it. He's here for me, so no checking him out."

Christian rejoined them in the kitchen, and the sweatpants were even more distracting than she thought they'd be. Between the fitted tee and the gray sweats that left nothing to the imagination, Mallory was struggling to have coherent thoughts, let alone speak actual words.

"What smells so good?" Christian asked before removing the lid from the pot of sauce and looking inside.

Dan's eyes were as wide as saucers as he watched the exchange. He took his wineglass to the kitchen island and made it a point to look from Christian to Mallory, no doubt waiting for her reaction. Mallory hated it when anyone got into her space while she was cooking, and Dan knew it. He had learned that even as her best friend, he was not allowed to interfere with any of the cooking process.

Mallory snatched the lid from Christian's hand and closed the pot. "Excuse me, sir. Hands off."

Christian's mouth curved into a smirk that she could only describe as devilish. Even though she suspected he was up to something, she was still caught by surprise when his hands gripped her waist, and he pulled her against him.

"Hands off everything? Or just what's on the stove?" His breath tickled her neck as he spoke.

"The food," Mallory managed to respond, ignoring the heat blossoming from her core.

Goosebumps spread across her flesh from the close contact. Even though he'd showered with her bodywash, she was surrounded by his masculine scent, and she wanted nothing more than to get close enough to be consumed by it. Remembering that they weren't alone, she turned and gave him a quick kiss, effectively dismissing him so she could finish cooking without either ruining the meal or embarrassing herself in front of Dan.

She was aware of Dan and Christian sitting at the table having a quiet conversation as she boiled the pasta and tossed some garlic bread into the oven. It didn't take long to finish cooking the meal, but by the time they sat down to eat she was able to relax and enjoy the fact that Christian and Dan seemed to be getting along. Crisis averted.

CHRISTIAN

Chris tried not to stare while Mallory was bent over the dishwasher adding their dinner dishes. She had refused his help telling him no guest was allowed to do any chores their first time over. Doing dishes sucked, so he wasn't about to argue. Plus, she'd taken a shower and changed into a tank top and some tiny shorts. He hoped she would bend over just a little further so he could get a glimpse of heaven.

"Have you heard from your brother?" Mallory asked while she dried her hands on a dish towel.

"Yeah. He said to keep him posted."

As an owner-operator, Robbie was able to park his truck and fly home if he had to, but it wasn't a simple thing if he had a load. They were counting on his mom to remain stable. Doctors were hesitantly optimistic. Chris still wasn't completely comfortable leaving her bedside, but she was right. He was exhausted.

"And your daughter?" Mallory had made her way over to him and seemed nervous to ask about her.

"Yeah. She's worried, of course. I explained that I would need to figure things out for her summer visit. Even if I use up all my PTO, I'm not sure I'll be able to get all those days off in a row. My ex is the one giving me shit about it, but that's no surprise." He looked up to find Mallory watching him closely. "I'm sorry. You didn't ask all that, did you?"

"Just because I didn't ask doesn't mean I don't want to know. I'm just trying to figure out how to navigate this. My piece of shit ex was the only serious relationship I've been in. We weren't married and have no kids so he's a non-issue. And I've never dated anyone with kids," Mallory sat beside him and looked down at her hands as she spoke. "What I'm trying to say is, I don't want to overstep."

Chris covered her hands with his. She looked up at him, her blue eyes a sea of uncertainty behind dark lashes. Without hesitation, he cupped her face and gently stroked her cheek with his thumb. A soft sigh escaped her lips as she closed her eyes and leaned into his touch.

"You could never overstep. I'm pretty sure that possibility ended today."

He wasn't sure when the change happened, but it felt silly to behave as though they had just started seeing each other, even though they had. The strange part wasn't that they'd apparently skipped the stage where things were new, it was that he wasn't bothered by it. Like Mallory, he'd only had one serious relationship, and that was with his ex-wife. Since then, he avoided them. But with Mallory, he wanted more.

"Stay the night."

Chris was torn. There was nothing he wanted more than to fall asleep with her in his arms. His discussion with Michael flashed before him. He was honestly able to deny sleeping with Mallory. He wasn't sure he'd be able to stay over and that still be the case. He also had to think about the fact that he was keeping things from her. She'd taken the news about Liliana in stride. She wasn't happy that he hadn't told her, but she was understanding. He wouldn't get that lucky twice. Finding out his best friend was married to her brother would be a different story.

"Please?" she prompted when he didn't give an answer.

"I really shouldn't," he hesitated.

"What are we doing here?" she asked. "I know we've skipped past acquaintances, but what does that mean? If you haven't noticed, I like to feel in control of the situations I find myself in, and I can't be in control if I don't know what's going on. Right now, I feel off balance and I don't like it."

Her vulnerability was disarming. He'd observed all of those things, but it was something else to hear her put it into words. They weren't acquaintances. They were much more than that, but he'd given his word to Michael that they weren't sleeping together. So, what were they?

"We're us," he said softly, brushing a kiss against her forehead. "I'll stay. But I'll take the couch. I'm glad you're here for me with everything that's going on with my mom, but don't feel like it has to be anything more. I backed out of my overtime, so I'm off this weekend. Keep me awake so I can get on a normal sleep schedule."

"Okay," she quickly agreed. "Find something to watch, and I'll get some sheets and blankets."

She disappeared down the hall and Chris went to the living room to turn on the TV. He'd had a feeling she would relax once she realized he didn't expect sex, and he was right. Truth be told, he relaxed as soon as sex was off the table. Even the thought of sleeping with her without being completely honest with her made him feel like shit. But he still wanted her. He turned Netflix on and waited for her to join him.

Her arms were piled high with blankets, sheets, and pillows. She could barely see around everything as she walked into the living room and set everything down. Wordlessly, she covered the couch with a sheet and folded a blanket on one end before placing a pillow on top.

"Sit," Chris requested. "Your day has been just as long as mine. Relax. I'll rub your shoulders. It's the least I can do since you cooked for me after the crazy day we had."

Season one of Grey's Anatomy started as she sat down on the floor between his legs. "Grey's? I didn't pin you for a soap opera type."

"It's not a soap," Chris argued. "It's prime-time TV at its best. You don't like this show? Believe it or not my mom watches religiously every Thursday night."

Chris felt her relax under his touch. Her head tipped forward before she responded. "Oh, I love it. But you know it's just a glorified soap opera. I'd think your mom would be a bigger Station 19 fan."

He kneaded her muscles, concentrating on the knots. Ignoring her sighs was impossible, since they spoke straight to his libido. Visions of her blue eyes looking up at him, her sighs of pleasure filling the silence as he buried himself inside her, flashed before him. Her eyes wide and glistening with tears as she took everything he was willing to give …

"Christian?" Her voice interrupted his thoughts.

"I'm sorry, what?"

"I said you don't have to sleep on this couch; I know how uncomfortable it is. I trust you," she said, turning to look at him.

Her words cut him like a knife. She shouldn't trust him. Just today he told her about an entire side of his life that she hadn't known about. And there was more. Her family situation was a large part of who she was and yet he was keeping things from her.

"You shouldn't trust me. You don't know me." His words were deathly quiet, but managed to slice through the thick silence.

Mallory turned around to face him. Sitting up on her knees, she placed her hands on his thighs for balance. "Explain."

"You know I'd never do anything or keep anything from you to hurt you, right?"

Her blue eyes somehow shined brighter as she tugged at her bottom lip with her teeth and watched him cautiously. Selfishly, he memorized everything about her gorgeous face just in case it was the last time he got to appreciate her from up close.

"Whatever it is, just tell me," she whispered.

He wanted to be honest. He wanted to tell her everything. He did. But when her blue eyes searched his, he would have done anything to make sure he never lost the chance to hold her in his arms and look into her eyes again. A partial truth wasn't a lie.

"I'm pretty sure I know who your brother is. Is he the reason why you chose not to get into emergency services?" Not a lie.

Her breathing faltered. "Yes."

"At this point, it feels ridiculous that I have to ask you this. You're Michael's sister? Is your last name Hunt?" He closed his eyes and waited for her response.

When he opened his eyes, she had lowered herself to the ground. Her eyes were closed, and she appeared to be holding on tight to the last shreds of her composure. Slow measured breaths were the only visible movements she made.

"Yes," she breathed. "Did you know that this entire time? Do you work with him?"

Chris wasn't sure how much he should say. He wanted her to know there was a connection, but how would she react knowing they were relatively close? He couldn't lie to her, but maybe complete honesty wasn't the best path.

"Yes, I know him from work. I wasn't sure, but I know he has a sister who he has no contact with. I also know he lost his mom. I didn't want to say anything, but I can't lie to you," he explained. "Is that a problem? I know you didn't ask, but he's never said anything bad about you."

Mallory cast her gaze downward. Chris used two fingers to tilt her chin up so she would meet his gaze. She briefly looked at him before closing her eyes.

"It's not a problem. I'm not surprised you know who he is. I just need to know if you knew the entire time. Secrets are the one thing I can't handle."

Chris rested his forehead against hers. "I didn't know. I only recently put the pieces together. But we're just us. None of that means anything as far as we are concerned."

Mallory sat up and held his face in her hands, taking him by surprise when she covered his mouth with hers. Desperate for contact, he pulled her up until she was in his lap straddling him, her soft heat pressing against him. When she rocked against him, they both shuddered.

He gripped her tighter and held her to him, grinding against her until she trembled beneath him. He was able to feel her heat through her shorts, but it wasn't enough. Loosening his hold, he slipped a hand into her shorts and slid his fingers against her wetness. She cursed under her breath and repositioned herself, giving him better access.

She was soaking wet and gasped in surprise when he slipped a finger into her tight core. It was his turn to curse under his breath. He'd taken sex off the table, but as he became uncomfortably hard, the only way he wasn't going to find out how tight she fit around his cock was if she was the one to put a stop to it.

Gripping her ponytail, he angled her head to grant himself full access to her mouth. She gasped in surprise when he tugged her bottom lip between his teeth and moaned when he used his tongue to soothe where he nipped.

"Christian, please," she breathed as she rocked against his hand. "More."

He added another finger and increased the motion even as he silently begged her to put a stop to things. Lord knew he needed to stop, but as she sighed into his neck and her pussy clenched around his fingers, there would be no stopping. He was only human.

He gently nipped at her ear before trailing warm kisses down her neck, stopping to concentrate on the space just above her collarbone when she began to tremble in his arms. She cried out when he bit and then sucked on that very spot.

"Do you want to come?" he asked her.

"Yes. Please."

He went still, the only movement coming from his ragged breathing. "Do you want to come on my hand or on my cock?"

"Please," she repeated, rocking against his hand.

"Tell me. How do you want to come?"

Mallory looked him directly in the eye. "On your cock."

"Fuck," he hissed.

"Condoms. In my nightstand."

He gripped her thighs and stood. He pushed all thoughts of her having condoms in her bedroom from another man out of his mind as he licked and sucked his way across her neck and shoulder while carrying her to the bedroom. When he reached the door, he kicked it open and tossed her onto the bed. She reached into her nightstand and tossed a few foil packets on top.

"Clothes off," he ordered.

He pulled his shirt over his head and waited for her to do the same. When she pulled her tank top off, his eyes landed on her full breasts and pebbled nipples. Without looking away, he removed his sweatpants and underwear in one move. Before she could do the same, he grabbed hold of her ankles and pulled her to the edge of the bed causing her to yelp in surprise.

Her cheeks were flushed, and she bit her lip as she awaited his next move. Seeing her tongue tease at her lip nearly shredded his last thread of control. He knew he should be gentle with her. It was their first time. He yanked her shorts off, tossed them behind him, then sank to his knees before her. Her smooth flesh glistened with signs of her arousal. Pressing his nose against the small strip of hair, he closed his eyes and inhaled her scent. When he opened his eyes to look at her, she closed hers and turned her head to the side, a blush creeping across her cheeks.

"Look at me."

Her eyes snapped open, and he held her gaze while he ran his tongue along her wet slit, circling her core with his tongue before moving up to flick her clit. She cried out and held him in place by his hair, arching her back for more contact.

"Not yet," he said as he stood and grabbed a foil packet off the nightstand, opening it with his teeth. "When you come, it's going to be with me buried inside you."

He looked down at her while he rolled the condom over his length. Her cheeks were red, and she was panting as she spread her legs and waited for him. He wanted to savor her, and there was no way he would last long if he took her standing up with her ankles over his shoulders. He was ready to come just picturing it.

"Slide up."

He climbed his way to the center of the bed as she scooted back, sealing her mouth with a desperate kiss before he pulled away and licked his way down her neck to her breast, taking her nipple into his mouth. She writhed beneath him when he sucked harder while squeezing her other breast, letting his thumb graze her nipple.

"Oh god!" she cried out. "I need to feel you."

He positioned himself at her entrance and searched her eyes for any signs of doubt. "Is this what you want?"

Holding his gaze, she nodded her head yes and with one thrust, he buried himself to the hilt. She closed her eyes, and her ragged sigh matched his own. He gave her a moment to adjust to his size before he began to move. Honestly, he needed a minute to gather himself if he was going to last longer than thirty seconds.

"Let me see you," he breathed.

Her pleading gaze met his and he began to move; slow, deep thrusts. He supported his weight with one arm as he used the other to explore. Starting at her thigh, his hand trailed a path up her body. Placing his hand on her neck, he held her in place while he once again claimed her mouth, capturing her desperate moan. He set a punishing pace as he thrust deeper and harder. She began to tense beneath him, and he knew she was close. He slid his hand up her arm and grasped her hand.

"Come for me," he ground out. "I need you to come for me."

His movements began to falter, and he felt her body go rigid as she came apart around him. A sheen of sweat covered his body and his skin prickled as he held her tight and tumbled to his own release with one final thrust, her name a whisper on his lips.

Chapter 10

CHRISTIAN

"Your mom doing okay?" James asked.

It was his first night back at work since his mom fell. She was still stable, and he couldn't afford to miss work if he didn't have to. Still, it wasn't easy to go to work knowing he could be delayed getting back to her if something happened.

"Yeah. She's doing better than they anticipated, actually," Chris answered as he navigated through traffic. "Am I clear your way?"

"Yeah, you're clear. I'm glad you're back to work. I was worried I'd be stuck with random per diems."

Chris gave him a dirty look. "So, you weren't worried about my mom, you just didn't want shitty partners. Nice."

"No, it's not like that. I was just as worried about your mom as I was about that."

"Dick," he mumbled before he keyed up the radio. "706 is on location."

"At 19:27. Be advised, this is going to be for the Altered Mental Status. ALS was notified," the dispatcher said.

"Received," Chris said before stepping out of the truck.

Chris stepped out and grabbed the stair chair from the side compartment while James gathered the bag and defibrillator. Altered mental status was such a broad term, there was no telling what they'd find once they got inside the second-floor walk-up. The paramedics pulled up while they were still waiting for someone to come down and open the door. Chris was surprised to see Michael and Alyssa making their way up the walkway.

"So, I take it *now* the husband-and-wife rule is no longer a thing?" Chris asked as he pounded on the door. "It seems like you two are together every other shift."

"It is in theory, but you know what a disaster the schedule always is," Alyssa answered. "Anyway, were you not planning to tell me about your mom? I would have come and sat with you at the hospital. You didn't have to do all that alone."

That was exactly why Chris hadn't told her. The last thing he needed was for Michael to show up at the hospital before he talked to Mallory. He still hadn't told her everything, but at least she had returned to work so he wouldn't have to worry about any awkward bedside revelations. His facial expression must have given him away, because Alyssa stood up straighter and pinned him with a look.

"You weren't alone," she accused.

"Says who? I was back and forth on the phone trying to reach my brother and I had to call my daughter and tell her and then deal with my ex. I had a lot going on."

Michael had his arms crossed and was watching Chris's response closely. Before he could say anything, the door finally swung open, revealing a young girl. Her hair was styled in two puffs and her brown eyes were wide with fear.

"Hi, sweetheart," Alyssa stepped forward and greeted. "Is there someone sick upstairs?"

The little girl didn't say anything. She nodded her head and turned around to go back upstairs. Chris shrugged and followed her up the steps and everyone else fell into step behind him. The girl stopped as soon as they cleared the top of the stairs.

"Pop Pop says I should never let strangers in the house. You won't tell on me, will you?"

Chris coped with the job by remaining aloof, but he could never maintain the façade when it came to kids. "Sweetheart, we're helpers. You did the right thing calling for help so there's nothing to get in trouble for. Where is your Pop Pop? Is he sick?"

She nodded her head and pointed down the hallway. Alyssa started walking in that direction before Chris reached out and stopped her. "Let me and Michael check it out. You stay back here with James."

"I'm not disabled. I can treat patients just as well as Michael can," she complained.

"You're pregnant and we don't know what we're walking into," Chris countered.

"He's right," Michael agreed before she had a chance to argue. "We'll be back."

They walked into the bedroom to find an elderly gentleman on the floor next to his bed. He was breathing; they could hear it. Chris crouched down next to him and shook his shoulder. He didn't stir, and Chris noticed the man's shirt was damp with sweat.

"Probably diabetic. I'll send Alyssa and James in and see if I can get any more info from the granddaughter," Chris suggested before leaving the room.

"Well?" Alyssa was standing in the living room with her arms folded, clearly annoyed.

"Probably diabetic. You guys are good to go in," he said before turning his attention to the little girl. "Does your Pop Pop take medicine? Do you know where it is?"

"I'll show you." She surprised him by taking his hand.

She led him into the kitchen and pointed at the refrigerator. On the front was a red sticker with the words "Vial of Life" across the top indicating his health information was inside.

"Awesome!" Chris said. "You did a great job showing this to me."

He opened the refrigerator and pulled out the medicine bottle. Inside he found a list of medications and his medical history. He was an insulin dependent diabetic and had high blood pressure. Chris carried the bottle into the bedroom as Michael held up the glucometer.

"We have a winner!" he announced. "Forty-two."

"He's an insulin dependent diabetic and has high blood pressure," Chris said, holding up the papers from the vial of life.

"Yeah, we figured," Alyssa said as she pulled a blue box from the med bag. "Hopefully we'll have him awake by the time we're ready to transport."

"Can I go with you guys?" the little girl asked.

"Of course, you can. We can't leave you here by yourself. What's your name?"

"Jasmine."

"Oh, like the flower?" Chris asked. "My little girl has a flower name, too. We call her Lily."

"No. I'm Jasmine like the princess."

"Oh well, yeah. I should have known that. Forgive me," he teased. "You should put your shoes on so we can get going. And go get anything you want to bring with you."

"Okay," she agreed. "I'm going to get Pop Pop a teddy bear so he isn't scared. And I need my purse. I'll be right back!"

Chris turned his attention back to the patient and the rest of the crew. "What do you guys need me to do?"

"We're about ready to carry him down. The IV is started. His vitals are good. We gave him an amp of D50 to bring his sugar up. He should be awake pretty soon," Michael answered.

Chris and James carried the patient down while Michael carried the bags and Alyssa looked after Jasmine. By the time they started driving to the hospital, the patient was waking up. He was groggy, but opened his eyes and looked at Jasmine which caused her to show off her dimples with a smile.

"Was my sister at the hospital with you?" Michael asked Chris as they stood at the nurses' station and worked on their charts.

Chris briefly closed his eyes. He had been counting on Michael forgetting about the conversation. He should have known it wouldn't happen that easily. He didn't want to lie, but he also wasn't ready to face the aftermath. Michael was protective by nature, and just because he wasn't close to his sister didn't mean anything.

"She was, but not because we were together when it happened or anything like that. I was taking a walk to get coffee and clear my head and I literally ran into her. She took it upon herself to stay with me."

Michael simply grunted and went back to working on his chart, which was fine by him. He'd take a grunt over the alternative. Things between Chris and Mallory already felt off without bringing the broody brother into it. After spending most of the night in bed tangled in each other's arms, he'd convinced her to keep her coffee date with her friend while he went back to the hospital. It wasn't that he didn't want her with him, he just didn't want things to move too fast because of the situation and not because they both wanted to move things forward. And now he was at work feeling like an ass.

MALLORY

Mallory was trying her best to pretend like everything was okay. She hadn't had a fight with Christian, but nothing seemed right ever since they spent the night in bed together. There had been no argument, no cancellations, and no to anything else that would make her suspicious, but she couldn't shake the feeling that something was off. Her phone rang as she was getting into Dan's car to head home from work.

"Hi, Christian," she answered.

"Hey. Want to come to my place for dinner? I know we had plans to go to my friend's house, but everything is crazy right now."

Her heart sank. The way things were going, she fully expected to look like an idiot, thinking things were more than they were. She'd been excited to meet his best friend. Everything would feel real once they existed beyond their little bubble.

"Text me the address," she requested as she put her seatbelt on. "I'll see you in a bit."

"Everything okay?" Dan asked.

Mallory did her best to put on a poker face. "Yeah. He just wanted to confirm our dinner plans."

"You're the worst liar I have ever met."

She expected him to see through her sooner than later. "I'm not. That's literally why he called. But he changed the plans a little, so I guess I'm disappointed about that part."

"Have you talked to him since he banged your back out?"

Mallory nearly choked, and she tried, to no avail, to keep the blush from rising up her neck. "Daniel. Could you not?"

"What?" He feigned innocence as he pulled out of the parking garage. "How should I say it? Fucked you senseless?"

"Oh my god. Yes, I've talked to him in passing since he spent the night. It's been hard with our schedules. He's been working at night, spending time with his mom, then sleeping until it's time to wake up and start the process all over again."

Dan kept quiet as he fought the heavy afternoon traffic. Saying the actual reason for their distance out loud made her feel silly for being so damned insecure. Christian wasn't her abusive ex. He also wasn't Aiden, the place holder. He was Christian.

"I'm being silly, huh?" she asked as he pulled into their driveway.

Dan didn't answer right away. He put the car in park and stepped out, locking it after she closed her door. Once they got to the front door, he looked at her and quirked an eyebrow. She already had a feeling what his answer was going to be before he even spoke.

"I would never say that," he began as he unlocked the main door. "Don't roll your eyes at me. Anyway, you feel how you feel. But I would wait until you've seen him before you decide what to do with those feelings."

She stopped in front of his apartment before going upstairs. She was struggling. Her solution to dealing with the breakup that wrecked her had been to shut down. Eventually she started dating, but she never let her entire being go into the dates. She'd put just enough of herself into her relationship with Aiden to make it last more than just a handful of dates, but never enough to give him the power to hurt her.

"What if I'm not sure what I'm feeling?" she asked quietly.

"More reason to wait and see. Don't give yourself an ultimatum. You're allowed to go along for the ride. You'll know what's right for you."

She watched him go into his apartment and shut the door before making her way up the stairs. He was right, as usual. She was too hard on herself. There was nothing that said she wasn't allowed to feel whatever she felt just like there was no rule telling her she had to act on every feeling.

The hot shower she took helped to wash away her weariness. Going to Christian's house for the first time should be exciting, not feel like she was walking the plank. He hadn't canceled, he simply adjusted the plans. There was no reason she should assume the worst, just because she was in her feelings.

She adjusted her white cotton tunic as she stepped out of her car and stood in front of Christian's apartment building. Her comfort clothing would always be a loose-fitting top over a soft pair of leggings, and at the moment she needed comfort. She gazed up at the older brick building with what looked like no more than two apartments per floor. A walk up. She double checked her phone before making her way toward apartment 2R.

"I've missed you," he greeted as soon as he opened the door.

He pulled her into a hug before kissing her cheek and pulling her inside. She was immediately enveloped in the scent she now associated with Christian, and she fought hard to keep from closing her eyes and inhaling a deep breath. Even knowing everything he was going through, it was hard for her to not feel like she'd been getting the brush off. His warm embrace combined with the heartfelt welcome were everything she needed.

"So, what happened with your friend?" she asked. The question had burned inside her since the moment he changed their evening plans.

"Would you like something to drink?" he asked when they stopped in his small kitchen.

The kitchen overlooked a narrow tree-lined alleyway. It was late spring, and many of the trees were in full bloom, creating a beautiful backdrop of pinks and whites to go with the luscious greens. Mallory immediately fell in love with the quaint building.

"I'll have whatever you're having."

Christian stepped away before returning with two small glasses and a bottle of whiskey. The hard stuff. Mallory's trepidation creeped back into play.

"Not a whiskey drinker?" Christian asked, picking up on her unease.

"It's not that. I'm just wondering if there's a reason why you're skipping wine and going straight to the hard stuff right after you decided against me meeting your best friend."

Christian's expression softened. His green eyes locked on hers and she felt as if he was looking through her. He set the bottle and glasses down on the small wooden table before closing the distance between them. Standing in front of her, he placed his arms around her shoulders and pulled her close. The warmth of his body gave her a sense of security when he held her close, and it also helped to calm her. Her emotions were all over the place and no amount of deep breathing and positive affirmations seemed to be able to help the way his arms did.

"Did you think I changed my mind about bringing you to meet her?"

Mallory was horrified to hear her insecurities spoken aloud. "No! It's not that. I just thought there must be a reason you changed things up."

"Alyssa's best friend is getting married in Vegas in two days. Kerry and Brian should have had their wedding by now but that was a whole thing. Anyway, she thought everything would be ready and she'd be able to have you over today. I tried to tell her there was no way everything was going to go as smoothly as it was in her mind and that she'd be packed and ready to go. The wedding is in Vegas, but the reception will be here next weekend. Worst case scenario, you'll meet her at the reception, if you'll go with me. I can't wait to show you off."

"Oh," Mallory breathed.

"Yes," he echoed. "Oh."

Christian sat down in one of the chairs at his table and pulled Mallory into his lap. She followed him without any resistance. The words of advice from Dan rang in her mind as she settled into his lap.

She shivered when he nipped at her neck, just below her ear, his nose teasing his way through her thick waves. She closed her eyes and relished his nearness, his breath a tickle against her neck. All of her insecurities vanished when she was safely in his hold.

"You hungry?" he asked.

The double meaning was not lost on her. Yes, she was hungry. She hadn't eaten dinner yet, and she was also hungry for him. She could practically feel his hands on her every time she closed her eyes and lost herself in memories from the other night, seeing everything as if she was a spectator and had been watching the entire thing. She was most definitely hungry in every sense of the word.

"Always," she finally answered.

"There is one thing I need to tell you."

Goosebumps spread across her flesh as his words sank in. She had a feeling he was keeping something from her. She had a fine-tuned gut instinct and learned not to ignore it, but sometimes it was hard to tell the difference between nerves and a true premonition.

"What is it?" she asked.

"Well," he said before pausing to run his hand through his hair. "I told you I know your brother."

"Yes?" she asked, not quite sure what the big deal was. "I'm sure plenty of people know my brother. I know how most of you cross paths at one time or another."

"I more than know him. Alyssa's last name is Hunt."

Realization hit her like a blast of cold air. "Is that why you changed the dinner plans? I should have known everything seemed too good to be true."

Christian shifted them in an instant. His firm grip on her arms as he angled her to look at him brought her attention back to what he was saying. "Mallory, that isn't why. I wouldn't lie to you, and I would never try to hide you. They are traveling tomorrow and needed tonight to get everything ready."

Christian placed her in the chair he'd been sitting in and kneeled in front of her. She watched his expression carefully. Believing him should be easy since he'd never lied to her before. It wasn't a lack of trust in him, it was lack of familiarity with her situation. She had avoided serious relationships for a reason, and it was just her luck that when she finally decided to go for it, the man was connected to her brother.

"So, he knows." It was a statement, not a question.

"He does. Of course, he does."

"Well, I guess this was fun while it lasted, huh?" Mallory kept an eye on the door, prepared to make her escape.

Christian watched her closely like she was a scared animal, ready to flee. If that was his assessment, he wasn't far off.

"I know things are complicated between you two. Honestly, that's why I hesitated to tell you. Please don't let that get between us." His gaze traveled over her.

In all of the scenarios that very quickly played through her mind, him pleading with her was not one of them. It still could be too good to be true. Men who looked the way Christian did could have their pick of women. It didn't make sense that he'd let himself get entangled in her drama, when he could easily walk away. More importantly, she wasn't even sure the drama was worth it.

"Trust me, Bunny. It's just us." He stood behind her chair and crowded over her, loosely wrapping his arms across her chest.

"Bunny?"

His quiet laugh washed over her. "Well ..." he hesitated. "When you get scared you run. Kind of like a rabbit. So, you're my little bunny."

Warmth spread from her chest, up her neck, finally heating her face and clear to the tops of her ears. As silly as it sounded, no one had ever given her an actual nickname before. It should probably be offensive, but she liked it. There was no fighting the grin that lit up her face.

"Are you blushing?"

"No," she answered, shifting so her hair would cover more of her face.

"Liar," he teased.

Taking her by surprise, he pulled her into his arms. His mouth tickled her neck when he kissed her; tiny nibbles until she squealed with laughter and moved away. The worries over having to be around her brother had nearly fled from her mind.

"You're trying to distract me," Mallory accused with even less conviction than she felt.

"That's not true. I know better ways to do that." He kissed her mouth. "Talk to me. What's worrying you the most? I don't want to ever put you in a situation where you feel uncomfortable or trapped."

She allowed him to lead her out of the kitchen and into his living room. A small sectional, a coffee table, and a wall-mounted television were the only pieces of furniture in the room. She broke off to take a closer look at the photographs. A large wall hanging with various sized framed photos took up most of the wall behind the sectional. Baby pictures of who she assumed to be Liliana were scattered amongst school-aged photos of her with Christian and a few with her, Christian, and his mom.

"She's beautiful. She has your eyes."

"Thank you. She's a good kid, too. Now sit and talk to me before dinner is ready."

She took a moment to sniff the air. She hadn't noticed the smell of food cooking when she walked in but thought maybe she just wasn't paying attention. After a moment, Christian started to laugh.

"Chinese food is on the way. I ordered you the steamed chicken and vegetables with brown rice. I hope that's okay. There's also lo mein, sweet and sour chicken, and pork fried rice if that sounds better."

"That sounds perfect. Thank you."

"Now. Talk to me. I know something is still bothering you," he said, bringing them back to the subject at hand.

Mallory sat on the sofa and tried to make herself comfortable. She wasn't quite sure how to explain her issues with her family without sounding childish and petty. Saying she was upset because her dad got remarried over-simplified things.

"I just don't want to be around my brother any more than necessary. I wouldn't say I'm mad at him, it just brings up bad memories. I shouldn't blame him and it's not his fault our dad replaced our mom, but it's hard for me to be around him. I used to come around for Christmas and stuff, but I had to stay away for my mental health. Is that going to cause a huge problem? I know you two are close." She rubbed her sweaty palms up and down her thighs.

Christian put an arm around her waist and pulled her closer. "It's not a problem. If you don't want to see him, you don't have to. Would it be weird for you to meet Alyssa? I think you'd like her. And I would like to bring you as my date to the reception, but if you aren't up to it because he'll be there, that's okay. Just think about it."

"I'll think about it," she agreed.

His fingers were warm on her chin when he gently turned her face to look at him. With the air cleared, she finally took a close look at him. His hair was bordering on wild, as if he hadn't taken time to style it after showering, and the scruff on his chin was new. She reached her hand out and stroked his face, enjoying the way his facial hair tickled her palm.

It wasn't until his breath hitched, that she thought about what she was doing. He covered her hand with his and pulled her into a kiss, his tongue teasing along her lips until she allowed him in. She slipped her hand beneath his shirt, wanting to feel as much of him as possible as he caressed her, the heat from his hands scorching her through her clothes. It was only a kiss, but she was already wet; her body aching to feel him everywhere.

She jumped at the sound of a knock on the door. It hadn't taken her long to forget that he'd ordered food.

"Awesome timing," he mumbled sarcastically as he straightened his clothes and headed for the door. "Remind me not to order delivery next time."

Chapter 11

CHRISTIAN

Chris stretched his legs out as he tried to get comfortable. No matter what, there was no such thing as a comfortable chair in a hospital, which made no sense considering the amount of time people spent at bedsides. He hoped to get an update soon. If modifications needed to be made to her house, Robbie would only be in town for a short time in order to help out. If she wouldn't be returning home, they would need to figure things out together.

He'd come straight from work and his mother was still sleeping, but he didn't want to risk going home and falling asleep. Watching her sleep so peacefully, it was hard to believe she was in a hospital bed and recovering from major surgery. With his arms folded, he settled into the chair.

As soon as he was settled, his phone vibrated in his pocket. Assuming it was his brother, he only opened his eyes enough to swipe open the call.

"Hello?" His voice was scratchy from lack of sleep.

"Chris. This is a disaster. I wish you'd listened to me and come here for the wedding. All Michael is trying to do is calm me down, and I don't want to calm down." He wasn't expecting to hear Alyssa's voice.

"Alyssa?" he asked as he hurried into the hallway. "What's going on? Isn't it four something in the morning over there?"

"I don't even know where to start, Chris. They had the wedding. Everything was okay until some bitch showed up to our table at the hotel bar and said the wedding wasn't legit because she and Brian were still married!" Alyssa explained in a rush.

Chris was doing his best to follow what she was saying, which was hard to do when behind on sleep. "He's married? Then how could they get a marriage license?"

"Exactly!"

He shook his head to clear the cobwebs but was still unable to connect the dots. Brian and Kerry had been engaged for what seemed like forever. How could they have overlooked an entire wife?

"It's been days since I've had decent sleep. Please spell it out for me because I'm lost."

"I'm sure they must be divorced, but that's not the point. He had a fucking wife, Chris!"

If she wasn't pregnant, he'd swear he'd fallen victim to a drunk dial. Since he really didn't want to drag the conversation out or ask her again to repeat herself, he did his best to connect the dots. Brian had been married and divorced. Kerry had no idea about an ex-wife. The ex-wife showed up in Vegas to stir shit up, and it worked even though the general consensus was that she was lying. And it worked because the bottom line was that he'd kept a previous marriage from Kerry.

"Alyssa, I know you don't want to calm down, but you need to. It's not good to get yourself upset. Wait till you have the kid before you decide you want to stab a bitch. Why don't you take some deep breaths and say some positive affirmations or something ..."

"Do what?" she half shouted. "What the fuck is that supposed to mean? If I wanted a voice of reason, I wouldn't have called you. No offense."

Chris laughed. "I'm just saying, maybe he forgot. Maybe it never came up in conversation."

"He forgot? Do you ever forget you were married to Vivian?" Alyssa asked.

"Maybe it never came up."

"In five years. In the five years they've been together he forgot to mention an ex-wife because it never came up in conversation. Sure. Makes total sense to me."

Chris couldn't help uttering a very loud and dramatic sigh. "I'm not trying to defend the guy. I'm just saying try not to let that woman ruin everything, which is obviously her plan. Finish out the trip. Leave the reception plans in place. Kerry doesn't need to rush into any major decisions, and as the maid of honor, it's your job to keep her calm."

There was a long pause. "Who are you and what have you done with Chris?"

Her reaction wasn't surprising. Of the two of them, he'd always been the one with the short fuse.

"We can't both lose our shit at the same time, so I guess it's my turn to be level-headed."

Another long pause. "I really need to meet this Mallory. It's only been a few weeks and you're like a totally different person. I think she's good for you."

"Okay," Chris began, ready to change the subject. "You need to get some sleep. Talk your friend down and then go to bed. You guys have a long flight tomorrow. You'll meet Mallory at the reception."

Chris disconnected the call as he walked back into his mother's room. She was wide awake and smiling at him. There was no doubt she'd heard his end of the conversation since he wasn't far from the doorway and wasn't as quiet as he could have been.

"Your best friend hasn't met your special friend yet? Why is that?" she asked as soon as he returned to the chair at her bedside. Even when confined to a hospital bed, she never missed a thing.

"Not yet. Scheduling conflicts," Chris responded with a shrug.

"Well, I hope they meet soon. She is good for you and I'm sure Alyssa will love her. How did her friend's wedding go?"

Chris was certain she'd been listening and already had a pretty good idea of how the wedding went, but he humored her anyway. "The wedding went great, but there's been some drama after it. Apparently, Brian has been married before, much to Kerry's surprise. Alyssa is out of her mind furious about it, and it's a mess. I'm hoping Kerry holds off on making any major decisions until she's rested and in her normal time zone."

His mom's eyes sparkled. She always did love a good soap opera. "That's terrible. When's the reception?"

"Next weekend. If it happens."

"Well, if it doesn't happen, then make sure to make up for it with your reception."

"Mom. What reception? I'm not even engaged," he pointed out.

"When's Robbie getting here?" she asked, completely changing the subject. Before long, she'd be playing things up as if she had dementia and didn't know what was going on. None of her strategies were new.

"Should be later today, Mom. Is there something you need?"

"Oh, I was just wondering, that's all. Has he said how long he's staying?"

He sat down and hoped his mom would stick with the subject change. "Well, that depends. We're hoping to get an update from your doctors. Once we know more, we'll decide from there."

"Okay. So, back to the wedding. Do you think they'll still have the reception?"

Chris shook his head. He knew she couldn't stay away from some good gossip. "I'm pretty sure they will since it's paid for. Now if it goes off without any drama may be a different story."

Chris stopped talking when he heard a light rap on the already open door. "Mrs. Ramirez?"

An older gentleman walked in wearing a long white coat over top of a sky-blue shirt and navy tie, along with a pair of tan dress pants. His expression was serious, but his eyes were kind. Chris decided he liked him.

"Hello, Doctor," his mom said. "Come on in."

"Hello everyone. How are you doing today? It's good to see you both."

Chris had been at the hospital at some point every day since she broke her hip. Aside from making sure his mom was okay, he wanted the hospital staff to get used to seeing him and to know that someone was there making sure she received the proper care.

"Do you have an update for us, Doctor?" He was aware of the meeting between his mother's entire care team to come up with an updated treatment plan. The doctor needed to get to the point.

"Yes. We had the meeting first thing this morning in order to discuss what's next. The good news is everything is healing very nicely. How has the physical therapy been going, Mrs. Ramirez?"

She shrugged her shoulders in a noncommittal way. "Okay, I guess."

"You guess? Are you able to do everything?"

She sighed. "I can, but I'm having too much pain, so I don't like to do it."

"Well ..." He hesitated as he appeared to search for the correct words. "I'm going to recommend you to be discharged to a rehabilitation facility. The physical therapist agreed that even though you are healing well, you aren't where we would feel comfortable with you going home."

"A nursing home," Chris chimed in. "I don't think so. I already told the other doctor I wasn't interested. You and I both know she'll be in the bed all day and they won't do shit for her. At least if she's home we'll know for sure when physical therapy is showing up."

Chris was starting to stress over the situation. He had been counting on Robbie being around for the conversation. He was getting tired of always having to deal with his mom on his own when he wasn't an only child. He loved her more than anything, but some help would be nice. And on top of that he was the one who would have to figure out how he was going to get time with his daughter this summer. Vivian never wanted to do anything to make the custody arrangements work.

"Not a nursing home. There are a few facilities specifically for rehabilitation," the doctor explained. The one I would most like to see her go to is great. There's an assisted living right across the street, so their goal is to at least get the patients well enough to go there. I'll see if the hospital social worker can work her magic. There are a few other places, but they are a little far from here, so we'll cross that bridge when we come to it."

Chris scrubbed his hand down his face. He never imagined he'd be finding a nursing home for his mom. She needed help, but she was stubborn and independent and didn't like admitting just how much help she needed. Sure, the doctor kept emphasizing that these were rehabilitation facilities, but it was the same thing as far as Chris was concerned.

"What did I miss?" His brother stood in the doorway looking like a scruffier version of Chris. They both had green eyes and shared the same hair color, Robbie just had more of it.

Mrs. Ramirez's eyes lit up as she looked past Chris to her other son. Of course they did. He was always too busy working to be bothered with his mom, but he was welcomed home like the Prodigal Son when he did show up.

"Everything, as usual," Chris answered once Robbie made his way to his side.

"I got here when I could, you know that." He leaned over to give his mom a kiss and a hug. "Hey, Mama. What are you doing in here?"

Their mother hugged him back before holding him at a distance to get a better look at him. "I'm so happy you're here. They want to put me in a home."

Robbie quickly turned to pin him with a fierce glare. Of course, he would have a problem with a plan that he didn't have any part in making since he wasn't there. Chris would do anything for his brother, but it was getting harder and harder for him to keep his mouth shut.

"Bro, you can have something to say when you are the one spending hours taking care of Mom. We aren't putting her into a home. She can't be by herself right now and she needs physical therapy. She's going into a rehabilitation facility," Chris explained as calmly as he was able, considering the simmering anger that was brewing within him.

"It's the same shit, man."

Suddenly Chris was on the doctor's side. He had shared the same misgivings at first, but facts were facts. "Are you going to be the one to take off work so you can stay with her twenty-four, seven? And are you going to keep track of her physical therapy sessions and make sure they are showing up when they are supposed to?"

"Boys," Mrs. Ramirez spoke up. "I'm right here, and there's nothing wrong with my ears. Stop your fighting."

"We aren't fighting, Mom," Robbie interrupted.

"I'm speaking." She didn't continue until everyone, including the uncomfortable looking doctor, gave her their attention. "I might be old, but I haven't lost my mind. I can decide what's best for me and I agree the rehabilitation facility is best. Maybe if I had more help, I wouldn't have ended up on the sidewalk with a broken hip."

"Mom!" Chris said slightly louder than intended. "I told you I'd take the trash out if you left it for me. I can't be more than one place at a time."

"I know, Christian. But it shouldn't be you all the time. I know you do the best you can and I'm thankful."

Chris was relieved that his mom was aware of how lopsided their share of taking care of her had been over the years. "Exactly. Robbie needs to do his part."

"Bruh. I got here when I could."

"That's not what I meant. It's better for me to go to a place where I don't have to worry about you coming to help me when you were already doing so much to help me. I'd just end up doing things I have no business trying to do. I want to go to this place for a while. And then when I'm as good as new I'll come back home."

Chris didn't have the heart to tell her how unlikely it was for someone to be discharged home from a place like that when they weren't completely self-sufficient. She would need to surpass where she had been before her accident. He used one of Mallory's cleansing breaths to stop himself from going down that rabbit hole. He got snippy when he was stressed, and his mom didn't need that from him.

"I think that's for the best," the doctor commented. "I have a few more patients to see. Please have the nurse page me if you need anything. In the meantime, I'll make sure the social worker gets started."

Chris watched in silence as the doctor left the room. Optimism was important, but he wasn't capable of faking enthusiasm on such little sleep with so much on his mind. He needed to make a quick exit, and the twinge of guilt wasn't as sharp knowing his brother was there. As soon as he had the opportunity, he'd make his escape.

"I still don't like it," Robbie said as they watched the doctor leave the room.

"Well," Chris began, barely containing his irritation, "until you come up with a plan that involves you doing more than showing up a few days a month, I suggest we go with what the doctor suggested."

Robbie sighed and shook his head in frustration. "I know what you and the doctor are saying is right, I just don't like it. Mom should be in her house."

"I'm still right here," their mom reminded them. "Pretty sure what I say should count for something."

Chris needed out. It was hard enough accepting what needed to happen, without getting pushback from his brother. He had to remind himself that he'd had more time to come to terms with things than Robbie had.

"Okay mom, I'm going to get going. Spend time with Robbie; I need to get some sleep."

Chris made his exit without waiting for any objections. He needed a minute. More than a minute. The world didn't revolve around him, and dwelling on how his mother's life-altering injury would affect his life was low, even for him. Certainly, he could remember something about those manifestations Mallory had gone on about.

Chapter 12

MALLORY

Why Mallory agreed to go to the reception was beyond her. No amount of yoga, cleansing breaths, or positive affirmations could get rid of the nerves that sat in the pit of her stomach like a brick. Christian had assumed she'd be struggling and insisted on spending the afternoon with her. He was due any minute. She wanted to look cute for him and treat it like two separate dates–an afternoon date and an evening date–but she hadn't gone beyond showering and putting on a t-shirt and a pair of leggings.

The last time she'd seen her brother was Christmas Eve five years ago. Everything had been awkward as hell, and she couldn't wait to get away. The entire dinner was filled with uncomfortable small talk. Her dad and brother had looked at her like she was a skittish animal, ready to bolt. Just because she felt like a trapped animal didn't mean they should have treated her like one. Treating her like family would have been just fine.

She did her best to tamp down her nerves as she buzzed Christian inside and stood at her opened door to wait for him to come up. He emerged at the top of the stairs looking nothing short of edible. A pair of relaxed jeans and a tight-fitting shirt never looked so good. Her mouth went dry and for a moment she forgot the reason behind her nerves.

They hadn't seen each other since she was at his house for dinner. A wicked smile spread across his face as he stalked toward her. As soon as he reached her, he dropped his bag on the floor and cradled her face in both hands before covering her mouth with his own. Completely consumed by his desperate kiss, she melted into him surrendering all control. His tongue danced along hers as he groaned, the timbre reverberating down to her toes.

He moved his hands to her waist, gripping her tight as he backed her into her apartment; kicking the door shut behind him. She wasn't expecting such an energetic greeting, but her response was quick and without hesitation. Her nerve endings were on fire and the heat of his body pressed against hers, set her ablaze.

In a frenzy, she tugged his shirt from his pants and slipped her hands under it, her fingers stroking the contours of his well-defined abs. His breath hitched, the sound fueling the ache between her legs.

"God," she breathed, shoving him against the wall.

"Not God. Christian." He chuckled just before he grabbed the back of her neck and returned his mouth to hers.

Placing his leg between her thighs, he used his knee to shove them apart. She gasped as her core clenched, anticipating his touch. He placed his free hand on her side at the top of her rib cage and slid it down her body, grazing her breast with his thumb as he went. Craving more contact, she turned her body into his touch.

"Don't move," he warned as he spun them around so her back was against the door.

Thankful for the support, she leaned against the door and waited as the sound of her harsh breathing filled the room. He continued moving his hand down her body, squeezing when he reached her hip. He moved his thumb back and forth, torturously close to her center.

"What do you want?" he asked. There was a dangerous edge to his voice that sent a delicious tingle down her spine.

"Touch me," she breathed.

"Where?"

Instead of speaking, she grabbed his hand and placed it between her legs, causing him to gasp in surprise when she grinded herself against him. The fabric was thin, allowing her to feel the heat of his fingers, but it wasn't enough. As if sensing her frustration, he slipped his hand into her pants and against her slick heat. She cried out and arched her back, trying to feel as much of him as possible.

"You're so fucking wet," he breathed, slipping a finger inside.

"Please," she whimpered.

She could hear the sounds from her wetness as he moved his finger in and out. Panting and no longer able to speak coherently, she tugged her shirt over her head and dropped it beside her, hoping he'd take the hint and follow her lead. Instead of removing any of his clothes he added a finger and placed his mouth on her neck, his bite toeing the line of pleasure and pain.

"Pants. Off," he ordered as he pulled his shirt up over his head then made quick work of his belt.

After stepping out of her pants she looked up to find him watching her with an expression that could only be described as hungry. His chest was bare, his belt unbuckled, and the top button of his jeans undone. They stared at each other, chests heaving, until he took her by the arm and brought her over to the couch. She was expecting him to toss her onto it, but instead he directed her to stand facing it, with her hands gripping the back as she leaned forward.

"On your knees," he growled.

Her knees nearly buckled at his command. Scrambling to follow his orders, she kneeled on the couch and faced the back, anxious to find out what he planned to do to her. The decorative mirror on the opposite wall revealed a glimpse of her kneeling on the sofa wearing nothing but a pink bra and matching thong, while he stood behind her fully clothed from the waist down. Right when she thought she couldn't get any wetter, he dropped to his knees on the floor behind her.

"I've missed you," he murmured as he ran both hands up her thighs and caressed her ass. "One night wasn't enough. I've needed more ever since. You know how many times I had to jerk off in the shower just thinking about it?"

Holy fuck.

He brought his hands to the top of her thong, running his fingers along the waistband, tugging until she heard the fabric rip. Looking over her shoulder at him in surprise, she found him watching her with that smirk that had hooked her the first time she'd met him.

"Hope you weren't attached to those."

Before she could respond, he shoved her forward and licked her from her clit to her ass. The unexpected touch of his warm tongue nearly made her come with one swipe. She spread her knees further and silently begged for more.

"Mmm. You want more?" he asked.

His tongue returned to her slit before she had a chance to respond, and she gripped the back of the couch hard enough for her knuckles to turn white. Every swipe of his tongue was a torturous form of pleasure. She was a quivering mess, but what she wanted most was to feel him inside her. As he continued to worship her with his tongue, she had no choice but to beg for more.

"Fuck me. Please," she cried out. "I need to feel you."

It wasn't like her to beg, but she was desperate. Christian cursed under his breath, and she heard the distinct sound of a zipper. She was trembling in anticipation and on the verge of tears. Clothing rustled and she turned to see him pull a condom from his wallet.

"No condom," she breathed. "I want to feel you."

Christian froze. "Are you sure?"

"I know you're clean. I'm clean and I'm on birth control. Let me feel you."

Another curse under his breath and then he was behind her. One hand gripped her hip while his other held on to the back of the couch beside hers. She didn't miss the slight tremble of his hand before he buried his face in her hair to kiss her neck.

The weight of his body against her made her absolutely feral. Her breath caught in her throat, and she arched her back, aching to be filled by him. Slowly, he ran his hand up her spine and back down, before gripping her hip and slamming into her in one thrust.

"Fuck!" she shouted.

He paused for a moment before he thrust into her once again. He felt deeper at that angle, and even more so when he gripped her hard and positioned her the way he wanted her. She met each thrust, crying out from the feel of him buried inside her, skin against skin. Every touch sent a jolt straight to her core.

The tears she'd been holding back now fell freely as they continued to take what they could from each other. Her breathing became erratic as she chased her orgasm. Sensing she needed more, Christian reached around and gently pinched her clit, sending her spiraling over the edge. White hot pleasure surged through her body as she pulsed around him. Before she returned to earth, he wrapped his arm tightly around her middle as he found his own release, emptying himself into her.

Christian collapsed onto the couch, bringing her with him. She lay on his chest as they both caught their breath. That was not what she had been expecting for the first part of their date. Not that she was complaining.

"That was ... unexpected," she said after a long moment.

"Sorry." He chuckled. "That wasn't my plan when I came over here, I swear."

"Wasn't it?" she quipped.

"No. But when I saw you, I just had to get my hands on you. Between our schedules not matching up and stressing about the reception, I guess I got carried away. Did I hurt you?"

She responded with a breathy laugh. "No. Did I hurt you?" she teased.

"No, Bunny. You did not."

CHRISTIAN

The bed and breakfast was smaller than Chris had anticipated. He'd booked two rooms in order to prevent World War Three from happening, but he wasn't thrilled to see what close quarters they would all be sharing. The only thing saving the evening was the fact that the Bridal Suite was the only other room on the same side of the house as their rooms. The other end of the house wasn't far, but at least they could spend time in the same room without anyone noticing.

He felt a rush of relief when he noticed Alyssa standing off to the side checking out the large bookcase in the corner of the parlor. After doing a quick scan of the room, he said a silent thank you to the universe for allowing him the opportunity to introduce Mallory without Michael breathing down his neck.

He let go of Mallory's hand so he could lead her to his friend by discreetly placing his hand at the small of her back. Alyssa turned as if she could sense their approach.

"Hey! This must be Mallory!" Alyssa beamed at them as she pulled her into an unexpected hug.

Mallory stumbled back a step before she recovered and hugged Alyssa back. Chris did his best not to laugh at the wide-eyed expression she flashed at him.

"I have heard so much about you," Alyssa continued. "I'm so glad Michael stepped out for a minute with Brian. In case Chris hasn't told you, I'm so excited about this entire thing. I feel like his big sister, proud to finally have him bring someone home."

"Really, Alyssa?" Chris interrupted. "Could you not?"

"I'm sorry, but I only have a few minutes to get my excitement out before I have to rein it back in. I'm sure you know how it is," Alyssa continued.

Somehow, that statement appeared to have the opposite effect Chris expected. Mallory visibly relaxed and looked more at ease than she had since they left the house. She smiled and fell into conversation with Alyssa while he stood back and watched. It wasn't until Mallory casually tucked her hair behind her ear that he noticed the bite mark he'd left.

He stepped forward and put his arms around her, planting a quick kiss on her cheek before whispering in her ear. "Untuck your hair."

She stiffened in his arms. "Why?"

Chris glanced at Alyssa, who was definitely eavesdropping to the best of her abilities. She wasn't even trying to hide it. Not surprising.

"Well, unless you want it to be obvious what we were doing before we got here, you should probably just do it."

At that she whipped around. "Christian!"

"You asked. I answered."

Alyssa was clearly enjoying the back and forth. Mallory? Not so much.

Alyssa had mercy on Mallory and changed the subject. "Mallory, would you like a drink? I can't have one so you can drink for us both. Come with me."

In the corner of the room stood a small bar with a single bartender. Chris stayed put while the two women made their way over, Alyssa engaging Mallory in conversation the entire way.

"Chris." Michael's greeting pulled his attention away.

Chris turned and gave him a nod. His expression was unreadable, so he decided it best to tread lightly. Before he could come up with any safe small-talk, Michael's attention was on the two women talking at the bar. It had to be difficult for him. Between not seeing his sister for several years and the idea of him dating someone who had a pretty bad reputation with women, Chris knew he had to be struggling.

"They seem to be getting along," Michael mumbled.

"I figured they would," Chris responded. "So, does this mean we're past where you tell me to leave your sister alone? Because that's not going to happen, and I really don't want to keep arguing about it."

"Fair enough."

Chris was surprised when he simply walked away and headed to the bar. He didn't follow. He already knew Mallory well enough to know she wouldn't want him to hover. This was something she needed to get through on her own. Being careful not to hover wasn't the same as abandoning her. He'd be watching.

"Hey, man." Brian walked over and clapped him on the back. "I'm glad you made it."

"How was the wedding?" Chris asked, even though he already knew how it went.

With a deep sigh, Brian led him to the other side of the room. Chris welcomed the distraction. Across the room from the bar, there was a table with hors d'oeuvres and pre-poured glasses of champagne. Brian made his way over to the table and Chris followed.

"Well, it started off okay." Brian's answer was cryptic.

"Until?"

"Until my crazy ex showed up. We were married for less than a year. I haven't even spoken to her in I don't know how long. She showed up after the wedding and said we're still married."

"Well? Are you?" Chris already knew the answer, but he had to ask.

"Fuck no."

Chris looked around to make sure there was no one around. He'd convinced Alyssa to talk Kerry out of cancelling the reception, and it would be his ass if he was the one to stir up drama. They were still fairly alone, and Mallory was still with Alyssa, while Michael watched from a distance. He'd investigate that later.

"So, she just showed up out of nowhere?" Chris snagged a small meat and cheese plate from the table. "Weird that she'd do that, but then ex-wives do weird things. So, is everything good now? Shouldn't be hard to prove you aren't still married."

He'd barely finished speaking when Kerry walked past, shooting daggers at them both. He had to bite his lip to keep from laughing. The timing was too perfect. Brian had his lips rolled in and was shaking his head.

"I never mentioned having an ex-wife. It's going over like a lead balloon."

It all made sense now. He had been worried about telling Mallory about his own ex-wife because he felt like he hadn't been up front. Kerry was probably livid, and with good reason. If he was honest, he'd be beyond pissed if he found out on his wedding day that his new spouse had been married before and never mentioned it.

"Oh man. I see where that look came from, then. You're lucky you're still alive," Chris said with a nervous chuckle.

Brian picked up a champagne flute and led them away from the table into the corner of the parlor, near the window. "It was really bad. It still is. I'm hoping tonight will help, but it's not looking good. I didn't intentionally keep it from her, I just didn't think it was important. She hasn't spoken to me since."

Chris's attention was drawn to the sound of laughter on the other side of the room. Kerry had joined Mallory and Alyssa, and the three women were having an animated conversation. Michael was still watching from a distance.

"Well, that's a good sign," Chris commented. "Maybe she'll warm up since she seems to be having a good time over there."

"Yeah, maybe. What's up with Michael? He's over there lurking."

That was the perfect description. He was lurking on the sidelines. Once again, he considered what might be going through Michael's head.

"Long story." He excused himself to go talk to him. When he approached, Michael barely spared him a glance before returning his attention to the women across the room.

"You good?"

Michael grunted in response to his question.

"You should talk to her," he suggested. "She's been so nervous about this night, but the fact that she's here is a good start."

"Did you really walk over here to give me advice about my sister?" he asked, pinning Chris with a lethal glare.

Chris wasn't going to back down. "I came over here because I could see you struggling. I gave you advice because I care about her and want to see her happy. You need to get over yourself."

"Get over myself?" Michael echoed, his voice rising. "I'm trying to give her space, not that it's your business."

"But it is my business. How many years of space do you plan to give her? How many has it been? Five? She's here. Don't waste it."

Michael didn't look impressed. Before he could pursue the conversation, the hostess stepped into the room and announced dinner. The small group filed into the dining room. A large wooden farm table took up the majority of the space. Chairs lined one side of the table, with bench seating on the other side. Chris tried not to laugh when Alyssa took the end seat, leaving Michael with no choice but to sit at Mallory's other side.

Chris had known Michael long enough to know the move wasn't going to go over well, but he watched in surprise as he sat down without any argument. Keeping his hands off Mallory was nearly impossible. He had to settle for a subtle touch here and there, but they both began to relax as the dinner went on.

Unfortunately, it seemed to be the opposite going on with Brian and Kerry. Kerry spoke to everyone except Brian, and Brian didn't speak at all. Somehow the tension between Brian and his new bride seemed much worse than the tension between Michael and Mallory. The siblings were at least politely ignoring each other and not actively freezing each other out.

Chris was a professional at tuning out uncomfortable situations, but just as he was reaching his limit, the hostess returned and announced that the wedding cake and dessert were ready to be served back in the parlor. He didn't think the situation could get worse, but he'd somehow forgotten about cutting the wedding cake.

"I really need to get some sleep," Chris began working on his exit. "I've either been working, or at the hospital with my mom for more days than I can count. Will you be offended if we head to our rooms?"

"Alyssa was telling me about your mom. Get some rest. We'll see you at breakfast," Kerry said.

"I couldn't take one more minute of that," he explained quietly once they were out of earshot of the others. "Are we sleeping in your room or mine?"

Chapter 13

MALLORY

Mallory awakened to Christian trailing kisses along her neck. Blinking the sleep from her eyes, she rolled to her side so she could look at him. His hair was a mess, and it was obvious that he had also just woken up.

"Morning," he greeted.

She smiled up at him in response. Once they had gotten back to the room, Christian took a shower and Mallory was asleep before he got out. All of the stress and emotions over the past several days must have taken their toll. As soon as her head hit the pillow she was out.

"You stayed."

"Of course I stayed. Where else would I go?" Christian asked, pulling her close.

"To your own room. Although Michael didn't have much to say to me, so I guess it doesn't matter."

Thoughts of the night before threatened to dampen her good mood. After five years of silence, Michael didn't seem to have much to say; not that she'd want a heart to heart in the middle of a wedding reception anyway. But still.

"I'm not worried about it; I just don't want to cause a scene. But we should be fine. We're next to the Bridal Suite, and I know Brian and Kerry don't care. They have their own shit they're dealing with," Christian said. "You taking a shower? Breakfast is in a little over an hour."

"Hopefully mimosas will be involved. I'm going to need one or three if everything is as awkward as it was last night." She stood up and made her way to the shower.

A shower would wash away some of the stress from the night before. A believer in fresh starts, she planned to go to breakfast with an open mind. Breakfast was less of a formal event, and she was determined to try again. After having some time to process everything, she already felt more comfortable with the idea of approaching him.

After stepping out of the shower, she wrapped the towel around herself and stepped out of the bathroom. Her heart rate picked up speed when she saw the expression on Christian's face. He was watching her with that irresistibly disarming smirk as his gaze traveled down and then up her body.

She adjusted her towel. "You haven't gotten ready for breakfast."

"I have time. Let's take a few minutes. Last night was a lot. And then we just went to sleep."

He voiced the same thoughts she was having in the shower. Last night was a lot. She still wanted to face her brother full on, but taking some time to gather herself wasn't a bad idea. She sat down on the bed next to Christian, resting her head on his shoulder.

"I'm glad you talked me into this. Even though Michael didn't seem interested in talking to me, it was nice to know I could be in the same room and the world didn't come to an end. So, thank you."

She gave him a quick kiss. Before she could pull away, he moved his hands to her face and held her in place, his tongue teasing its way past her lips as he deepened the kiss. Once again, her response was immediate. She reached for the waistband of his boxer briefs and gave them a tug, but instead of helping her to remove them he placed a hand over hers and held her still.

"Not yet, Bunny. I want to take my time with you."

She stilled at his words. The time before had been hard, fast, and hot as hell. They had never taken their time with each other, not even their first time together. The idea of savoring the moment caused her to pause.

He returned his mouth to hers, his hands trailing down her body. When he reached the point where the edge of the towel met her thighs, instead of removing the towel, he slipped his hands beneath the damp fabric and stroked her heated flesh, spreading her legs as he pushed her to lay back on the bed. She melted into his languid caress, her anticipation climbing.

Her hands wandered back to him, but he grabbed both her wrists in one hand, forcing them above her head. "Don't move."

His words vibrated through her, sending a rush of heat to her core. She tried her best to be still, but when his tongue trailed down her body, she gripped the sheets beside her.

"I said don't move," he growled.

He straddled her and used both hands to hold hers above her head. The motion elicited a gasp, to which he chuckled in response. He flashed a grin before returning his mouth to her neck. Using one hand, he untucked the towel from across her breasts before diving back in. His tongue singed her skin as he licked and sucked his way across her neck and down her chest.

"Move again and I'll have to tie you up."

Determined not to move, she relaxed under his hold and concentrated on the feel of his mouth. He let go of her arms and continued his southern descent. She bucked when he reached her center, his tongue making small circles around her clit as she cried out from the pleasure.

Her breathing increased as her pleasure continued to build. She wanted to touch him, to hold him tight against her body. His gentle touch was a stark contrast from the rough way he'd taken her before. Her body was coiled tight, the promise of release getting closer as he continued to devour her. Just as she was nearing the point of no return, he pulled away.

Her eyes flew open, and she opened her mouth to protest but before she could utter a word, he covered her mouth with his, the tang of her arousal coating her tongue. Moaning into his mouth, her hands made their way to the back of his head, finally unable to resist holding him close. He didn't punish her for moving. Instead, he positioned himself at her entrance and filled her in one slow thrust.

Hanging on to her control by a mere thread, she met each thrust, desperate to feel more. It wasn't a feeling she was used to. Christian shoved into her harder and faster, seeking his own release. The headboard knocked against the wall in time with his thrusts as he chased his release, but at that moment she didn't care. Everything he was willing to give, she would be willing to take. His hand covered her mouth, muffling her cries.

"Quiet. They'll hear."

He slid his hand from her mouth to her neck and she came undone when he gave a gentle squeeze. She came with a rush of curse words and then finally his name on her lips, her thighs squeezing him tight.

He followed, holding her tight as he emptied himself into her. No words were needed as they lay in each other's arms waiting for their breathing to return to normal. They needed to get ready for breakfast, but Mallory had no desire to leave the safety of Christian's warm embrace.

"Wow," Christian muttered after a moment.

Mallory giggled in response. Giggled. She even caught herself by surprise.

"We're going to be late," Mallory pointed out.

"Yeah. I left my suitcase in the other room." He climbed out of bed and pulled on his pants from the night before. "I'll be right back."

Mallory followed him out of the bed and made her way back into the bathroom to clean up. She'd packed a short sunflower yellow sundress to wear to the breakfast, and going with sticky thighs wasn't going to work for her. She left the bathroom door cracked open, and before she turned on the faucet, raised voices caught her attention.

"What the fuck? I knew you were lying when you said the two of you weren't sleeping together, but Jesus Christ." Michael's voice could be heard loudly from the hallway.

She couldn't hear Christian's response, so she slipped on her robe and made her way closer to the door so she could listen.

"Who cares what room I was supposed to be in? That's my sister and you two were loud enough for the entire fucking place to hear."

She'd heard enough. Listening at the door was as far as it was supposed to go, but that statement infuriated her. The audacity. She swung the door open and stormed into the hallway, an uncharacteristic rage taking over her actions.

"Who do you think you are?" she shouted. "Now you want to be my brother? You ignored me during the entire reception, not to mention the past five years!"

"I was giving you space, Sammy!" Michael shouted back at her.

Mallory was surprised steam wasn't rising from her head. Space? Space was a few days or a few weeks. She might not have been receptive, but it hurt her more than she cared to admit that he hadn't even tried.

Devastated by the warm tears that stung her eyes, she turned to blink them away. Her vision was only slightly blurry when she turned back and pointed a finger in his direction.

"Do not call me that. And you don't get to be a protective brother after pretending I don't exist." She turned on her heel and charged back into the room.

She was beyond washing up. She turned on the shower, hoping the warm water would once again soothe her racing thoughts. After tossing her robe onto the floor, she stepped under the cascade of hot water. Her old tactics of cleansing breaths did little to calm her anger, so she quickly soaped up and rinsed off, before reciting some positive affirmations.

"Are you okay?" Christian was standing in the doorway when she stepped out.

He wore fresh black dress pants, and his yellow shirt was unbuttoned. He was looking at her like he thought she might run. She wasn't going to, but a few minutes to regroup would do her some good.

"I will be."

He stepped the rest of the way into the bathroom and pulled her close. His warm embrace soothed her and this time her deep breathing did what it was supposed to do.

"We can leave if you need to," he suggested.

"No. I'm not letting him ruin what should have been a nice getaway," she answered. "I'm tired of always running."

He held her at an arm's length, his green eyes studying her closely. After a moment he nodded his head in agreement. "Okay. Let's do this then."

She breathed him in for an extra moment before releasing him so she could get dressed. His arms felt like home, and she didn't want to move, but she couldn't use him to hide. Hiding wasn't any better than running. It was time for her to face things.

Chapter 14

MALLORY

"Can you take this next patient?" Jenna asked. "I'm supposed to go on break."

Mallory finished up her paperwork and headed out to the lobby. When the double doors opened, her heart stuttered, and she felt as though she was looking at a ghost; freezing her in her tracks as goosebumps spread across her flesh. She hadn't seen her father in person since Christmas five years ago. The fact that he was standing there just days after she'd seen her brother couldn't have been a coincidence.

"I need to talk to you," he said after a moment.

"I have a patient," she said before looking behind him and into the waiting room. "Henry Lasko?"

An older gentleman stood when she called the name and made his way toward her. She directed him through the automatic doors but stopped to address her father.

"You need to go. I'm at work."

"I'm here for bloodwork," he argued.

"Then someone else can do it."

She paused on the way to her chair to tell Jenna that she wouldn't be able to take that patient. She didn't explain why, figuring Jenna would get it out of her later, if she really wanted to know.

As she prepared Mr. Lasko's labs, she heard Jenna call her father back. It took everything in her to not react; but she was listening. She made her normal small talk as she found a vein and started drawing his blood.

"Have you ever had blood drawn before?" She heard the question come from the other side of the curtain.

"Plenty of times. I get checked out every year. I just haven't been here before," her father's voice traveled to Mallory's ears.

Mallory filled the first tube and picked up the next one.

"Ever since I lost my wife, I make sure I get checked out. Even though my children are grown, I don't want to leave them before it's truly my time."

Mallory filled the second tube and reached for the next one.

"My wife had a heart condition. We didn't think it would be fatal, but her biggest concern was that the kids could be left without parents. I'm a retired police officer, and she was determined that I remarry as soon as possible if anything happened to her. She knew that with my job, anything could happen in the line of duty. Even after I married my current wife, I still get my well visits and labs done like clockwork."

"Oh wow," Jenna's voice carried over to her. "Your kids are lucky to have you care so much."

A long pause.

"I wouldn't say that. They never knew their mother was sick. One day she was gone and then one day I got remarried. I just wish they knew I only wanted what was best for them. If something happened to me there wouldn't have been anyone to take them."

"I'm sure they are grateful," Jenna responded. "Big pinch."

Tears escaped Mallory's eyes as she gripped Mr. Lasko's arm. Her mother had been sick? He'd only been obeying her mother's wishes when he remarried, not pretending she never existed. While the new knowledge made her angry for different reasons, she'd still been wrong. Her stomach dropped when she thought about what a jackass she'd been. Their mother hadn't been replaced; she'd been honored.

"I just hope my children know that everything I've ever done has been for them."

There was no slowing her tears. She finished filling the last tube of blood and put a bandage on Mr. Lasko while on auto pilot. She was vaguely aware of him asking if she was okay, but she was unable to do more than nod. Her heartbeat was erratic as she processed everything she'd heard. How many years had she lost with her family? Shoving those thoughts aside, she finished up the charting after sending her patient on his way.

"Are you okay?" Doris asked from the computer beside her.

Okay was relative. She would manage just like she always had. A few cleansing breaths followed by a positive affirmation or two and she'd be okay.

"I will be," she said with a slow nod. "We'll talk about it later. I just need a little time."

Instead of her feelings subsiding as the day went on, she felt worse. It was busy enough that she was able to avoid both Jenna and Doris for most of the day, but any time she had a break between patients, she found herself blinking back a fresh set of tears.

"Talk to me." Jenna stood beside her while she entered the information for her last patient.

"There's nothing to talk about." She'd made it to the end of the day without tears, and she didn't want to start.

Jenna grabbed both arm rests of her chair and spun her around. The compassion in her brown eyes was nearly her undoing. With a ragged sigh, she covered her face with her hands and tried to regain her composure.

"Was that patient—"

"He was nobody," she lied, losing the battle over her tears.

"Mallory?"

She took her time before she responded, doing her best to collect herself. "Yes. That was my dad."

Jenna's eyebrows shot up in surprise before she regained control over her facial expression. "Oh wow. I didn't think you were in contact with any of your family. Are you okay?"

"Not really," Mallory admitted. "I saw my brother the other day. It was the first time I'd seen him in five years. This was not what I needed."

The tingling in her chest reminded her to take a few deep breaths before her anxiety took over. After years of trudging through, she was exhausted. As much as she wanted to ignore this new information, holding on to resentment was exhausting, and she was so tired.

"I didn't know my mom was sick. Dad never told me."

"I'm sorry, hun. Do you want to go for a drink? Get your mind off it?"

Mallory considered the offer. "It sounds amazing. But I'll pass."

"You sure?"

Hesitating for a moment, she considered backing out of what she knew had to be done. "I'm sure."

CHRISTIAN

Chris sat on the cold tile floor of his mother's bathroom. He'd been there all day and was exhausted from working the night before. Robbie had stuck around to help make some adjustments to the house. Modifications had to be made in order for her to safely return home. They were still awaiting the final plan, but whenever she came home, they wanted her to do it comfortably.

He tightened down the bolts of the new toilet, before turning on the water and watching for a leak. With her hip, they wanted to get rid of the old one. Not only was it too low to the ground, but it shifted any time someone sat down. He couldn't buy her a new house, or pay for a full-time private nurse, but he could replace a toilet. Having an aging parent was hard, even knowing the only alternative to getting old was dying young.

His phone began vibrating in his pocket as he washed the grime off his hands. His ex-wife's name lit up across the screen and he heaved a long sigh before he answered.

"You need to come down here and get your daughter," she said without preamble.

He sat up, giving the call his full attention. "What's going on? Is she okay?"

He stood and paced the floor as he listened. "She's been acting out. I don't know what's going on with her and I don't know what to do anymore. She's refusing to do anything to help out around here and she's either yelling at me or she's crying."

"She's a teenager, I'm sure it's just hormones," Chris reasoned.

"You say that like you spend every day with her." A dagger through his heart. "I know all about hormones. This isn't that. There's something going on with her and she won't talk to me. I can't keep leaving work because I'm worried about her being home with the neighbor lady."

His daughter needing him while he was so many hours away had been his biggest fear, even before the move was complete. He should have fought harder to keep Vivian from taking his daughter so far away. It wasn't Liliana's fault that he and Vivian couldn't work things out, and she shouldn't have to suffer for it. He ran a hand through his hair as he tried to quickly figure out what to do.

"Can you take a couple days off work and bring her up here? I can give you some money toward a plane ticket. I've got a lot going on right now," he said as he tried to work out a plan in his head.

"No, I can't just drop everything and come up there so that you can be a father. You need to figure it out," she snapped.

Fuck!

Chris had a temper, and although he'd promised himself that he would always keep things civil with his ex, she was really pushing it. It didn't take a psychologist for him to know his breakup with Vivian was the reason he changed women nearly as often as he changed his clothes. Until Mallory. The end of his marriage caused him more pain than he thought possible. Liliana had his entire heart, and Vivian took her away when she up and moved. She could have stayed local. No matter what she told him, he was certain she moved away out of spite.

"You're the one who moved. It's bullshit that you take my daughter away and then it's up to me to figure shit out. I'll let you know what I come up with." He hung up without giving her a chance to respond.

Nearing his breaking point, he stormed out to his car after yelling over his shoulder to his brother and headed to the gym. He needed to hit things, run, sit in the sauna—something. Anything to dull what he was feeling. Even after so many years of his daughter living away from him, nothing could dull the searing pain of not being able to get to her when she was in trouble or hurting. Lily needed him, and he was sixteen hours away. There had to be a solution.

Seeing the crowd at the weight stations, he went straight for the cardio area. There was a treadmill available, so he settled for a jog. He was thankful he had thrown on a t-shirt and some basketball shorts to work at his mom's house. He was nearly finished with his warmup when he heard a familiar voice call out to him.

"So, you do workout more than once a week," James said when he finally looked over.

A pang of guilt briefly distracted him from the reason behind his impromptu gym visit. "Sorry I've been skipping our after-work gym visits. Everything's been crazy. I wasn't planning on coming today or I would have sent you a text."

"I know. Just giving you shit."

Chris hiked the speed up and started his run. He wasn't usually much of a cardio guy, but running relieved stress. His concentration moved from his feelings of frustration to the steady rhythm of his feet on the treadmill. The front of his shirt was damp and sweat dripped down his back before he finally slowed back down to a walk.

"How long do you plan to work out?" he asked James once he caught his breath.

"Until I'm done," he answered with a smirk. "Wanna hit some weights?"

He did. Any physical activity that might tamp down his feelings of anger and frustration would be a good idea. After wiping up behind themselves, they went down to the weights. The area had mostly cleared out, so they had their pick of equipment.

"Spot me?" Chris asked, walking over to the bench and selecting a few weights to add to the bar.

James stood over him as he lay on his back and lifted the heavy bar. He lifted more weight than usual because he craved the burn his muscles felt as he pushed himself. Instead of blocking out his reason for being there, he used his time to work on a solution while he counted out each rep.

"One." He could buy Liliana a plane ticket and have her travel as an unattended minor.

"Two." How would that work with his schedule? Liliana wasn't old enough to stay home alone all night.

"Three." He could see if anyone on days would be willing to trade shifts.

"Four." Even during the day, twelve hours was a long time for a thirteen-year-old to be home alone.

"Five." He could fly down to Florida and spend a couple days with her.

"Six." A couple of days might not be enough.

Chris continued thinking everything through while he lifted. The more his muscles shook as he lifted the bar, the clearer his thoughts became. His arms strained under the weight and sweat beaded on his forehead as the realization hit him while he counted out his last rep.

"Ten!" He needed to go to his daughter by any means necessary.

Chapter 15

MALLORY

The house looked exactly as she remembered it. True, five years wasn't very long, but it was a long time to avoid something. Memories of walking up the sidewalk hand-in-hand with her mother flashed unbidden across her mind. That was another thing that bothered her as she got older. Not only did her father replace her mother, but the new wife just moved in and literally took her mom's place.

A cold chill washed over her, despite the early summer heat. Giving her head a small shake, she slowly made her way up the cracked sidewalk and to the door. Without having a plan, there was no telling what she was going to say if her father was home. She was wrong and needed to remember that when anger began to creep back up; even though it wasn't right that he had kept things from her. Would she have accepted that information when she was younger? Probably not, but it wasn't up to other people to decide what she could handle. As a child, maybe, but not as she got older.

"Sammy?" Her stepmother's voice tore her from her thoughts. "Sammy, it *is* you!"

She looked up to find Sheila bounding out of the front door. As usual, her graying hair was pulled into a bun, and she was dressed in jeans and a long tunic. The smile on her face was genuine and her eyes crinkled as she stopped in front of Mallory, reaching her arms out but stopping short of pulling her into a hug.

"No one calls me Sammy anymore, remember?"

"I'm sorry, dear. Mallory. I'm so glad you're here. Will you come inside? Your dad should be out of the shower by now. He just came in from mowing the lawn. He'll be happy to see you."

Mallory fell into step behind her and followed her into the house. Not much had changed in the five years she'd avoided the place. The distinct scent of "home" threatened to overwhelm her, but she was able to blink back the tears that filled her eyes. A paperback book lay face down over the arm of the recliner opposite the window, so she assumed Sheila had been reading when she noticed her making her way to the front door. The television was on but muted.

Declining a seat in the living room, she sat down at the kitchen table and let the memories wash over her as she waited for her father. The wooden table hadn't been replaced since she was a kid. She rubbed her fingers over the lightened spot from where she'd spilled nail polish remover. Even though she wasn't supposed to use the nail polish remover by herself, she had been too impatient to wait for her mom to finish what she was doing. Instead of her mom yelling, she'd helped clean up the mess then treated her to a manicure.

The refrigerator was new, but if she closed her eyes, she could see her artwork hanging by magnets. Her mother used to save everything. Even just the quick doodles she made while sitting down and waiting for an af-ter-school snack had made their way to the refrigerator and bulletin board. She smiled to herself remembering the good times, before life stepped in and snatched everything away.

"Sweetheart? You're here?" Her father stood in the doorway as if he was afraid she might disappear if he came any closer.

"Why didn't you tell me?" she asked.

He slowly walked toward her, and her breathing grew faster with each step until she worried she'd hyperventilate. She wanted his arms around her. She craved the security that could only be brought to a daughter by her father.

"You were so young ..." he trailed off, his icy blue gaze looking above her and out the window. "Then suddenly it seemed like it was too late. I didn't want you to be upset with your mother, but I never imagined it would cause such a wedge between all of us. I just wanted you to be cared for and happy. Please know that."

Relief washed over her as she listened to his words. She believed him. After so many years of running and avoiding, she was ready to stop. Running was exhausting. There was no more fight left in her and her shoulders slumped as she looked at the floor and took a slow, unsteady breath. Staying angry would not bring her mom back.

"Okay," she breathed.

Her dad's eyebrows shot up. "Okay?"

She nodded her head and repeated herself. "Okay."

The next thing she knew, she was on her feet as her father held her close. Warm tears ran down her face and onto his soft cotton shirt. He smelled like sandalwood and fabric softener as she tried to take deep breaths in order to regain some ounce of composure. She squeezed him tight as she fought the sobs that shook her body.

"It's okay," he soothed. "Please don't cry."

"I'm sorry," she choked out as she tried to catch her breath. "I'm so sorry I was awful to everyone."

He squeezed her tighter as they rocked side to side. He was tall and her face barely came to his chest. "Don't be sorry. You didn't know, which is my fault. I'm just glad you're here now. Will you stay for dinner? Sheila is making lasagna."

Her initial reaction was to refuse, but for some reason she agreed. All the years that she'd lost with her family because of hurt feelings, pride, and misunderstandings wouldn't be regained if she didn't work hard to break the cycle. She craved the closeness of family. Spending time with Christian and his mom made her feelings undeniable, even to herself.

As soon as she agreed, Sheila appeared out of nowhere and began making a fuss over her. Cheese, crackers, wine, and water arrived at the table before she even knew what was happening. It was attention she didn't deserve. She'd treated the woman terribly even though she never did a thing to warrant it. Her eyes welled with fresh tears as Sheila poured her a glass of wine.

"I'm so sorry, Sheila," she uttered in a strangled whisper. "You shouldn't be doing all of this for me."

Sheila set down the wine bottle and placed her hands on Mallory's shoulders, giving a comforting squeeze. "Honey, don't you dare apologize. Just let us sit here and enjoy you."

And just like that, things were different. They had all said what they needed to say and agreed to move on. Just like that. They sat at the table talking and catching up. She sat in the seat she'd claimed as a child, and her dad sat across from her. Sheila flitted about the kitchen, pouring refills and checking on dinner as the three reacquainted themselves. A comforting warmth draped over Mallory as she took it all in.

All awkwardness had dissipated by the time dinner was served. Conversation was smooth and Mallory nearly forgot how long it had been since she'd sat at that table and shared a meal with these people. Her father was retired and adjusting well, and Sheila was relieved to not worry about him every time he went to work.

"We've been taking cooking classes together," Sheila went on. "Michael bought us a few classes over a year ago for our anniversary, and we decided to keep it up. It's a lot of fun."

The mention of his name sent a wave of pain through her. One thing remained on her mind. "Did Michael know?"

"No, sweetheart. Just Sheila. She wanted me to tell you, but you know how I can be. I thought I knew what was best. My mistake caused both of you pain. I want you to forgive me, but if you have to be mad at someone it should be me, not your brother or Sheila."

"God," Mallory muttered.

As she recalled the last time she'd seen her brother, her heart sank even further. Getting everything off her chest had been a long time coming, but she had been pretty terrible to him. Had she known the entire story, she might have reacted differently. It wasn't necessarily what she'd said, but how she said it.

"What is it?" her father asked, his eyes creased with concern.

"Did you know I saw Michael the other day? Is that why you showed up at work looking for me?" she asked.

He swallowed. "He mentioned it."

"Did he tell you what a bitch I was to him?"

Her father chuckled nervously. "He didn't use those words. But he did say things didn't go well."

Her cheeks flushed as she realized what started their argument. If her dad knew Michael had overheard Christian and her having sex, she would die right then and there. She immediately regretted mentioning that interaction.

"It's okay. You didn't know. And neither did he. Don't be too hard on yourself."

His statement made her feel confident that he wasn't privy to the details surrounding their disagreement, which allowed her a sigh of relief. The interaction had been so charged with emotion she completely forgot the reason behind it.

"Do you think he'd talk to me?" she asked quietly.

Her dad reached across the table and took her hand. "Talk to him. I know for a fact there's nothing he would want more. All he ever wanted was a relationship with you. I should have told him. If I did, I know he wouldn't have allowed all this time to pass. I'm so sorry for that."

Talking to him was definitely up next on her agenda. It just couldn't be the same day. She needed some time to process everything; time to catch her breath. What she needed was Christian's comforting embrace, and she hated that she allowed herself to get there.

"I'll talk to him," she promised. "I will. Just not yet."

CHRISTIAN

Chris felt like a complete dick for giving Mallory the brush off the past couple days. She'd mentioned wanting to see him, but he was too caught up in his own shit. He finally told her she could stop by if she wanted. That was one of the reasons he hadn't allowed himself to get into any serious relationships. When he was going through something, he shut everyone out and handled it himself. Alyssa had been the first person to break through any of his walls, and then Mallory managed to slide in through the cracks.

He left his bedroom to open the door when he heard Mallory knock. He hadn't told her that he was leaving for Florida, but he couldn't keep avoiding her. He opened the door to find her standing on the other side holding a bag of takeout. The unfamiliar sensation of guilt rose from his chest.

"Hey," she said with a shy smile. "You said you were going through something, and I thought maybe you haven't had a chance to eat. I picked up sandwiches from the deli around the corner."

He was a jackass. "Thanks. Come in. I haven't eaten all day, actually."

He took the bags from her hands before leading the way to the kitchen. It wasn't until he set the bag down on the table that he turned to look at her. Her eyes were filled with uncertainty as she watched him. He could tell she was reading his mood. She knew something was up.

"What's wrong?" she asked after a long silence hung over the room.

He remained quiet while he removed everything from the bag and took down a couple paper plates. He wasn't sure how he wanted to navigate this. It would be a total dick move to shut her out, but he really needed to handle things himself like he always did. After a heavy sigh, he turned to face her. Her unease was palpable. Without thinking about it, he pulled her into a comforting hug, squeezing her tight to comfort himself as much as to comfort her.

"I need to go away for a few days," he said hesitantly.

"Is everything okay?"

"Not really," he admitted. "But let's eat, and I'll tell you about it. It's kind of a long story."

Chris started from the very beginning as he explained the situation. The fact that he and his daughter were inseparable before Vivian moved them clear to Florida was important, so she could understand the situation. She listened attentively as he described the phone call. Even after having time to digest everything that was going on, he couldn't think of anything worse than his daughter needing him while he was unable to get to her immediately.

"You're right to go," Mallory said once he'd finished. "What can I do to help? I have some vacation time left if you want me to come with you."

And there was the question he'd been dreading. How could he explain to her that he didn't want her help? She'd been there for him while he dealt with his mom's fall and resulting surgery. He hadn't even told her about the nursing home, yet.

"There's not really anything you can do. If Lily's going through something, I really need to handle it myself. But I didn't even tell you the update on my mom. There's also that. Everything is just a lot right now."

"What's going on with your mom?" Mallory immediately snapped to attention.

"She's not coming right home, but I've been working with Robbie to get her house ready for when she does," he explained after finishing a bite of his food. "They're putting her in a glorified nursing home. She's not doing well enough to go home so she needs a rehab facility until she's ready."

Mallory stood and began cleaning up. She hadn't uttered a word since hearing his mother wasn't coming home. He'd been around her long enough to figure out that the news about his mom stressed her out. She kept fiddling with her hair like she did every time something was on her mind.

"Do you think she'll be there long," she finally asked once everything was cleaned up.

She cared about his mom as if she was her own family. The realization made his chest ache. There she was ready to drop everything to be there for them, and he couldn't be bothered to keep her updated. It was no wonder his marriage hadn't worked out and even less surprising that he hadn't had a serious relationship since the failed marriage.

"I hope not. The doctor keeps insisting it will only be until she's ready to be home by herself, but I have no idea," Chris answered.

"How long will you be away? Will you be back before they move her?"

He wasn't sure. He'd be gone as long as he needed to be. After speaking to the powers that be at work, he'd been cleared to take all the time he needed. As long as he kept them updated, there was no rush for him to return.

"A few days," was his answer.

His answers were vague. A quick glance at Mallory told him she wasn't interested in a guessing game. It didn't make sense that he was struggling with including her in his life as a father, but old habits were hard to break. He stretched his neck from side to side in an effort to relieve some tension.

"I'm not trying to be vague," he explained. "To be honest, I'm having a hard time having this conversation, but I'm really not sure how long I'll be gone. I'm not even sure what's going on with her or if I can fix it."

For what felt like the millionth time, his heart sank at the thought of not being able to help his daughter. Whatever it was, he had to find a way to fix it, even if he landed back in family court with a custody battle. The warm touch of Mallory's hands on his shoulders snapped him out of his dark thoughts. Leaning into her gentle touch, he forced himself to relax. He hadn't taken a moment to breathe since receiving that phone call.

"I know you're having a hard time. I didn't mean to sound like I was grilling you. If you're going to be gone while your mom gets moved, I can be there to help get her settled in. That's why I was asking."

Slowly, he turned to face her. Even after getting to know her, she always managed to surprise him. It was rare to find someone who was genuinely kind, and yet there she was giving him a shoulder massage and focusing in on ways to help. Even years in an abusive relationship hadn't tarnished her kind heart. All things considered, finding out his daughter was in trouble and knowing it was his fault for being so far away really put things into perspective.

"You don't have to go out of your way. They plan to move her within the next few days, so Robbie should still be here. But thanks for thinking of her."

She pinned him with a look. "Is this you telling me to stay away from your mom? Because if it isn't, give me the details so I can be there."

A rumble of laughter escaped him. That was not the response he had been expecting. It would appear that finally standing up for herself to her brother was only the beginning. The fire he always knew was smoldering within her was finally beginning to burn. She wouldn't be anyone's doormat.

He stood from his chair and turned to face her, looking down to meet her fierce gaze. "My mom loves you. I wouldn't tell you to stay away from her."

"Good," she breathed.

"Good." He watched her mouth, waiting for what she'd say next.

One corner of her mouth turned up as she continued to stare back at him. Her gaze bounced from his mouth to his eyes, and he adjusted himself as his cock hardened and strained against his zipper. With things being so up in the air he needed to keep his distance. It was the right thing to do.

He gripped the back of her neck and held her in place as his mouth found hers. Using his thumb, he tugged her mouth open enough for his tongue to meet hers as he lost himself in the kiss. He should keep his distance.

"I leave in the morning. Stay the night," he requested before diving back in to devour her mouth.

She sank into him, her body soft and warm against his taught muscles. As much as he knew he should stay away until he knew where life would take him, he needed her. She wrapped her arms around him, and this time it was her mouth seeking his. He placed his hands on her face and held her tenderly as he answered her kiss.

Every time they'd been together had been a desperate rush to get their hands on each other. Once things had started, neither of them could slow down. They were like fire and gasoline. This time, Chris needed more. He traced the outline of her face before gliding his hand down her neck and to her shoulder, pausing to breathe her in.

"Will you stay?" he asked again. If the answer was no, he'd allow her to walk away.

"Okay." Her answer was so soft he nearly missed it.

Hands on her hips, he backed her toward the bedroom. His heart hammered in his chest as he peppered kisses across her cheek and down her neck, breathing in her scent again once he reached her hair. With so much uncertainty, he needed to lose himself in the one thing he knew was real.

"Are you sure?" He paused to nudge the bedroom door open with his foot.

In typical Mallory fashion, instead of answering him she began undressing him. She tugged his shirt up until he pulled it the rest of the way over his head and then made a move for his belt. He smiled against her lips as she fumbled with his belt.

"Slow down, Bunny."

Once they reached the bed, he returned his hands to her face and kissed her slowly, pouring out everything he couldn't find the words to say. Her mouth was eager against his, but he kept things slow, savoring her taste; willing himself to live in the moment. He dropped to his knees and looked up at her as he slid her pants over her hips and down her legs. She gripped his shoulders for balance as she stepped out and the raw emotion in her eyes as she looked down nearly shredded him.

He remained on his knees and gently caressed the back of her thighs, resting his forehead against her leg as he closed his eyes and tried to gather himself. His breath hitched when he felt her shiver against him. What was she doing to him? He stood, moving his hands up her body as he went, and sealed his mouth to hers.

"Touch me." He'd removed the rest of his clothing and made his way to the center of the bed.

Without any hesitation she straddled him and rested her hands on his chest for support. She looked down at him as if she was unsure what to do now that she was there. Chewing on her bottom lip, her eyes lingered on his face.

"Touch me," he repeated.

Her soft hands moved slowly down his chest and to his stomach, heating his skin every place she touched. His breath caught when she swiped the patch of flesh below his navel. Her eyes snapped to his, both heated and unsure. She licked her lips, and it took every ounce of his self-control to keep from grabbing her hips and setting her on his cock. He closed his eyes to regain control, before returning his gaze to hers.

She never looked as perfect as she did right now; the steady rise and fall of her breasts as her breathing grew heavy. He did place his hands on her hips, but he didn't reposition her. He did some touching of his own, skimming his hands up her body and toward her breasts. She shivered and her nipples hardened under his gaze.

"What are you doing to me?" he breathed.

Her lips tugged into a ghost of a smile before she leaned forward and covered his lips with hers. Her tongue teased at his lips until he let her in, groaning as she explored his mouth. She only broke the kiss long enough to move to his neck, carefully licking and sucking her way to his collar bone. She used the tip of her tongue to lick her way over to his shoulder, where she nipped.

"Fuck," he groaned.

The bite went straight to his groin and that quickly, he'd reached the end of his control. He moved his hands up to her breasts and squeezed, skimming his thumbs across her nipples. She threw her head back and let out a guttural cry, squeezing her eyes shut.

"Are you ready?" he asked as he dug his fingers into the soft flesh of her hips.

She kept her eyes closed and nodded.

"Look at me," he growled.

She opened her eyes, her blue gaze crashing to his.

"Are you ready?"

Once again, she licked her lips. She kept her eyes on his and nodded. "Yes."

He lifted her hips and positioned her above his length. Slowly, he lowered her until he reached her entrance. She was hot, wet, and ready for him. Using his last shred of control, he slowly lowered her inch by inch, until he filled her completely. She shuddered on top of him and squeezed her eyes shut.

"Look at me. I need to see you."

She opened her eyes, looking at him. He gripped the nape of her neck, threading his fingers through her hair, and pulled her to him. His mouth crashed against hers as he continued to grip her hip with his other hand and thrust into her. His movements began to falter with the new sensation of her on top, and he knew he wouldn't last long in that position.

In one movement, he flipped her so she was on her back and he was looking down at her. She gasped in surprise as he thrust into her from the new angle. He was still unable to regain control, but he felt less vulnerable in this position. Her cries matched his and he could tell she was close. With her nails in his back, she held on tight, her body trembling against his. Once again, his movements began to falter.

"Come for me," he demanded.

She detonated around him, her core squeezing him as she shouted his name. He gripped her hair and tugged hard as he followed her to his own release, calling her name as he spilled into her. His hand trembled as he released her hair and held her face, kissing her as if his life depended on it.

Chapter 16

MALLORY

Mallory was alone when she woke up. Reaching her hand over, she felt the bed to find it was empty aside from her. She sat up and rubbed the sleep from her eyes as she smiled at the memories from the night before. A white sheet of paper on the nightstand caught her eye and trepidation sank heavily to the pit of her stomach.

Mallory,

You were sleeping so peacefully I didn't want to wake you. My flight is early. I'll probably be almost to Florida by the time you get up. Stay as long as you want, just lock the door when you go. I'll see you soon.

Love,

Christian

She reread the note several times before sliding her legs over the side of the bed to begin the process of getting ready. *Love, Christian.* Surely, she was reading into it, but that one word took the sting out of waking up alone, even if she did feel strange about being in his apartment without him being there. After making the bed, she washed her face and threw on her clothes from the night before.

There was only one thing she could think of that she could do from the sidelines that could make things a bit easier for Christian once he was back. Looking at the time, she realized she needed to get going so she wouldn't have an excuse to put it off for another day. She locked up behind herself and headed home to take a quick shower and change clothes. Knowing mornings were the best time to reach someone who worked nights, there wasn't much time before she would risk waking them up.

Less than thirty minutes later, she double checked her phone to make sure she was at the right address. She took a slow cleansing breath before stepping out of the car. It was hard to keep walking when her sense of self-preservation screamed at her to turn around. In the past, she wasn't strong enough to handle the confrontation. She was strong enough now, and it was time to finally move forward.

"Mallory?" Alyssa stepped out of the house, closing the door behind her. "Is everything okay? What are you doing here?"

Instant regret washed over her. She shouldn't have shown up unannounced. "I was hoping to talk to my brother."

Alyssa rested her hand protectively across her stomach as she turned to look at the closed door. "He worked last night …"

"I should leave," she blurted out. "Can you tell him I'm sorry? That's all I really came to say."

She turned on her heel to make her escape, but was stopped by Alyssa who grabbed hold of her arm. "Wait. Don't leave. He's not asleep. I'm sorry for not inviting you in, I just thought maybe there was going to be a continuation of the morning after the wedding reception."

"I'm really sorry about that, too," Mallory began her apology.

"Wait," Alyssa held up a hand. "Come in. It's really none of my business. Blame hormones for me being a bitch."

Her smile was so genuine that Mallory found herself smiling with her as they walked inside. Michael was lounging on the couch looking at something on his phone when he looked up in surprise.

"Sam—Mallory? What are you doing here?" He stood and walked over, looking at her as if she could be a mirage.

"I'm sorry," she said. "Mom was sick. Dad didn't replace Mom, and even if he did it wasn't your fault."

She looked up into blue eyes that matched her own. His hands were unexpectedly gentle when he gripped her shoulders. "What are you talking about?"

Mallory gave her head a shake, an attempt to clear her thoughts so she could make sense of what she needed to say. "I talked to Dad. I was wrong. Please forgive me."

Without a word, Michael urged her to the couch where he sat beside her, keeping an arm around her shoulders. For such a big and intimidating man, there was nothing but kindness in his expression.

"Can you start from the beginning?"

She was aware that she still wasn't saying things as clearly as she had hoped. "Dad didn't talk to you?"

He sat back, crossing one leg over his knee. He was quiet for a long moment before he responded to her question. "Talk to me about what?"

She took a deep breath to calm her nerves. Hearing the truth was one thing; repeating it was another. "Dad told me everything. Honestly, I am an asshole. What he said shouldn't have made a difference. The way I treated you was shitty. Mom was sick. No one expected her life to end when it did, but she knew it was a possibility. She always told Dad she was worried for us since she was sick, and Dad had a dangerous job. He loved Sheila, but only married her as quickly as he did to honor Mom's wishes."

Michael sat stock still. Even after being away from him for as many years as she was, she knew he was digesting what she had said. He took things seriously. He took everything to heart. He always had.

"Mom was sick?" he repeated what she'd said as a question.

"She had a heart condition. I don't think they were expecting anything to happen the way it did, but still. They were worried about where we would end up if something were to happen to her and then something happen to Dad on the job," Mallory explained.

Michael uncrossed his legs and leaned forward. "I can't believe I'm just now finding out Mom was sick," he muttered. "I mean, it doesn't change anything, but still. I had no idea Dad was keeping things from us. Did Mom pick Sheila out? Because that would be a whole different level of weird."

Mallory couldn't fight the bubble of laughter that erupted from her. "Oh, god, I don't think so. That would be super weird ... but I didn't ask how they met."

"So, does this mean we can start over?" Michael asked, turning to face her. "I should have made more of an effort before, but I'm here now. I'm willing to start over if you are. Can you forgive me for not reaching out? I wish I could get those years back."

Mallory was beyond grudges. She hadn't realized how tired she was until she began to let go of some of the baggage. She felt so much lighter after the conversation with her father that she wanted to see what else she could accomplish. Forgiveness took strength and courage, and with each decision she made to move forward, she felt stronger.

"I'm tired," was what she managed to put into words.

Instead of responding verbally, he pulled her into a hug. His embrace was warm and strong, and she felt completely safe for the first time since she was a child. Christian's arms felt like home, but there was something different about a hug from a protective brother. He may be younger than her, but he would never let anything happen to her. She squeezed him back as she inhaled his comforting scent.

"I've missed you," he said softly as he buried his face in her hair.

"So, where do we start?"

He sat back and looked at her; studying her as if trying to memorize her every feature. "I'd say this is a pretty good start."

"Okay in that case, what's next?" she asked, refusing to spiral into a bout of self-pity over all the time they had lost.

"Have you eaten? Stay for breakfast. Your sister-in-law happens to be an amazing cook."

She didn't want to intrude. It was already out of character for her to show up unannounced, and it felt like a huge imposition to stay for breakfast, invited or not.

"I shouldn't. You worked last night so I should let you sleep. But let's make plans for dinner or something."

"You are staying." Alyssa appeared in the doorway holding a box of pancake mix. "I'm making pancakes. I didn't work last night so you don't have to feel bad. We all have to eat. Please stay. Please ..."

Mallory caved. Alyssa was genuine and likeable. It was no wonder she and Christian had grown so close. As she looked into large hazel eyes, there was no way she could say no. Mallory looked down and smiled to herself.

"Okay. I'll stay for breakfast. But then I have to get home."

It was Saturday, but she had plans with Dan. They'd rescheduled their weekly dinner because they'd both made plans with their significant others. She felt much better about moving their plans around when they both needed to do it. Tonight would not be getting cancelled no matter what. She still had to finish catching Dan up on everything with her dad, and now add to it the fact that Christian was out of town for an undetermined amount of time, and here she was clearing the air with Michael.

They moved the conversation into the kitchen so Alyssa wouldn't be stuck in there making breakfast alone. She flitted around the kitchen talking and cooking as if she did things like that all the time. The sister-in-law who had avoided the family for years and years showed up on their doorstep after a particularly loud argument in a public place... and she was humming and talking as she made pancakes. Mallory was beginning to relax a lot more as she watched how relaxed her sister-in-law was as she whipped up breakfast.

"Do you need any help?"

"I'd rather you just sit back and relax," Alyssa answered quickly. "I've got it."

"You hate anyone in your way while you're cooking, don't you?" Mallory knew that response all too well.

Alyssa gave her a sheepish grin. "Guilty. You aren't offended, are you? Nothing against you, I'm just weird."

Mallory laughed. Maybe she had more in common with her sister-in-law than she realized. Michael gave her a knowing look as if he knew she was the same way. It was possible since she started cooking while she was a teenager and still living at home, but she was still surprised he remembered how annoyed she used to get when anyone came into the kitchen while she was cooking. He probably remembered more than she realized.

"If that makes you weird, then I guess we're both weird."

Michael chuckled at his wife's look of surprise. "I told you."

"Told her what?" Mallory asked, quirking an eyebrow.

"I told her sometimes she does things that remind me of you."

This was even more surprising than the fact that he remembered anything about her at all. After already getting a wakeup call that she had been wrong, seeing it up close and personal really brought it all home. The feeling of anxiety was replaced with a feeling of regret as she realized how terribly she'd treated everyone. Her grief was not anyone else's fault, and it was no one's cross to bear but her own.

"I'm really sorry for everything," Mallory repeated. "Why I was invited inside and to stay for breakfast is beyond me."

"Stop," Michael warned. "We're moving past it, remember?"

"Yes. Be kind to my sister-in-law," Alyssa joined in.

Shifting in her chair, she realized how unaccustomed she was to these new feelings of happiness and contentment. She spent so many years training herself to not feel her emotions, yet within the past few weeks she felt as though she was constantly feeling all of them at once.

"Are you going to stay on the road until you go on leave?" Mallory changed the subject.

Michael's eyes flashed while he looked at his wife, waiting for her to answer. When she stayed quiet, he prompted her to answer. "Alyssa?"

With a deep sigh, she turned around. "This past week was my last week on my normal truck. I'll be working the airport detail."

Mallory looked from Michael to Alyssa, trying to read the unspoken words that passed between them. He folded his arms and sat back in his chair, clearly amused by Alyssa's response. Obviously, her going to work at the airport was not her idea.

"I'd rather she come off the road all together, but the airport was an acceptable compromise. It's not as busy and a lot safer with police and security everywhere," he explained. "She'll realize I'm right. It's hard enough with them not allowing us to be permanent partners, but with what happened a couple years ago I can't take the chance of someone hurting her while she's pregnant."

"You know I'm still standing here, right?" Alyssa said as she set a plate stacked with pancakes onto the table.

"Sorry, hun. I was just trying to explain to Mallory that I'm not being an asshole and bossing you around, I just need you safe."

"I heard about what happened. I'm so glad you're okay, Alyssa. Christian told me about it when we first met."

Alyssa's lips pulled into a smile. "I think it's the cutest that you call him Christian."

Mallory was startled by the subject change. It was unexpected enough that she forgot to feel self-conscious over what was said. Instead, she was curious. "Well, that was quite a change of subject. Is it really that strange? His full first name is what I used when we introduced ourselves the very first time I met him, and he never corrected me."

"Not strange," Alyssa corrected as she placed a plate of bacon and bottle of syrup next to the pancakes. "Cute."

Mallory rolled her eyes and helped herself to a few pancakes and a slice of bacon. Her eating habits had really gone downhill since getting a social life. The realization made her chuckle to herself. The old her would have been very upset by that, but learning that it was okay to feel had slowly lessened her need to have control over every single thing in her life.

"That was delicious, thank you," Mallory said as she finished her last pancake. "At least let me help clean up."

Alyssa finished up her food and then sat back in her chair, rubbing a hand over her stomach. "Now that's something I won't argue with. Cleaning up sucks and you're family so have at it."

"Alyssa," Michael complained. "You aren't going to put her to work the first time she comes over here. Or ever, for that matter."

"It's okay, Michael," Mallory said as she stood and began gathering dishes. "She wouldn't let me help cook, so cleaning up is the least I can do."

"I'm so glad you stayed." Alyssa joined her at the sink and helped load the dishwasher. "How long is Chris going to be gone?"

It shouldn't have been a surprise that Alyssa knew he was going out of town, but the question caught her off guard. Since she had only found out the night before, he must have spoken to Alyssa about it before he spoke to her. Doing her best to mask her irritation, she finished loading the dishwasher before turning to Alyssa.

"I'm actually not sure. By the sound of it, I don't think he even knows."

"We should do a girls night or something," she suggested. "I mean, you don't have to. I always wanted a sister, and a sister-in-law counts. Pregnancy has apparently made me soft."

Mallory chuckled. Once again, the pair of large hazel eyes won her over. The not-so-subtle caress of her pregnant belly was also a nice touch. No way could Mallory say no. "You already have a couple sisters-in-law."

"Yeah, but not the infamous Sammy." She lowered her voice and glanced at the empty chair where Michael had been sitting before going on. "Even if you don't go by your middle name anymore ... He loves Liz and Rebecca, but they aren't you."

"I was already going to say yes. No need to butter me up," Mallory teased. "What did you have in mind anyway? I have plans tonight, but until Christian comes back, most of my evenings are free."

"I know you work during the week, but I'm off until Thursday. You should take a 'mental health day' so we can get our nails done. And eat food. And get facials. And eat food."

Mallory laughed. "I take it food is important to this excursion? I'm in. I haven't gotten my nails done in a while, but the place I go to is right next door to the best Mexican food you've ever eaten."

"Perfect! Tuesday?"

Mallory agreed. The smile that tugged at her lips was unavoidable. A new sister. Sure, she had stepsisters, but there was something different about a sister-in-law. Someone there by choice who wanted to spend quality time? Yes, please.

Michael had returned to the kitchen in time for her to start her goodbyes. Mallory was grateful for the space he'd given so she could spend a few minutes with Alyssa. She really did like the woman. After kissing Alyssa on the cheek, she confirmed their plans before making her way over to Michael. He stood several inches taller than Mallory, but his size didn't intimidate her. Since making up, his size was a comfort. She stepped into his arms and hugged him goodbye.

CHRISTIAN

Chris hated Florida. If it wasn't so hot, humid, and miserable, he would have considered moving closer. If he was honest, he likely would have endured the ridiculous heat if it didn't mean leaving his mother in New Jersey to fend for herself. But regardless, he was not a fan.

The baggage claim was clear on the other side of the airport, making him wish he went with his original plan of only packing a carry-on. Even in the air-conditioned airport, his shirt was clinging to him from the humidity. He stood amongst the throng of impatient travelers and watched as his suitcase came around, shouldering his way through to the front as it came closer. After grabbing his bag, he turned to head for the door and walked straight into Vivian.

"Shit! What are you doing in here?" he asked, looking behind her for his daughter. "I thought I was meeting you guys outside. And where's Lily?"

Vivian looked him up and down before answering. "Her attitude was out of control, so she's at home. I wasn't going to reward her behavior."

Vivian was dressed in a pair of cutoff denim shorts, a halter top, and an entire face of makeup. Some things never changed. After taking a moment to tamp down his irritation, he responded to both what she said, and the situation.

"Lily hasn't seen me in months, and you don't let her meet me at the airport because she has an attitude? Ever heard of choosing your battles, Vivian?"

"You can dictate rules and punishment when she lives with you. For now, she's my problem so I'll decide what I'm willing to accept." Vivian turned on her heel and walked toward the doors leading to short term parking.

"I'm not paying for your parking," he informed her.

Once they made it across the walkway and into the parking garage, Vivian turned to acknowledge what he'd said. "You think I expect you to voluntarily pay for anything?"

It was going to be a long trip. The amount he paid in child support was more than enough, but he never complained. She was getting more than he paid in rent and utilities every month, so for her to insinuate that he was a dead-beat had him seeing red. She was baiting him. He knew that. But it still took an impressive amount of restraint for him to hold his tongue.

"So, what's been going on with her?" he asked once they were in the car.

"If I knew that, you wouldn't be here. She hasn't been easy to be around for a while, but now I'm at a loss. You need to figure it out. Be a dad."

Chris closed his eyes and did his best to breathe through all the red he saw. She was the one who moved out of state. She was the one who made it so hard for him to spend time with his daughter. She could have used some vacation time to bring his daughter up for a visit, but that was too much of an inconvenience. It wasn't that she was a bad mother, but she sure liked to put herself first.

He closed his eyes and used his time in the car as a chance to cool off while regretting his agreement to stay at her house. Everything in him said to just pay for a hotel, but with all the things he had going on he needed to save money, and there wasn't much point in rushing down there if his time wouldn't be spent with Lily.

It wasn't too long of a drive from the airport, but long enough to lose some of the tension. He didn't speak for the rest of the ride home, and neither did she. They pulled up to the small house as the early afternoon sun beat down. He swore he could see the heat.

Vivian popped the trunk then went into the house, leaving him to grab his stuff then awkwardly waltz into a house that didn't belong to him, even though between the divorce settlement, spousal support, and child support, he probably paid for it. He shook his head in an effort to clear those thoughts away. Bitterness solved nothing.

"Lily?" he called out as he walked through the front door. "Liliana?"

Hearing a door creak open, he looked down the short hall to find his daughter, dressed in all black, watching him from the doorway. She stared at him without blinking for several moments before her shoulders slumped and she lowered her head.

He dropped his suitcase where he stood and made his way over. Her sobs grew louder as he approached, but they could barely be heard over the sound of his heart breaking.

"Sweetheart? What's wrong?"

"You're here," she choked out. "I didn't think you'd come."

Forcing down his emotions, he reached out and tilted her chin, causing her to look up at him. "I said I'd be here. I'm here."

They watched each other in silence. Chris moved his hands to her shoulders and held her at a distance as he appraised her. She had changed a lot since he'd seen her last. In mere months, she'd grown a couple inches and filled out. Instead of a lanky little girl, he was looking at a teenager; beautiful, even with the troubled expression in her gray eyes.

Wrapping her arms around him, she surrendered to her tears as Chris did everything possible to keep himself from falling apart. The hope that things weren't as bad as he thought shattered around him as he held her tight and whispered soothing words.

"Do you want to talk about it?" he asked gently.

She looked up at him then glanced past him down the hall. It was obvious that whatever it was, she wasn't comfortable talking about it in front of her mother.

"Let's sit outside for a bit," he suggested. He could endure the heat.

Without a word, Lily walked past him and down the hall to the door he'd walked in moments before. He followed her and closed the door behind them, joining her when she sat on the stoop. The silence was loud as he gave her all the time she needed.

"Can I live with you, Dad? I don't want to be here."

"Lil, I would love to have you with me all the time. But I know you'd miss your friends and even your mom. How about a visit? Some time away? A week or so now? And then at the end of the summer?"

Lily was quiet. He watched as she dragged her bare feet back and forth across the warm sidewalk, obviously unhappy with his response. He waited in silence for several moments, until it became obvious that she wasn't going to respond.

"Well? If it's okay with your mom, do you want to come back with me for a week?"

"Just forget it." She stood and walked into the house, leaving Chris sitting alone on the stoop.

Despite the heat, he didn't follow her inside. He knew better than to expect to get down there and immediately solve everything. Sure, he'd always been close with her, but teenagers were a different animal. Knowing in his heart a change of scenery would be good for her, he stood, brushed himself off, and headed inside to find Vivian.

Chapter 17

MALLORY

It didn't take Mallory long to spot her sister-in-law when she walked into the nail salon. She was wearing a long sun dress with a cardigan, looking like the definition of a glowing pregnant woman. Her tight curls fell below her shoulders, and she was balancing at least six different bottles of nail polish in her hands. She chuckled to herself as she made her way over to her.

"Going for a pattern?" Mallory asked.

"This is the hardest part of going to the nail salon," Alyssa said with a laugh. "They tell you to pick a color like you can just walk over and pick one. Which one should I go with?"

The dress she wore was yellow with pink flowers. Her sweater was also pink. The colors popped against her brown skin, so Mallory pointed to a pink bottle.

"That's what I was leaning toward! Thanks. What color are you going with?"

Mallory looked in her hands to see if there was one that she liked but there wasn't, so over to wall of colors she went. Opting for simplicity, she went with a shimmery coral color, then took the seat beside Alyssa and waited to be called back.

"Isn't this better than being at work?" Alyssa joked.

"I like my job, but literally anything is better than being at work," she responded with a laugh.

"You ladies can come," the woman announced from behind the counter. "You can follow me. We'll do your pedicure first. Did you pick a color?"

Mallory and Alyssa looked at each other with a grin before holding up their polish at the same time. As they did, they burst into a fit of laughter. As hard as she tried, Mallory couldn't hold back her laughter. Even though she was aware they were being as annoying as two giggly schoolgirls, it only made her laugh harder.

They giggled the entire way back to the pedicure area. Mallory stepped out of her shoes and rolled up her leggings before sitting down in the leather chair and placing her feet into the warm water. The tub was still filling, and the woman sitting on the stool in front of her added a blue powder. A floral fragrance filled the air as bubbles began to form in the water.

"How much is Chris hating life?" Alyssa asked after she got herself situated.

Mallory hadn't talked to him much over the past couple days, but she assumed Alyssa had, by her comment. Looking at her, she could tell it was a genuine question. "He didn't seem too thrilled when I talked to him, but we haven't talked a whole lot. Does he not get along with his ex?"

The woman pulled one of Mallory's feet out of the water and began clipping and filing away. She was normally a bit ticklish for that part, but she was too focused on Alyssa to notice. With one eyebrow raised, Alyssa looked her up and down before answering.

"They wouldn't be exes if they got along."

"What aren't you saying?" Mallory asked.

Alyssa chuckled. "He doesn't like being around her any more than he has to be. And he really hates Florida."

"Well, that would explain his tone when I talked to him. I just hope he gets things situated with Liliana so he can come home. Have you heard anything?" Mallory closed her eyes and enjoyed the foot massage while she waited for her to answer.

"I only talked to him just before he left, so I have no idea what's going on with her. But I was hoping he'd be back by now since they're moving his mom soon. Tomorrow?"

Mallory sat up straight in her chair. She had nearly forgotten about it. Her plan was to work for at least half a day since there was no telling what time transport would show up, and then get to the new place so she wouldn't feel so lonely. It was a good thing Alyssa mentioned it, or she might have just worked straight through the day.

"I'll be there."

Alyssa's eyebrows raised as she looked at her. "Oh, wow."

"Wow, what?" Mallory asked.

"I just didn't realize things were *that* serious. Not a bad wow. Just surprised. I can go with you if you want," she offered. "I love his mom."

"I'm not even sure what time everything is happening, but I won't tell you not to come. I'll be fine either way. You don't need to go out of your way unless you really want to be there."

"Hmm," was her response.

They were quiet as the pedicure went on. Mallory closed her eyes and relaxed as the lotion was massaged into her legs and feet. A little pampering was exactly what she'd needed to take the edge off. The water was warm and the firm touch on her legs caused her to sink down in her chair.

"Mallory?"

She looked up to find Alyssa standing next to her pedicure chair. "Hmm?"

"Damn, I wish I could have gotten the foot massage. You were out." Alyssa giggled. "It's manicure time."

Mallory felt heat rush to her face. She couldn't believe she'd fallen asleep. Sleep hadn't come easy the past few nights, so it was no wonder. She gathered her shoes and her purse, foregoing the flimsy foam sandals they provided, and followed them to the manicure chair.

"So, what's the story with Vivian. I wasn't going to ask but ..."

Alyssa hesitated for a moment before responding. She looked up at the nail tech, who didn't appear to be paying them any attention, before heaving a sigh. After watching Mallory closely, she finally spoke.

"There really isn't much of a story as far as I know. Sounds like he fell hard and fast and didn't see how they brought out the worst in each other. I've only met her in passing, but from all the shit I've heard, it sounds like she's a self-centered bitch."

Mallory sat on that bit of information, telling herself she didn't need to know more. Telling herself it was none of her business ... telling herself not to pry information from his best friend.

"So, they don't get along even though there are thousands of miles separating them?" Mallory blurted before she had a chance to listen to herself.

Alyssa turned to her with a smirk. It was no surprise, since she was not being the least bit stealthy as she pried for information. "What is it you want to know? You aren't very good at this."

Mallory hid her face behind her arm and attempted to stifle a giggle. "Am I that obvious?"

"Yes."

"Okay, fine! I'm trying not to let this whole situation bother me, but I'm not loving the fact that he's staying with his ex. Or the fact that he's so far away." She sighed, realizing how she sounded. "I'm pathetic. Ignore me."

Alyssa's gaze softened. "It's not pathetic. If Michael was staying with an ex or even someone who he used to have a crush on, I would be losing it. But you don't need to worry about him. He loves you. You don't have to worry."

Choking, she struggled to catch her breath. Those words had never been spoken. He didn't love her. Love was a big word. The fact that she might also love him had nothing to do with anything.

She watched as her nails were painted the neutral yet sparkly color she picked out. As much as she tried to focus on her girls' day, her mind kept wandering to what Alyssa said. He loved her? Only time would tell.

CHRISTIAN

Chris lay in bed, exhausted. He hadn't gotten a decent night's sleep in several days. It was getting late, and he needed to reset. He needed to catch up on sleep. There was officially no way around having a conversation with Vivian. He'd been there for three days and still had no idea what was going on with Liliana. The only thing he could do was bring her home with him and hope she either opened up or had a change of heart after spending time away.

He was just drifting off to sleep when his phone lit up with a video chat request. Recognizing the name on the screen, he hit accept.

"You're up late," he greeted once Mallory's face lit up across his screen.

"Am I?" she asked. "I haven't slept since you left. All the days and hours run together."

Chris could tell she was in bed. The dim lighting reflected off the white comforter she kept tucked under her arms not far below her shoulders. Swallowing hard, he tried to decide where he wanted the conversation to go. The distance that appeared to be growing between them could be a good thing, especially if he ended up bringing his daughter home with him. His time would be for her, or it would be pointless to bring her home to New Jersey with him.

"Need some help getting to sleep?" he asked.

He didn't miss the unmistakable spark flicker across her expression before she quickly masked it. "I wish you were here so you could help."

"Assuming I was there, what would you have me do?"

Chris watched in amusement as she sat up, nearly dropping her blanket. She didn't respond until she had leaned against the headboard and had the blanket safely tucked back in place. "What?"

"You heard me. Tell me what you would do with me."

Her mouth dropped open before her cheeks turned a gorgeous shade of pink. She was nervous. And embarrassed. "I, um ... I'm not sure."

This was going to be even better than he imagined. Confident in his decision to take it there, he pushed her further. "If I was there in your bed, would you want me to touch you?"

"Yes," she breathed, her face growing more flushed.

"Where?" He found her shyness arousing as fuck.

"Everywhere."

"I want you to tell me," he growled.

She squeezed her eyes shut, and he knew he wasn't going to get an answer. "I can't."

Sliding himself up, he leaned against his headboard, so they were looking at each other from the same angle. It felt wrong on every level to be sitting in the bed in the guest bedroom of his ex-wife's house talking dirty to his girlfriend. Keeping his voice low, he continued the conversation.

"The next time I'm in bed with you, I'll use my hands and touch every part of your body. Starting at your neck, I'll work my way down, stopping only to spend time on your perfect tits, listening to the gasps you make when I play with your nipples. Would you like that?"

"Yes." She was panting.

"I'll follow the same path with my tongue. Licking and sucking down your body. Sucking on each hard nipple until you cry out and beg for more. Would you like that?"

Leaning her head against the headboard, her lips parted as a soft moan escaped her mouth.

"Drop the blanket and touch your nipples the way I touch them."

She looked as though she was going to argue, but instead she let the blanket fall before dragging her hand across her chest and squeezing her nipples; first one, then the other. Her broken sigh sent all his blood flowing to one place.

"Does that feel good?"

She nodded her head as she tugged on her nipple. He was already rock hard and he hadn't even touched himself yet. As much as he wanted to, he wanted them to get there together.

"Are you wet for me?"

She nodded again and shifted.

"Tell me."

"I'm so wet," she whimpered.

Unable to hold off, Chris reached a hand under the blanket and gripped himself. "Get rid of the blanket and show me how you touch yourself."

Her eyes were unfocused as she stripped the blanket away and did as he told her. She spread her legs, giving him the perfect view of her slit. Signs of her arousal glistened. She was wet for him. She propped the phone up, freeing her hands and giving him a better view.

"Fuck," he groaned when she finally moved her fingers and began touching herself.

Biting her lip, she spread her thighs even further apart, circling her clit before dipping a finger inside her pussy. She groaned loudly and slid down in the bed. "Shit!"

She looked fucking incredible. He licked his lips, wishing he was there to replace her fingers with his tongue. "Does that feel good?"

"Oh shit. Yes."

Chris moved his hand in slow strokes as he watched Mallory bring herself pleasure. The only place he wanted to be was buried inside her, but his hand would have to do. Phone sex was something he never had the desire to do before, but he couldn't seem to stop himself. His plan to sit back and watch the show had gone out the window.

He tossed his blanket to the side, putting himself in view of the camera. "Look at me."

She looked at the screen, her eyes widening when she saw what he was doing. Her mouth opened, but he didn't hear any words. He smiled at her as he continued to stroke himself.

"This is what watching you does to me. If I was there, I'd be inside you already."

Without taking her eyes off the screen, she circled her clit faster and inserted a second finger, her back arching as she moved. When she closed her eyes, he knew her orgasm was close. His skin prickled as his own release drew nearer.

"Look at me. I want to see you."

Her eyes snapped back open and the heat he saw in her eyes was nearly enough to send him over the edge. But he held on, determined to wait for her. His breathing grew ragged as he stroked himself faster, keeping in time with Mallory.

"Come for me," he demanded, feeling his control crumble.

She bit down on her lip and cried out, her body tensing as her fingers made slow deliberate swipes while she rode out her orgasm. He held her gaze and found his own release, warm ropes of liquid hitting his stomach. He groaned softly, giving himself a few last strokes as he pulsed in his hand.

Her cheeks took on a rosy, red hue and she was back under the blankets before he even grabbed his t-shirt to clean himself off. Her eyes drooped; fatigue winning out over embarrassment.

"Don't hide from me. I've seen everything and I love every part of you." He winced as he realized the first time he allowed that word to slip was after having phone sex. The timing didn't make his words any less true, but still.

"That was ... not what I was expecting."

Chris chuckled under his breath. "What we did, or what I said?"

"Both? I've never done that before."

He breathed another laugh. "Well, I was also surprised."

"By which part?" she asked, her lips tugging into a small smile.

"Both."

Her blankets were pulled up to her chin, but she was finally smiling. "We should get some sleep. Will I see you soon?"

Whoever came up with the phrase "absence makes the heart grow fonder" wasn't lying. He needed Mallory. There was no other way to describe it. He had been stressed over whatever it was that was going on with his daughter, and being away from the woman he loved only made him feel things more acutely. He'd tried to create some distance before he left, knowing how stressful being under the same roof as his ex would be and needing to focus any energy he had left on Lily. He was lucky she even reached out to him after how standoffish he'd been.

"God, I hope so. Get some sleep. I've about reached my limit here. I'll be home soon."

Chapter 18

MALLORY

Mallory was having a hard time looking the woman in the eye. It had been nearly twenty-four hours, but she thought Mrs. Ramirez might be able to sense the filthy things she'd done with her son. Even after all the hot actual sex they'd had, phone sex seemed taboo. Her cheeks flushed at the memory of him coming undone under his own hand as he watched her do the same.

"You feeling okay? You seem flushed," Mrs. Ramirez asked once the EMTs had transferred her to her new bed.

She knew it. She could tell. The phone sex was written all over her. Her face heated even more. "Oh, I'm fine. Just feeling a bit run down from not sleeping well the past few nights, that's all. But how are you? How was the ride here?"

"The ride over was fine. I'm not an invalid, though. They could have let me get up and walk over to the bed," she said, glaring in the direction of the EMTs as they left the room. "With Christian being away, I would think you'd be getting more sleep."

If there was any doubt as to what she meant, the exaggerated wink cleared it up. Just as she thought she couldn't blush any harder, heat rose from her neck all the way back to her ears. Closing her eyes, she took a moment to regain her composure.

"Don't look so surprised. I was young once, and I've seen the way you two look at each other."

Mallory struggled to find something to say. Some way to change the subject. Anything. "Oh, uh ..." She laughed nervously. "Is there anything I can get you? I'm sure you must be tired from the move."

Mrs. Ramirez shook her head and laughed. Things were not going the way she'd planned. She figured she'd go there, spend some time with Christian's mom while she got settled, then leave.

"Don't be so nervous. I like you and I love you for my son. I'm no prude, so I won't pretend my son doesn't have sex."

Oh god. That explanation somehow made her feel even more awkward. In just a matter of days, Christian's best friend told her that Christian loved her, Christian himself said he loved everything about her, and now his mother said she loved her for him. Overwhelmed was an understatement. It was officially time to go. She'd seen that she arrived okay. Spent a few minutes. Her job was complete.

"Well, Mrs. Ramirez, I'd better get going. It's getting late and I'm sure if I'm tired, you must be tired as well. I wrote down my number in the notebook by the phone. Call me if you need anything."

She walked over to the bed and gave her a friendly kiss on the cheek before digging her keys out of her purse. She really did need to start carrying a smaller bag. The bigger the purse, the more shit she loaded it up with. She was still digging for her keys when she heard Mrs. Ramirez speak.

"Christian! What are you doing here? I didn't think you'd be back yet."

Mallory looked up and saw Christian standing in the doorway. Her heart skipped a few beats and she felt butterflies in her stomach. Her body reacted to him the same way it did when they first met. Before she could come up with a reasonable greeting, he moved to the side allowing a little girl to step into the room. Little girl probably wasn't the best way to describe her. A young teenager with dark hair and haunted gray eyes looked back at her. Her dark hair hung loose past her shoulders, and she was dressed in black leggings and a black t-shirt. She was gorgeous, even with the somber expression on her face.

She pulled her gaze from Mallory and directed it behind her. "Abuela? Are you okay?"

Mallory looked up at Christian who already had his eyes fixed on her, his expression unreadable. Instead of his usual clean-shaven look, he was sporting a few days' worth of facial hair. It would have been a good look on him if he didn't look so tired. As if on autopilot, Mallory walked over and wrapped her arms around him in a supportive hug. He held her tight and rested his chin on her head, likely watching the interaction behind her.

"I didn't expect to see you here today," she said before breathing him in.

After giving her a quick squeeze, he pulled back to look at her. "I didn't expect to be here." He quickly looked behind her before continuing. "I'll tell you about it at some point. Thank you for being here for my mom."

Taking the cue, she stepped out of his embrace, immediately missing the warmth of his body. His daughter was completely focused on her grandmother, which was good. As much as she wanted to meet Liliana, it wasn't the time or the place.

"I'm going to get going so you two can spend time with your mom. When do you go back to work?" she asked as she stepped around him to the doorway.

"I did a switch just in case, so I'm off until the weekend."

"I'd love to meet Liliana. Maybe bring her over for dinner tomorrow night? You know how I like to feed people. No pressure. Think about it and let me know." She kissed him on the cheek and then stepped into the hallway.

"Okay. Sleep well," he called after her.

When she stopped to turn around, she didn't miss the gleam in his eye. He was definitely referring to the night before. Turning around before he could see her blush, she made her way to the exit and out to her car.

CHRISTIAN

He had spent the last four days with his daughter and was no closer to figuring out what was going on with her than he was before he took off to go to Florida, and he had no idea what he was going to do about returning to work. He was low on vacation days, and he'd already made a switch in order to be off until the weekend. Lily still wasn't back to her old self, but she was in better shape than when he first saw her. He just wished she would talk to him.

"Anything fun you want to do today?" he asked as they sat at the small table eating cereal.

"No," she said without looking up from her bowl.

"Shopping?" he suggested.

"Nah."

He was determined to find something to help snap her out of whatever this was. He needed his little girl back. Even if she overcame whatever it was that she was going through and he never knew what it was, he could live with that.

"Mani pedis?" he tried.

This time she looked up at him with a raised eyebrow. "Seriously? No. I'm not going to the nail salon with my dad. That's weird."

"Well, how bout we go to lunch?"

She took another bite of food before answering. "We're literally eating breakfast and you're talking about lunch." It wasn't a question. It was a statement.

Chris stifled a laugh. There she was. "If you knew where I wanted to have lunch, you might not think it was strange to think about it this early."

Finally, her ears perked up. She looked up at him and squinted her eyes, waiting for him to continue. Chris pretended like he didn't notice and went back to his cereal, trying not to laugh as she stared at him.

"Just tell me. Where are we going?"

Chris finished his cereal and shoved the bowl away, folding his arms over his chest. "I'm in the mood to go into the city and grab a pie from Luigi's, but if you don't want to go ..."

"Yes!" she exclaimed, with more animation than he'd seen since laying eyes on her in Florida. Maybe this was what they needed. Maybe she would finally open up to him.

It had been a long time since Chris had gone into Manhattan. He enjoyed it every now and then, but it wasn't something he liked to do often. Lily, on the other hand, absolutely loved it. Every time he brought her into the city, her eyes lit up and a smile spread across her face. This time was no different.

The subway train jerked and swayed as they sped toward their stop. It wasn't very crowded since they were heading in during an odd time, too late for the morning commute and too early for the lunch rush. Chris sat back and watched as Lily tried to hide her excitement, but as they announced the next stop over the speaker, her smile broke free.

"I'm not even hungry yet," she said when she caught him looking at her.

"Good thing we aren't going straight to Luigi's. Thought maybe we should take a detour first."

"Where?" Lily asked, forgetting to hide her excitement.

"Central Park. Unless you don't want to."

She clapped her hands and screeched. "Really?"

"Really."

She quickly tamed her excitement and sat back in her seat. She said nothing else, only smiled to herself as she did whatever it was she was doing on her phone. Chris took the opportunity to send Mallory a text letting her know they would be there for dinner. He had no doubts that one of the most important people in his life needed to meet *the* most important person.

When the train slowed, Chris knew they were nearing their stop before it was spoken over the loudspeaker. And it was a good thing, since it was nearly impossible to understand the garbled words that came over it. He stood and reached a hand out to Lily so they could quickly exit the train before the doors closed.

Summers in New York City were often hot and humid, as the buildings seemed to trap the heat. Fortunately, the weather was on their side, granting them the perfect day. The sun was shining, but it wasn't beating down on them. As they crossed the busy road and headed into the park, a cool breeze welcomed them.

As they walked further into Central Park, the classic sounds of traffic, cars honking, people shouting, and buses squealing to a stop, began to fade. Couples stretched out on large blankets, talking and enjoying the mild temperatures. In the distance, a small family enjoyed a carriage ride. Chris chanced a glance at Lily and found her taking in the scene with a content smile on her face. Some color had returned to her cheeks and her eyes had brightened.

They took their time walking around and even stopped to watch a dance battle. Lily was into it, watching the dancers with laser focus. She always loved music and dance, so it was no surprise that she would be immediately sucked in. Chris wasn't enthralled by the scene, but he would endure anything to see Lily glow with happiness the way she did when she was passionate about something.

By the time the dance battle ended, it was time for lunch. As much as he wanted to ask her what had been bothering her, there was no reason to risk ruining their day. She would tell him when she was ready. Not being in control was something that took getting used to. His first instinct had been to swoop in and save the day, and he was still itching to do just that. Even knowing how teenagers were, he just wanted to fix everything. But he couldn't.

Chapter 19

MALLORY

Mallory rushed around the kitchen feeling more anxiety about cooking than she ever had. As soon as she read the text message, she broke out into a cold sweat just thinking about preparing dinner. Cooking was her love language, so the nerves were a new feeling. She had been genuine when she extended the invitation, but she wasn't ready for the stream of nerves that followed.

Liliana had seemed like a sweet girl when she'd seen her in passing at the nursing home ... but even without having children of her own, she knew how things could be. All she could do was hope the girl had no preconceived notions about her. Meeting a future stepchild was stressful enough. Future stepchild? Where did that come from?

Overthinking again! After taking several deep breaths, she realized she was cooking dinner for people she loved, not performing an audition. Cooking was something she could do in her sleep. And yes, she really was cooking for people she loved. She hadn't yet formally met Liliana, but she already loved her, knowing she was a part of someone she loved more than she was willing to admit.

Lasagna was something she made all the time. Sometimes it was vegetarian, other times it was traditional. Either way she could make it without following a recipe, so her fear was irrational. After giving herself a quick pep talk, she got back to it, pushing all worries about meeting Liliana to the back of her mind.

She was singing show tunes and cleaning up after herself when she heard the buzzer. A quick glance at her phone told her it was actually a little later than when she expected them. They weren't late since she never specified a time and neither did they. Lasagna was something that didn't have to be eaten right away, so the timing wasn't a big deal. She walked over to the panel by her door and buzzed them in, taking one last look at herself even though there was no time to do anything about whatever she found.

Just as she was taking the lasagna out of the oven, she heard footsteps outside her door. Instead of knocking, Christian opened the door and walked right in. It made Mallory smile. She couldn't help but wonder if he'd act like he normally did around her or if he would behave like a stranger. The reaction her body had to him walking into her apartment made no sense. Her skin was on fire, and it was as if she could feel him the closer he got. Ridiculous.

"Mallory?" he called out softly as he stopped just short of the kitchen.

She turned and met them with a grin. "Oh my gosh, you must be Liliana," she greeted. "It's so good to finally meet you!"

Mallory set the pan of lasagna on a cooling rack then stepped around the island to greet her guests. Liliana was standing slightly behind her father. Even though she seemed uncertain about everything, she still looked to be in a better state than she had been when Mallory first laid eyes on her. Her sad gray eyes now had a gleam to them. Liliana wasn't exactly enthusiastic, but she nodded a distinct hello.

"I hope lasagna is okay. There's also cookies and brownies. Are you hungry? If you want to eat now, you guys can have a seat at the island. I'm rambling. Sorry. Make yourselves at home." She covered her mouth in order stop herself from talking.

Liliana finally cracked a real smile. "It's okay, I'm nervous too."

Both Mallory and Christian looked at her in surprise. Mallory was surprised to hear her admit to being nervous, and judging from Christian's reaction he was just as surprised. Mallory resorted to taking a few calming breaths before she responded to what Lily had said.

"You're nervous? My house is nothing to be nervous about."

"I'm not stupid. I know you're my dad's girlfriend. I was nervous you might be a bitch," Lily said simply.

"Liliana!" Christian immediately warned. "Language."

Mallory tried her best to keep a straight face, but laughter bubbled out. She liked this kid. And it would seem the kid might like her as well. Hopefully she did, anyway. With a clearing of her throat, she went back to setting everything out for dinner as Christian had a quiet discussion with his daughter. If she listened closely, she would probably be able to hear what was being said, but it wasn't her business.

By the time she finished moving around the kitchen setting out food, dishes, and silverware, Lily and Christian were seated at the island. It startled her to see them there. Even though they were right in front of her, she had been so focused on what she was doing that she didn't even notice. She let out a nervous chuckle.

"I guess this means you're ready to eat?"

"Mallory." Christian reached out a hand and covered hers. "It's okay. It's just us. We're ready to eat if you're ready to sit down and eat with us."

The touch of his strong hand above hers was exactly what she needed to feel grounded. Tension eased from her shoulders, and after a moment she served up plates and sat down at the island. It wasn't often when she had dinner guests, aside from Dan, and she had to fight the urge to run around serving everyone instead of enjoying the meal with the people she cooked for.

"This is really good," Lily gushed, once again surprising both Mallory and Christian.

Mallory didn't acknowledge Christian's reactions to his daughter. As her first time meeting Lily, she had no idea what her normal behavior was, and it wouldn't be fair to judge based on his reactions. Lily seemed sweet, and by the time they finished their meal, she was certain she liked the girl. She was genuine and respectful.

Taking her up on her request to make herself at home, Lily plopped herself on the couch and took out her phone, leaving Christian and Mallory alone at the island. She propped her feet up and inserted earbuds, completely off in her own world.

"So? How's that been going?" Mallory asked quietly as she stood to begin clearing dishes.

Christian began helping, moving the empty dishes to the counter so Mallory could load them into the dishwasher before he took it upon himself to hand wash the larger dishes. As they were side by side, doing dishes, he finally answered her question.

"I'm enjoying our time together, but I have no idea what's going on with her. She still isn't herself, but she's been getting closer since we got back to New Jersey."

"She still hasn't talked to you?"

"Not really," he said with a sigh. "All she keeps saying is that she doesn't want to be in Florida with her mom and wants to live with me."

Mallory was quiet while she finished loading the dishwasher. Wishing she had something helpful to say, the only thing that came to her mind was what she'd needed when she was struggling at around the same age. But still, she felt out of place offering any form of parenting advice.

"What is it?" Christian coaxed.

"It's not my place." She hesitated.

"Please?" he asked before glancing over his shoulder and lowering his voice. "I'm at a loss here. I feel like I'm losing her right in front of me."

His admission stunned her. She blinked back unexpected tears as she tried to put her thoughts into words. She didn't know how to help his daughter, but she did know what would have helped her when she was younger.

She glanced over her shoulder to make sure she wasn't listening to them. They were being so obvious, but she didn't want to risk Lily overhearing their conversation.

"I just needed someone to be there. Someone who wouldn't leave or get upset no matter what I did or what I said. I'm not a parent but I would say just keep doing what you're doing," she said gently.

"It's so hard," he said, his voice cracking. "I just want to fix everything for her. I want to shield her from the world."

Mallory dried her hands on the dish towel before wrapping her arms around him. Touching him while his daughter was around wasn't something she planned to do, but at that moment she didn't care. Lily wasn't stupid. She knew they were more than just friends.

"I'm so sorry," she breathed. "How are you going to manage work this weekend? I know she isn't staying home by herself."

Christian stepped back. "I'm not sure yet. I'll figure something out."

"She can stay here," she offered. "I don't mind and I'm here anyway. It'll be a reason for me to get the guest room ready, it's really not a big deal."

He hesitated. "You don't need to do that. I can figure it out."

"Christian. I wouldn't offer if it was a problem. It'll just be me here. She'll be fine. Most we'll do is go downstairs to Dan's for coffee. Ask her. If she's good with it, I am."

Mallory finished wiping down the counters and straightening up while she pretended not to watch him walk over to Lily and sit down beside her. Lilly didn't move beyond pulling her earbuds out. She said something and shrugged before replacing them and then continued to do whatever she was doing on her phone.

"She said she's fine with it. I still feel weird, though. You really don't have to."

She took his hand and led him back to the island to sit. Lily was back doing her own thing, so they had a few minutes to sit and relax. She poured them each a glass of wine then sat down to join him.

"It's fine. Here," she said, passing him a glass. "I know everything is a lot right now, so just take a minute. It's okay to do that."

She felt like she was giving a motivational speech, but she didn't know how else to get through to him. It was obvious that he was on edge. And being on edge was the worst thing he could do if he wanted Lily to open up to him. Mallory wouldn't tell him that since she drew a hard line at giving parenting advice.

"I'm not trying to lecture you. I just want to help. You don't need to do everything alone."

Saying nothing, he nodded in agreement. His shoulders relaxed as they sat in companionable silence and sipped their wine. Lily looked as though she spent every day on that couch listening to music and playing on her phone. The thought of seeing her on the couch daily brought a smile to her face. Sure, it might be a little early to start thinking like that, but she liked her.

"What are you smiling about?" Christian asked.

"I'm just glad we're doing this."

He placed his hand on her thigh, giving it a gentle squeeze. Of course, her thoughts flashed to their night together on the phone, but she blinked the images away. His daughter was right there. With her hand covering his hand on her thigh, she continued to sip her wine while enjoying being near him.

CHRISTIAN

Chris held the door open and watched as Mallory padded into the hallway. He needed to talk to her in private, and the bedroom didn't feel right with Lily sitting there. They really would be talking, but Chris was well aware of how the teenage mind worked. Hell, he knew how his mind worked, and teenagers were even worse.

"What is it?" Mallory asked once the door was shut.

Christian sighed as he tried to figure out how to explain what made him leave Florida. "I'm not sure exactly what's going on with Lily, but whatever it is, Vivian doesn't want me to know. I thought she was as clueless as I am, but as soon as Lily started to open up to me, Vivian barged in and interrupted, clearly not wanting Lily to tell me."

Mallory covered her gasp with her hand. "Do you think it has to do with her mom?"

Christian bristled at the thought. "I'm not sure. But if it does, I'm going to jail."

Her warm touch on his forearm took some of the edge off. "You don't mean that. Why don't you figure out what's going on before you let your mind go there …"

Chris ran his hand through his hair in frustration. He was trying to keep calm. He was trying to be patient, but once he found out who was hurting his baby girl, he couldn't promise to keep such a cool head about things.

"It's so hard doing this alone," he admitted. "Even though Vivian and I weren't anywhere close to friends, we didn't do terrible with the coparenting thing. But now? I just don't understand. I know she'll talk when she's ready. But still."

"You have me," she reminded him. "And I'm here however you need me."

"I could use a distraction about now."

Mallory stepped closer and rubbed her hands across his chest, effectively distracting him. The heat from her hands traveled beyond where she touched and he wished he could lose himself in her, but they only had a few minutes. He pulled her into what was meant to be a quick kiss, but as soon as their lips met, he needed more.

She sighed and melted into him, her sounds reminding him of that night over Facetime. Holding her tighter, he deepened the kiss, exploring her mouth with his tongue. God, he wanted her. When she moaned into his mouth, he forgot about control and shoved her against the wall, pinning her with his hips as he ran his hands over her body.

"Lily is right on the other side of the door," she breathed.

"Then you'd better be quiet. Not being able to touch you isn't going to work for me."

He returned his mouth to hers, swallowing her cries. He felt the moment her last bit of control snapped. Wrapping her arms around him, she pulled him closer and threaded her hands into his hair, tugging as she pressed her body into his. It took everything for him to remember that they were in the hallway outside of her apartment and her neighbor was downstairs and his daughter on the other side of the door. But another minute or two wouldn't hurt.

He gripped her waist with both hands before sliding one hand up her body, over her breast, and stopping at her neck. With a gentle squeeze, he held her back so he could look at her. Her bright eyes shined with emotion as she looked back at him. She was breathing heavy, and her lips were swollen from their stolen moment. The feel of her delicate neck in his hand

and the way she responded when he squeezed nearly caused his desperation for her to override all common sense.

"Fuck," he breathed, leaning his forehead against hers. "I don't think I've ever needed anything as much as I need to be inside you."

Mallory's breath hitched. "You can't say things like that. Not when we have to walk back through that door without any of that happening."

She was right. He adjusted himself as he realized Mallory wasn't the only one being tortured. "Sorry. I guess we should get back."

Even without getting everything he needed from Mallory, feeling her touch against his anxious body made him feel a hundred times better. Mallory had her hand on the doorknob, and he had to stop her from opening the door. She looked at him in confusion, but started laughing to herself when he straightened out her clothes and used his fingers to comb out her hair. After fixing his own clothes, he nodded for her to go ahead and open the door.

Chapter 20

CHRISTIAN

"So, welcome back?" Michael half said and half asked from his seat at the table across from Chris.

It was a painfully slow night, so Chris and James met up with Michael and his partner. In need of food, they skipped their usual coffee routine and settled on a diner. Chris ate his fries while his cheeseburger sat untouched. The slow night was not keeping his mind occupied the way he'd hoped.

"Thanks, I guess. I'm glad I'm back, but I'd feel better if Lily was with my mom," he admitted.

Michael's brows creased in confusion. "Oh, I didn't even think of that. Where is she?"

Chris tilted his head, surprised Michael didn't know. Mallory and Alyssa appeared to be as thick as thieves. He assumed Michael would know everything Alyssa did. "She's with Mallory."

Michael coughed in surprise while the other two continued eating. James had already heard all about it and Michael's partner was new, having no idea who they were even talking about. Even if he did, they would have immediately shut him down if he attempted to join in the conversation. Fortunately, he knew better and made himself as inconspicuous as possible, scrolling his phone and eating his food.

"That's—" Michael began before pausing to find the right words. "That's a big step."

Chris sighed as some of the tension left his body just knowing someone else understood what he was feeling. It was a big step. Aside from the fact that his daughter had never stayed overnight with anyone but his mom during his parenting time, it felt like a big fucking deal to have his girlfriend step in and take care of his daughter. He wasn't looking for a stepmom for her.

"Yeah," he agreed on a sigh. "Honestly, I was against it. I don't want Mallory to feel obligated and I don't want Lily to feel like I'm passing her off to my girlfriend."

"I know my sister well enough to know she wouldn't have offered if she didn't want to. Does Lily get along with her?"

Chris already knew she wouldn't have offered if she didn't want to. She valued her peace and tranquility, and doing something she wasn't comfortable with would get in the way of that. But even knowing that, he couldn't shake the feelings of guilt.

"It's fine," Michael reassured him once again. "Mallory has never done anything halfway. They are probably in the middle of a movie marathon or a spa night. You'll see."

Chris finally took a few bites of his burger. Michael was right. He knew his daughter was fine. She was a mature thirteen-year-old who had plenty of practice entertaining herself. What worried him most was that she wasn't actually comfortable staying with Mallory, and all the progress they had made would be erased. Helping her get through whatever it was she was going through was still his number one priority.

"Unit 706 for the assignment. 706," the dispatcher's voice crackled over his portable radio.

"Go ahead," he answered.

"706: North Main Street and Adamson Road for the motor vehicle collision with injuries. ALS has been notified."

Chris heaved a sigh. "Received."

The others were already standing and closing up their to-go containers as Michael and his partner's pagers chirped. Any time they ate at a restaurant, they ordered their food to-go so they would be ready to make a quick exit if they needed to.

"706 is responding with MIC 1," Chris announced over the radio as soon as they stepped out onto the sidewalk.

"At 22:27."

A few minutes later they arrived on scene to find the road already blocked off by police. There was a trail of parts leading to what appeared to be a mangled motorcycle in the distance. Just beyond the motorcycle, a car had smashed into the concrete barrier.

"What do we have?" Michael asked once he caught up to Chris and the police officer.

"Car vs motorcycle. Single rider. And the fire department is working on extricating two from the car," the officer answered.

"The motorcyclist?" Chris asked.

The officer shook his head. "Looks like a DOA, but obviously that's not my call. In the car we have one conscious."

Chris looked at Michael and nodded in the direction of the wreckage. Wordlessly they separated to assess what was going on. James and Chris made their way to the car, while Michael and his partner stopped at the motorcycle. Once they made it to the car, they were able to see a woman in the driver's seat slumped over the wheel and a child in the passenger seat.

Chris's heart dropped when he saw the child. Usually, he was able to disconnect while he was working, checking his personal life at the time clock. But when he looked at the frightened child sitting in the front seat crying for her mother to wake up, it was his daughter's face when he closed his eyes to gather himself.

It was the firefighter's voice that snapped him out of it. "Two occupants. The driver is unconscious but the juvenile in the front seat has been responding the entire time. We'll have the roof off in about five more minutes."

"You should grab another board from the truck," Chris suggested to James.

"On it."

Before James made it back, Chris had the bags on the ground and the stretcher dropped to the ground, ready for rapid extrication. Michael and his partner joined him just as the roof was removed from the car. Michael shook his head, and Chris was able to see a white sheet covering the patient from the motorcycle.

In the sudden quiet, the child's screams could be heard loud and clear. "Mom! Wake up!"

Chris sprang into action, desperate to comfort the child above all else. While Michael quickly moved to the driver, Chris went around to the other side of the car and leaned into the window. A quick glance inside and he could see what appeared to be an empty liquor bottle. Anger rushed through him, but he tamped it down in order to focus on the girl.

"Hi, sweetheart. My name is Chris and I'm here to help you. Can you tell me what hurts?"

She looked up at him with her tear-stained face. "Someone help my mom, please. She needs help."

He leaned into the car and pointed a finger to the opposite side of the car. "You see that tall guy right there?"

She turned her head to look just before James straightened her head and secured a c-collar around her neck. "Yes."

"Well, he is here to help your mom, and James and I are here for you. Let's worry about you, so they can help her. Now, can you tell me what hurts?"

"My arm hurts, and it kinda hurts when I breathe."

As much damage as the car had suffered, it was likely there were more injuries that she would feel once the adrenaline wore off. "Okay. We're going to get you out of here. We need to keep you still in case you're hurt in places you don't notice yet, so try not to fight us."

She sniffled as tears ran down her face. "Okay."

Once they had the girl moved out of the vehicle and secured onto the stretcher, Chris looked across the car and made eye contact with Michael as he was covering the woman with a sheet and talking into his radio. Chris muttered a curse to himself as he tried to figure out what to say to the little girl. He preferred not to break the news, but he wasn't going to have a choice. The fact that the other occupant in the car was dead, automatically made the little girl a critical patient, requiring the paramedics; the paramedics he said would be taking care of her mother.

"Fuck," he mumbled again before he climbed into the truck behind his patient.

"You good?" James asked.

Chris took a slow breath. "I will be."

He sat on the bench seat beside the girl who watched him with eyes wide. "Is my mom okay?"

Chris cleared his throat. "I'm not sure how your mom is since I've been paying all my attention to you. Is it okay if I check you over and make sure we find everything that needs fixed?"

She closed her eyes and nodded.

"Perfect," Chris said softly. "What's your name, sweetheart?"

"Rayne," she answered without opening her eyes.

Chris did his head-to-toe exam, noting how she winced in pain when he checked over her ribs and abdomen. Her arm appeared to be broken so he splinted it while James took a set of vital signs. Just as Chris began cutting her shirt off to take a look at her abdomen, the side door of the ambulance opened. His body tensed when Michael stepped inside. They could no longer brush off Rayne's questions.

"Is my mom okay?" she asked after straining to see who Chris was looking at.

"Why don't we worry about you." Chris attempted to distract her. "Does your stomach hurt, or just your side?"

"Just tell me. Please?" she pleaded, her tears resuming. "She's dead, isn't she?"

Michael stepped the rest of the way inside and sat in the seat across from Chris. "I'm sorry. There was nothing we could do."

Michael explained that her mother was already dead when they got to her, likely dying on impact. Rayne didn't look at Michael as he explained. She continued watching Chris with pleading eyes and he knew she wanted him to say something that would change what Michael was telling her. He wanted to. He wanted nothing more than to tell that little girl that her life as she knew it wasn't over. But it was.

Swallowing hard, he looked over at Michael who held one of her hands in both of his, rubbing it soothingly. He and Mallory knew all too well the effects of losing a mother as a child. Chris no longer just saw his daughter when he looked at Rayne, he also saw a young version of Mallory.

"I'm so sorry, Rayne," Chris choked out. "I'm sure your mom would want to make sure you're okay. Let's get you taken care of and to the hospital. Okay?"

Rayne closed her eyes and gave a nearly imperceptible nod.

"I'm going to start an IV. You'll feel a big pinch, but it'll only hurt for a couple seconds," Michael said as he got started.

Rayne didn't speak another word to them. Both Chris and Michael were careful with her, admittedly being more cautious than usual. The pain of the accident and the pain of losing her mother was more than enough. If Chris could have taken all of her pain for himself, he would have. The occasional eye contact she made with her large brown eyes was the only way Chris could be certain she was conscious.

Chris was cleaning up and restocking the truck when Michael climbed in through the open back doors. "That was tough."

"Yeah," Chris agreed as he continued doing what he was doing.

"You good? I know your kid is the same age."

Chris slammed the cabinet door and turned around. "Yeah, I'm good. If I had a breakdown every time I had a patient the same age as my kid or someone who reminded me of my mom, I'd be in the wrong business."

Chris moved on to the bag, replacing what they'd used. When he zipped the bag and looked up, Michael was watching him with his arms folded. There was no reason for him to respond the way he did, and he knew it. Michael had to be affected by the call as well.

"Are *you* good?" Chris asked in place of an apology. However Michael decided to interpret the question was on him.

He expected a quick retreat. Michael was a man of few words. Having long conversations about feelings was not something he was known for. Chris raised his eyebrows in surprise when Michael sat down on the bench seat and leaned against the wall.

"I don't remember my mother," Michael admitted. "I was very young when she died. Mallory, though; she remembers. Sometimes I think it would be easier if neither of us remembered her."

Chris sat down on the opposite seat. He wasn't big on talking about feelings either, but he got the sense that Michael needed to talk and that he needed to hear what he was saying. He closed his eyes, pushing all thoughts of Lily to the back of his mind, before opening them again.

"I hate calls like this because I know from experience how fucking awful her situation is," Michael explained. "We at least had a dad who gave a shit. He may have gone about things the wrong way, but ultimately, he wanted us happy and healthy."

"I hope she has a dad who gives a shit," Chris said mostly to himself. "Mallory told me about everything. I was being a dick a minute ago. Are you okay? I kept picturing my daughter so I'm sure you were having a hard time too."

Michael stood up, grabbing hold of his monitor. "I'll be okay. All we can do is our best. As cold as it sounds, Rayne isn't our family member. All we can do is make sure we do our best and get them to the hospital in one piece even when it's something that hits close to home."

He was right. Stressing himself and envisioning his family members wouldn't help anything. He had always done his best to treat every patient as if they were a family member, so any similarities wouldn't make a difference. It was very difficult trying to separate things sometimes.

Michael stepped out of the back of the ambulance just as James was approaching. Judging by the look on his face, he was also having a hard time with that call. They weren't usually the ones to break bad news to their patients, but they also wouldn't lie. He stopped at the back doors.

"Coffee?" he suggested.

Chris nodded. "Yeah. I need it."

What he needed was a stiff drink and to get home to his daughter, but both of those things would have to wait until morning. He finished up and closed the doors, making his way to the driver's seat with what felt like lead in his stomach. Hopefully coffee would chase away some of the heaviness.

MALLORY

Mallory woke up to the sensation of someone watching her. After rubbing her eyes into focus, she found Christian standing in her doorway. She had given him a key so he could let himself in, assuming they would be up late, which they were. Sensing something was wrong, she sat up quickly.

"What is it?" she asked.

Without a word, Christian stalked toward her, his face becoming clear as he got closer. A face that was obviously troubled. He leaned forward and placed his hands on either side of her on the bed, caging her in. After studying her face for several moments, he finally closed the gap and found her mouth with his. His kiss was desperate. She could feel his need and when she reached for him, he pulled her closer. She was still under the blankets but found herself sitting on the edge of the bed with her legs between his, desire coursing through her. She needed him as much as he needed her.

"You should close the door."

He broke the kiss and leaned his forehead against hers. "As much as I want to get you naked, we can't. Not her first time sleeping over. The last thing we need is for her to think you watching her was just an excuse for me to come over for sex. But I needed to touch you."

Disappointment overshadowed the desire that she still felt. Things had felt slightly off between them ever since he started trying to figure out what was going on with Lily, and sex would reassure her that they were okay. She knew how ridiculous it was, but she craved that connection. As if he could sense her thoughts, he reached out and tucked her hair behind her ear in a gentle gesture.

"I want to be inside you so bad I can barely think straight," he breathed before reaching for her hand.

She gasped when she felt the unmistakable bulge beneath her hand. They needed to figure out some alone time or she'd go crazy. She wanted him; needed him. Needed that connection as much as she needed her next breath.

"Fuck," she hissed in frustration.

He stepped back, breaking their contact. "I'll go make coffee while I still have the ability to walk out of here."

Needing a moment to cool down, she went into her bathroom, brushed her teeth, and splashed cold water on her face. What she needed was a cold shower. Actually, what she needed was to have sex, but maybe some cold water followed by hot coffee would help take the edge off.

When she stepped into the kitchen, she found Lily sitting at the island eating a bowl of cereal. Her hair was a mess as if she rolled out of bed and into the kitchen. It was probably a good thing Christian hadn't listened to her when she suggested they take things further.

"Good morning," she greeted as she accepted the coffee Christian offered. "How did you sleep?"

Lily glanced up from the bowl and looked her up and down before shrugging and returning her attention to her bowl. Mallory didn't blame her. She wasn't much of a morning person either.

"Sorry," Christian began to apologize.

"Nope," Mallory interrupted. "Don't worry about it. She just opened her eyes, I get it."

Christian uncrossed his ankles and repositioned his stance against the counter so he was facing Mallory. "Alright then. How did last night go?"

"It was fun," Lily mumbled with her mouth full of cereal, catching Mallory by surprise.

She chuckled to herself before agreeing. "We did have a good time. We watched the Golden Girls, ate ice cream, and did our nails."

As if they planned it, they flashed their nails. Lily showed off a midnight blue polish, while Mallory had gone for a cheerful pink. She really had enjoyed her time with Lily. Instead of things feeling awkward, they had gotten along as if they spent evenings together all the time, laughing and talking with no guards up.

"Did you have a bad night?" Mallory asked, noticing his quiet demeaner and recalling their moment in the bedroom.

"Yeah, it wasn't great," he admitted.

"You should take a nap here. We'll find something to do and stay out of your hair. That way you don't have to worry about coming back or feel like she's fending for herself while you sleep."

After putting his coffee cup in the sink, he scrubbed his hands over his face and stepped away from the counter. "That sounds amazing, but I'm sure you have things to do. Not to mention she'll be here tonight, too. We'll get out of your way."

"Christian," she said, cutting him off. "I wouldn't offer if it was a problem. The only plans I have for today are to get caught up on laundry and to go have brunch at Dan's, which he already invited Lily to last night."

Sensing his hesitation, she reminded him that Dan is a child life specialist and was therefore more than qualified to spend time around his daughter. Not to mention he was probably the perfect person for her to be around. His inviting demeaner could make anyone feel comfortable, and feeling comfortable was key to opening up and beginning to heal. Mallory knew that firsthand.

"Go into my room and close the door. Take a shower then get some rest. We both know Lily will have much more fun hanging with us than she would sitting in your apartment while you sleep."

She watched in silence as he fought and lost an internal battle. He sighed deeply as his eyes softened in resignation. "Okay."

"Great!" She clapped her hands in triumph. "You don't mind if I take her for a girls' day, do you?"

"No," he breathed with a confused smile. "I don't mind."

She felt as confused as he looked. She knew she wouldn't have a problem keeping an eye on Lily while he worked, but she actually *wanted* to spend time with her. The idea to swoop Lily off while Christian napped excited her more than she expected it to.

"This was supposed to be a girls' day," Mallory teased Dan as they made their way from the bookstore to the coffee shop.

"You think I was going to let you two have all that fun without me?" Dan asked with one eyebrow raised. "Today, I'm one of the girls."

Lily giggled beside her. Laughing more than Mallory had seen her laugh since meeting her, she seemed to have been enjoying herself the entire morning and didn't appear to have the weight of the world on her shoulders. It was a nice change. Hopefully it wasn't a temporary one.

"I'll grab us a table since it looks busy in there," Dan offered. "Order me a small caramel macchiato."

Mallory hadn't been to the coffee shop in at least a year. Not much had changed. It still had a warm welcoming environment. The far wall was lined with alternative seating. There were couches, beanbag chairs and even large pillows to sit on. The counter was in the middle of the room with multiple people working. Even though the line was long, it went pretty quick.

"You seem to like Dan," Mallory pointed out, leaning to the side to give her a friendly nudge.

"He's pretty great. I see why you're friends with him."

"That he is," she agreed. "He pretty much saved me when I was going through a rough time. He insisted on coffee every morning so I would have to get myself dressed and so he knew I was okay. He's easy to talk to. Even though I no longer need him to check up on me, we still have coffee every morning."

Mallory hadn't realized how fast the line had moved until she looked up in time to see the person in front of them step to the side, revealing an expectant barista looking at them with a cheerful smile. Mallory placed their order then moved over to wait.

"Have you met his boyfriend?" Lily asked, peeking up at Mallory through dark lashes.

It wasn't a question she'd been expecting. "Yeah. He seems pretty amazing, too. You'd probably like him."

Lily shifted on her feet as she chewed on her bottom lip. Mallory didn't know her well yet, but she could tell she was holding something back, her internal battle nearly loud enough for her to hear.

"It doesn't bother you?"

For a moment, Mallory was genuinely confused. "What? That he's gay?"

"Shh." Lily looked around nervously before continuing. "Yeah, I guess."

"Why would it bother me?" she responded honestly. "I don't care who anyone loves."

Eyes wide and filled with an emotion Mallory had yet to see, Lily agreed with what was said. "Yeah. Love is love."

Before Mallory could ask any questions, her name and order number were called out. Mallory and Lily picked up the cups and headed to join Dan, the moment over. She shrugged off the interaction as Lily not being around a lot of different people. She obviously didn't have a problem with Dan. Curiosity maybe, but not a problem.

Dan had managed to find a small table meant for two, and an unused chair which he'd pulled over. He smiled fondly as they made their way to him. Somehow, the coffee shop had a way of being crowded without feeling crowded. It was one of the many things Mallory had always liked about it.

"What do you ladies have planned for the rest of the week?" Dan asked as Mallory sat down and passed the drinks around.

"I'm not sure. Christian hasn't said how long Lily will be here," she answered before turning to the girl. "Is there anything you want to do while you're here? Just in case it isn't much longer."

"Can you talk my dad into letting me stay for the summer? I don't want to go back," Lily responded, taking Mallory by surprise.

"I'm sure he would love that, but it might not be that simple. I'll talk to him, though, okay?"

Lily took a sip of her drink, eyes welled with tears as she attempted to blink them away. "Should be easy. Mom doesn't want me around, anyway."

Mallory swallowed down the lump in her throat. She knew all too well the feeling of not being wanted. It didn't matter if the feelings were justified or not. It didn't matter if she was both loved and wanted. If she didn't feel loved, that was all that was important. Another piece of her heart broke for the child. She would give her all the love she had if it could erase some of her pain.

"Well, I can't speak for your mom, and I can't speak for your dad, but there's nothing I'd like more than to spend the summer with you."

Lily swiped at the few tears that had escaped. "Will you talk to Dad? Please. I can't go back home."

"I'll talk to him," Mallory repeated through the tightness in her throat.

"I'll talk to him, too," Dan said, giving a cheerful wink.

Lily giggled and looked down at her cup. They spent a few minutes quietly enjoying their coffee in comfortable silence. Mallory wasn't bullshitting. She really did enjoy spending time with Lily. She was funny, mature for her age, and generally easy to be around.

"Why don't you and Christian go to dinner or something Monday night? I'll come up to your place and have a movie night with Lily. You can talk to Christian about Lily staying. I'm off Tuesday because I have to work Saturday, so stay out as late as you want," Dan suggested after a few minutes.

Mallory hesitated. Some alone time with Christian? That sounded amazing. It hadn't been terribly long since they'd had some time alone together, but she missed him. Balancing a relationship around a child was completely new to her. She felt like a selfish bitch, but she did miss having Christian to herself.

"Please?" Lily asked.

"It's not up to me. It's up to your dad."

"Yay!" Lily exclaimed, a smile spreading across her innocent face. "I'll ask him."

Chapter 21

CHRISTIAN

Christian reached over and gripped Mallory's thigh as he drove toward the restaurant. He was grateful for some alone time with her, but he couldn't stop worrying about Lily. Never before had he left her with anyone aside from his mother, and here he was leaving her with yet another stranger.

"She's fine, you know," Mallory said, as if reading his mind. "Not only is Dan a professional, but she begged me to talk you into this. She really likes him."

She was right. He was being ridiculous. Lily was nearly old enough to take care of herself. She would be fine spending a few hours with a man whose job was to deal with children. And if he still had doubts, the fact that he was Mallory's best friend should have eliminated them.

"I'm glad we get a night to ourselves," he said after a moment.

She turned to him and pinned him with a smile that lit up her entire face. "I've missed you. I've been looking forward to this since Dan offered."

Chris gave her thigh another squeeze. As hesitant as he'd been to leave Lily with Dan, he was dying to spend some time with Mallory. He wanted much more than a dinner date, but alone time was alone time, and beggars couldn't be choosers. Figuring on their dinner dates being few and far between, he chose one of his favorite restaurants just across the river in New York. Living close to a bridge and tunnel leading into New York City did have its perks.

"Where are we going, anyway?" Mallory asked as they entered the lane for the George Washington Bridge.

"One of my favorite restaurants. It's in Brooklyn, so we should be able to find parking."

Mallory turned to face him, placing her hand on top of his where it still rested on her thigh. "I'm glad I took a vacation day for tomorrow."

Chris chuckled to himself. This was what he missed. The two of them setting out to do something new without anything to worry about. They couldn't stay out all night, but at least with Lily and Dan being at Mallory's place, they didn't have to rush back before bedtime.

"I suppose you might need a day of rest."

With an eyeroll, Mallory reclined her seat and sang along to the radio as they drove into the city. Between the singing and the conversation, Chris didn't feel like he was driving for long at all before he began circling the block to find parking. As expected, the area wasn't crowded, and he was able to find a space.

"This is such a cute neighborhood," Mallory commented as they walked hand-in-hand down the quiet street.

"Tourists flock to Manhattan, but Brooklyn has always been my favorite," he responded.

The street was lined with brownstones and quaint mom and pop shops. Beside the bookstore stood a small Mediterranean Restaurant. It wasn't Chris's favorite type of food, but he absolutely loved their grape leaves and falafel, not to mention the atmosphere, and he thought it might be something Mallory would enjoy. She had been very much into healthy living and healthy eating, even though she often let him derail her eating habits when they spent time together.

"I wasn't expecting Mediterranean food," she said as he stepped forward to open the door for her.

"Is it okay?"

He took her hand and led the way to the hostess desk. Her broad smile was all the answer he needed. Even though the only windows were at the front of the restaurant, the bright colors combined with fairy lights throughout made the inside feel bright and airy without the use of harsh lighting.

"It's perfect," she confirmed once they were seated in a back corner.

Chris would have preferred a seat at the front near the window, but the table in the back gave them a level of privacy. The pink sundress she wore was simple, but sexy as hell. She'd been wearing a thin white cardigan over it, but when she slipped it off and draped it over the back of the chair, he nearly forgot how to breathe. The dress was sleeveless and fell to mid-thigh. The olive skin of her toned thighs was a brilliant contrast against the dark pink. His fingers ached to reach out and touch her.

"You look amazing," he breathed.

A tinge of pink spread across her cheeks as she smiled and looked over the menu. Chris didn't need the menu. He ordered the same thing every time he was there, so he took the opportunity to take her in. The floral scent of her shampoo drifted his way as she flipped through the menu. He was no longer hungry for food.

"You know what you're ordering already?" she asked when she looked up to find him looking at her, his menu sitting unopened.

"Grape leaves, hummus, and falafel. I'm not sure if they go together, but they are the reason I love this place."

Mallory stifled a laugh. "Good choices. I'm getting the tabouli salad. I'm sure you'll let me taste whatever you get, right?"

"I'll let you taste anything you want."

The flush across her cheeks grew deeper and she returned her attention to the menu even though she already said what she wanted to order. Chris did his best to remind himself that they were out for a few hours for quality time. Dinner was quality time. Conversation was quality time.

"Thanks for bringing me here," Mallory said after a few minutes of comfortable silence.

"I had a feeling you would like this place."

"Pretty confident that you know me, huh?" she retorted.

"I know you like control, and that the food you eat is one thing you can control. I know when you get anxious, you recite phrases that make you feel more in control," he said before pausing and lowering his voice. "I know how you sound when my cock is buried deep inside your tight pussy."

She gasped in surprise. He watched as she shifted in her chair and tried her best to focus on something, anything besides what he said. No matter how cool she tried to play it, the flush of her cheeks and the change in her breathing gave her away. She was affected by his words.

"Do you two need a minute?" the waitress asked before either of them had realized she was standing there.

Chris chuckled to himself. They needed a minute, alright. "I think we're ready. Right, Bunny?"

Mallory cleared her throat and gave her head a small shake. "Yeah. We're—I mean I—um. I'm ready to order. Tabouli, please."

Chris placed his order without looking away from Mallory. "I'll have the grape leaves and falafel, and an order of hummus and pita to share, please. We're good with water to drink."

The waitress gave a polite nod before writing down their order. "My name is Serena, if you need anything. I'll get your order right in."

Once she had gone, Chris reached across the table and covered Mallory's hand with his. She jolted at the contact and locked eyes with him. "Shit," she breathed, before laughing to herself.

"What is it?" He had a feeling he knew what she was referring to. Just the feel of the back of her hand beneath his sent a shock of electricity through him. It was his turn to shift in his seat as his pants grew tighter around his arousal.

"Obviously it's been too long since we've been together," she answered with a laugh. "I'll be back. Is the restroom in the back?"

"On the left. Just past the coatroom."

He watched as she stood and walked away. The dress swayed as she walked, giving him a taunting view of the back of her creamy thighs. He needed to get his hands on her. The short hallway leading to the restrooms was just on the other side of the coatroom, which was unused for the season. Chris gave her a minute before he stood and headed that way.

MALLORY

Mallory turned the sink off before taking a moment to stare at her reflection in the mirror. Despite splashing some cold water on her face, careful to avoid her eye makeup, her face was still flushed. The touch of his hand over hers shouldn't have made her squirm with need, but it did. The vibration of his voice when he called her "Bunny" shouldn't have reached her core ... but it did.

"Get it together," she whispered to herself in the empty bathroom. "You can survive without sex."

After drying her hands and patting her face dry with a paper towel, she took one last cleansing breath and pushed the door open. She was making her way down the dim hallway when someone grabbed her arm and pulled her into a dark room, covering her mouth so she couldn't scream.

"Shh. It's me," Christian's familiar rasp washed over her, his breath tickling her neck.

Once she stopped struggling, his grasp loosened, and his hand drifted down her neck and rested on her chest slightly below her collar bone. Even that simple touch had her pulse skyrocketing.

"What are you doing?"

"Whatever I want," he growled into her ear, causing goosebumps to spread across her body.

Before she could respond, she found herself with her back pressed against the wall. When she parted her lips in a gasp, he covered her mouth with his, claiming her mouth. Sighing into him, she swiped her tongue along his as he thrust his hips, pressing his erection into her while pinning her firmly against the wall.

This was what she needed. What she craved. He slid his hands down her body over the soft fabric of her dress, stroking her curves along the way. She began trembling in anticipation once he reached the hem of her dress and slipped his hands underneath, tracing his fingers over the bare skin of her thighs before finally stroking her over her panties.

"Touch me," she pleaded. "Please."

He placed a leg between hers and used it to nudge her thighs apart before slipping his fingers inside her panties and stoking her aching center. She bit down on her lip to keep from crying out.

"You're so wet for me, already," he said before slipping a finger inside her.

She whimpered and thrust forward in search of more friction where she needed it most. She didn't care where they were, she needed to feel him inside her. She needed more.

"Please," she pleaded once more, not quite sure what she was asking for.

When he withdrew his hand, she opened her mouth to protest until she realized he was working to undo his belt. She grasped his shirt, untucking it from his pants as she heard the jingle of his belt.

"Turn around. Hands on the wall," he commanded, his voice barely above a whisper.

Without hesitation, she turned and placed her palms on the wall in front of her, dizzy with anticipation. Gripping her hips with both hands, he pulled back until her ass was pressed against his length. She was wet before, but now she was soaked as she waited for him to take her. She felt a chill from the cool air when he lifted her dress up to her waist, snaking his hand up her back before sliding it around to her stomach.

"You're shaking," he said into her ear. "Is this okay?"

"Yes."

"Good," he breathed.

He slid his hand further down, pushed her panties to the side, and stroked her slit. His wet fingers circling her clit nearly pushed her over the edge and she once again chewed her lip to keep from crying out. She needed more. She arched her back and pushed back into him, in a silent plea.

When he slipped two fingers inside her, she was unable to hold back her moan. Without warning, he pulled his fingers out and replaced them with his cock. She opened her mouth to cry out, but he slipped his fingers inside her mouth, spreading the salty tang of her arousal over her tongue.

"See how good you taste? Now lick them clean," he instructed.

Tasting herself on his fingers only fueled her arousal. She sucked on his fingers, swirling her tongue around to clean them as he thrust into her, making it a point to keep quiet as she met each thrust.

"Good girl," he praised.

Everything about what they were doing felt wrong. From that angle, she was beyond full, and it wasn't long before her breathing increased, and all of her focus was on that one place in her body. She was wound tight, and desperate for release.

"Please," she begged. "Harder."

With that, he slipped his fingers out of her mouth and gripped her hips. "Don't make a sound."

He plunged into her, deep and fast. She met each thrust as she chased her release, her breaths coming out in harsh pants. Keeping quiet was nearly impossible. Tears stung her eyes as the tightening in her core released into the most intense orgasm she'd ever experienced. Christian released her hip with one hand and wrapped her hair around his hand, pulling her head back as he emptied himself into her.

"Fuck," he breathed as he continued to pulse inside her.

After a moment, she felt him pull out before moving her panties back into place. She was a mess; wet and sticky from their love making.

"I'll go out first," Christian said as he zipped up and buckled his belt. "Don't clean up. I want the mess we made to remind you where I've been."

Chapter 22

MALLORY

Mallory woke up on her couch, wrapped in Christian's arms. The blanket was half on the floor, and she was sweating from the heat of his body. When they had gotten home from dinner, Lily was already asleep. Somehow, Christian had managed to carry her to bed without waking her.

Not wanting to spend another night apart, and not wanting Lily to feel uncomfortable by finding them in bed together, they settled on sleeping on the couch. True, there wasn't much of a difference between sleeping in the bed fully clothed, and sleeping on the couch fully clothed, but it made Mallory feel better.

She had barely become fully awake before she heard soft footsteps coming from down the hall. Fighting the instinct to sit up and out of Christian's embrace, she instead waited for Lily to come into the room.

"Good morning," she whispered before holding her finger over her mouth and pointing to a sleeping Christian. "You hungry?"

Lily smiled and nodded, seemingly unbothered by the sight of them curled up together. Mallory carefully untangled herself from Christian's arms and stood from the couch, covering him up before she made her way to the kitchen.

"How was it last night? Did you have a good time with Dan?" Mallory asked as she started a pot of coffee.

"Yeah, it was fine. What about you and Dad?"

Mallory hoped her blush wasn't noticeable as her mind immediately flashed to the coatroom. "We had fun, too. I've never been to that restaurant before."

She pulled the electric griddle from the cabinet and set it on the counter. "Pancakes okay?"

Lily smiled and took a seat at the island. Mallory took that as a yes and took out the pancake mix, eggs, and milk. Making them from scratch felt like entirely too much work. She was tired from the evening's activities and staying up late. She and Christian had talked for over an hour about nothing and everything once they had settled on the couch. It was a great night.

Pancakes were quick, so it wasn't long before Mallory set the large serving dish on the island before serving up to plates and sliding one over to Lily. "So, what did you guys do? Anything fun?"

Lily smiled before answering. "We played Mad Libs. I thought it was a stupid suggestion, but it was actually really funny."

Mallory chuckled around her fork as she shoveled in her first bite. "That sounds like fun. What else?"

Lily started eating before she answered the question. "I don't know. We just talked a lot. Watched TV. I don't need a babysitter, you know. So, we just hung out."

"Nice. Well, I'm glad you had a good time. I think it was good for all of us to have a change in scenery."

"You guys don't have to sleep on the couch, you know. I'm not a baby."

Mallory nearly choked on her food. The kid was mature for her age, but she never expected her to come out and say that. Without children of her own, she wasn't sure what the appropriate response was. Once she stopped coughing, she tried to quickly think of something to say since "I'm glad you're okay with me banging your dad" didn't seem like the thing to say.

"Good morning sweetheart," Christian said from behind Mallory. She had been so wrapped up in trying to think of a response that she hadn't even noticed that he moved from the couch.

He placed a kiss on top of Mallory's head and squeezed her shoulders as he spoke over her and to his daughter. "You sleep okay?"

"Yeah. You going to eat some pancakes? They're really good."

Mallory stifled a laugh as she reached for the last plate and stacked it high with pancakes before passing it to Christian. Every time she was around this kid, she liked her even more. It was a shame she didn't get along with her mother, because she really was a great kid.

"Thanks," he said as he sat down and began to dig in. "So, how was your night, Lily? You guys have fun?"

She rolled her eyes, obviously annoyed to be asked the same question all over again. Mallory failed at holding in her laugh and attempted to cover it with another cough.

"She had a great time," she answered for her. "They played games, talked, and watched TV."

Christian looked at her with an eyebrow quirked up. "Sounds like fun."

"It was." Lily said with a shrug. "Did Mallory talk to you about letting me stay the rest of the summer?"

Mallory didn't. She had hoped Lily would forget she asked her since she was trying very hard to stick to her rule of not interfering. Helping out so he could go to work was one thing, but talking to him about parenting things was another.

She could feel him looking at her as he answered his daughter. "As a matter of fact, she didn't. Why don't we talk about it now."

"I don't want to go back. There's no reason I can't stay here all summer. It's not like I have school, and Mom doesn't want me around anyway. Even Dan thinks it's a good idea for me to stay."

That was news to Mallory. And not the most welcomed news to Christian, judging by his scowl. "Oh, does he?"

"Yeah," Lily answered eagerly. "He listens when I talk. I was telling him how much I'd rather be here, and he said staying for the summer sounded like a good idea."

Mallory quickly jumped into the conversation, sensing Christian's displeasure with what he was hearing. "When we were out with Dan the other day, she brought it up. I forgot to say something to you, I'm sorry. And Dan said he'd say something too, probably knowing I'd forget."

"I'm gonna go get dressed," Lily said, taking that as her cue to leave.

Mallory stood to clear plates, using it as a way to buy herself some time before thinking of an explanation. Her skin grew warm as she started to panic, knowing Christian must be upset. She didn't blame him if he was. Lily was none of her business and certainly wasn't Dan's business just because he kept an eye on her for a few hours one night.

"Stop panicking. I'm not upset," Christian said, wrapping his arms around her and nuzzling her hair from behind. "Talk to me."

"She doesn't want to go back," she answered without turning away from the sink.

Christian gently turned her to face him. With nothing but concern and sincerity etched across his features, he reiterated his request. "Tell me everything. Please. I know you feel like it's not your business, but I promise you it is."

"She wants to stay the summer. She doesn't feel like her mom wants her around, and obviously whatever is going on with her is back there. I don't think it's a bad idea. She's happy here, and I love having her around. She can stay with me when you go to work."

Christian roamed her body with his hands, his firm touch continuing to calm her. "I just wish she would talk about it. It can't be good for her to keep everything inside. I know I'm not much better, but I'm old and already disillusioned with life in general. It's not too late for her."

Mallory laughed quietly at his words. He had summed up his personality in one sentence. "If it makes you feel better, I think she may have talked to Dan about whatever it is that's going on with her."

"Oh yeah? Good. Once he tells me what it is, I can work on fixing it."

She wasn't sure it would be that easy. If she knew Dan at all, she knew he'd probably keep whatever Lily told him in confidence. Even if he wasn't at work, one of the things he prided himself on since she'd met him was being a safe place for whoever needed it. Mallory knew he would never tell anyone all the things she had told him. He also never judged. That's what made him so easy to talk to; he was trustworthy.

"Yeah, we'll see," she said noncommittally.

"Why do I get the feeling there's something you aren't telling me?" he asked.

Mallory considered her options. She could mention how unlikely it was that Dan would divulge everything and face the aftermath, or she could change the subject.

"I'm more than happy to keep helping out however long you have her. She's a good kid and we have fun. Keeping an eye on her while you're working isn't a problem at all."

Christian was quiet for a moment before he spoke. His expression was serious, and she could tell he was choosing his words carefully. "I don't want to put you out," he said in a quiet voice. "You didn't sign up for this."

She appreciated that he didn't want to take advantage of her kindness, but she committed to all of it. The way she felt about him? She was on board with anything that had to do with him.

"Don't say that," she warned softly. "I signed up for you and everything that comes with you. I'm not sure what she is afraid of back home, but if she can stay then I'm here. And I mean that."

"I'll talk to Vivian."

Before she could respond, he was heading off to grab his daughter. She only hoped he took what she said to heart. Anything he needed; she was there. She wasn't exaggerating, she was being honest. Their short time apart taught her that she would indeed do anything for him. And if she hadn't been certain before, the coatroom proved it.

CHRISTIAN

"Still like it here, Mom?" Chris asked.

He had stopped by to check on her every day before and after work, but it was only his second time bringing Lily with him. The staff seemed friendly, and the place was clean. If she liked it, he loved it. But he was still anxious for her to go home.

"I do like it. Everyone is nice and they tell me I've been doing great since I've been here."

Lily sat in the chair at the far side of the room and played on her phone, completely uninterested in what was going on. She greeted her abuela with a hug and a kiss, asked her how she was feeling, then parked herself in a chair before mentally checking out. Chris couldn't blame her. He wouldn't have been interested when he was her age either.

"Any idea when you can go home?"

"I'm not sure I want to go home," his mom said after a moment. "I heard they might have a spot available in the assisted living building. It doesn't sound bad having people check on you and a full-time staff so if something happens, they can help me."

"I can help you," Chris interjected, offended by the implication that he wasn't there for his mother. He had always been there as much as he could. If she ever needed anything, he was there without question.

"I know you can, honey. But I would rather not bother you if I don't have to. Plus, I have friends here. Take my house. No need to live in that small apartment. And if for some reason I decide I want to come back, then I know I have a place to go back to," Mrs. Ramirez reasoned with him.

"Mom, it's your house. I don't need all that space. My apartment is fine."

"Not for you and Lily," she pointed out.

"We're fine for the amount of time she gets to stay with me. And once you're home then she'll go back to spending a lot of her time there."

His mom sat forward in her chair and covered his hand with hers. "I'm not coming home, Christian. And Lily wants to stay with you, so this could be the perfect opportunity."

Her warm hand soothed him, but the words she uttered came as a surprise. He didn't expect his mom to bring up Lily staying since he had purposely avoided the topic whenever he came to visit. He knew how she was; she wouldn't rest until Lily was permanently living with him and he wasn't sure that was possible.

"Mom, I'm not going to –"

"Don't argue with me, please," she interrupted. "They have an apartment for me in the assisted living, and I'm going to move into it as soon as I'm ready. I'm also telling you that child needs to be with you. Don't ask me why I'm so sure if it, just know that I am."

It wasn't often his mother took that tone of voice with him, but when she did, he knew not to argue with her. The thought of her not returning home made his body feel cold from the inside out. He grew up in the modest home, but he wouldn't feel right living in it without her being there. There had to be another solution.

"Christian, I can hear you thinking way over here. What is it?"

"It's just—" He paused to clear his throat when his voice unexpectedly cracked. "If you don't come home, nothing will be the same."

"Things can't stay the same forever. I'm old. I never would have admitted it then, but it was hard for me on my own. Even before the fall. It's time."

He blinked back tears and chanced a glance at his daughter. She was no longer in her own little world ignoring the rest of them. Now sitting up straight in her chair, she watched the interaction with wide eyes.

"Abuela? You really aren't coming back home?" she choked out.

His mother's eyes softened as she looked at Lily. "My apartment will be my home. I'm not staying in this nursing home, but I need something smaller where people will always be around if I need them. Your dad has a life to live. It isn't fair for him to have to be ready to drop everything in case I need something."

"I know it's not my job, but I want to be there for you. Me. Not some strangers," he interrupted.

"I know. I know you want to. And you can. But now you don't have to worry about something happening while you're at work. If you want to go away for a weekend, you'll know I'm okay. Trust me. This will be good for everyone."

Chris tried to slow his racing thoughts. Even if she was right, he didn't want strangers taking care of her. Assisted livings were for old people who didn't have families, or whose family didn't want anything to do with them. His mom had a family.

"Abuela?" Lily began. "How did you know I don't want to go back to Florida?"

"Abuela knows these things, sweetheart," was her answer.

"Did Mallory tell you?" Chris asked.

Her hesitation was answer enough. It wasn't a surprise that she'd been by to visit his mother without him, but he wasn't sure how he felt about her talking about his personal issues without him knowing about it. Even if it was his mother.

"She thought I was asleep." When Chris said nothing, she continued on. "Mallory comes by almost every day. She came in one evening and I must have been asleep when she got here. I woke up while she was going on about the weather, but before I could turn and tell her I was awake, she changed the subject. I know Lily asked her to talk you into letting her stay."

Another wave of surprise washed over him. He'd known Mallory was visiting his mom while he was in Florida, but he hadn't realized she continued her regular visits even after he'd returned home. A glance at Lily told him his mother wasn't making anything up. She really was doing everything she could to stay. Before he made his decision, he'd need to speak to Dan and figure out what all this was about.

"Lily," he said, giving his daughter a weary look, "we'll talk about it later. And I'll think about it, Mom."

"Have Manny draw up the paperwork. You know who I'm talking about, right? He did my will."

"Mom," he said, heaving an exasperated sigh. "I said I'd think about it. That isn't a yes."

"I'll still need the papers ready. If you don't want it, then I'll just sell it and leave you the money. I have plenty of money saved in case I needed to come somewhere like this, but I don't want this place to get my house or the money I make selling it. You should really think about it before you make a decision."

Just like that, everything became real. And along with it came the realization that only Mallory could make him feel better about the decisions he needed to make. If he was honest with himself, he wanted Lily to stay just as much, if not more, than she wanted to stay. If he looked beyond emotions, his mother's house would be the perfect place to live with Lily and Mallory. *And Mallory?* He needed to get out of there before that idea made itself comfortable in his mind.

Chapter 23

MALLORY

Mallory sat on her couch and tried to listen to what Christian was saying, but she was incredibly distracted by his large hands as they absently stroked her legs. Lily had excused herself into the bedroom to watch TV, so it was just the two of them. The anxiety she felt weighing her down upon hearing the words "we need to talk" was finally beginning to let up.

It was Friday night, so she was able to relax without having to worry about being at work the next morning, and Christian had the night off. It was nice. It was comfortable; until the time came to talk about real things.

"What should I do?" Christian asked, his gaze fixed on hers.

"What?" Mallory stammered.

"What should I do? My mom wants me to take her house, and apparently everyone wants me to keep Lily for at least the summer, but knowing my ex it won't be that simple."

Mallory forced herself out of her daze so she could respond. "If she doesn't want Lily around, why won't it be that simple? Seems to me she'd be ecstatic to get her out of her hair."

Christian's hands momentarily paused on her legs before he let out a soft chuckle. "It won't be simple because it's something that I want."

"After all this time?" Mallory asked incredulously.

A slow nod was his only response. As a woman who never had children, it was hard for her to imagine being in either situation; a single mother, or a father having to deal with a single mother. As far as Mallory was concerned, it seemed like the perfect solution. Lily's mother was tired of dealing with her and her father wanted more time with her. It should have been simple.

"Even if Lily is right and Vivian doesn't want to deal with her, she'll never admit it. Saying something like that out loud would make her a bad mother. She'd rather fight me tooth and nail and get the chance to make my life hell while also looking like a mother who is fighting for her kid, than admit she needs a break."

Mallory gaped at him in horror. There was no way a mother could behave that way. She opened her mouth to speak then closed it several times before Christian squeezed her ankle, bringing her attention back to him.

"I over-simplified that statement. While I do think she'd still go out of her way to make me miserable, she isn't necessarily a bad mom. She's tired. Raising a teenager and working full time isn't easy. Unfortunately, she'd get raked over the coals if she admitted to needing a break. Why do that, if I can be punished while also helping her look better?"

The standards that women were held to were ridiculous. Add in being a mom, and she couldn't be happier that having children hadn't been in the cards for her. She had a hard enough time feeling adequate, without anyone judging how well she kept another human alive.

"So, what do you think?"

His question jolted her from her thoughts. "What?"

Christian went back to lazily stroking her legs. She knew he was just trying to ease her anxiety, and it worked. "What do you think I should do?

Should I start that fight with Vivian? And what about Mom's house? I just don't know what I should do."

"Oh," Mallory fumbled as anxiety lanced through her. "It's really not my business. You should do what you think is right."

"I want it to be your business. Doing this without you isn't going to work for me. Florida made me sure of that."

She whipped her head over to look at him as her heart continued to pound. He looked back at her with a look of uncertainty. His face was free of his nearly constant smirk, and he was studying her face carefully. Either her heart skipped a beat, or she was having an actual heart attack. His expression told her he meant every word he spoke.

"Christian," she hesitated.

"It's. Your. Business."

She took a deep breath to steady her voice and her racing thoughts. "Fight for her. She's worth it. And your mom's house is the perfect place to raise her. Fight for more than just the summer."

Christian exhaled as if he'd been holding his breath the entire time. His shoulders slumped slightly before he returned his gaze to hers. "I know she is. Maybe I should talk to your friend and find out what's going on."

"I wouldn't recommend that," she warned.

Christian's shoulders stiffened as he looked at her with his eyes narrowed. "What's that supposed to mean?"

Mallory let out a frustrated sigh. Christian worked in healthcare. He should know better than to think Dan would tell him everything that Lily said. While it was true, Dan wasn't at work when they spoke, it still wasn't a good idea to get the one person who she'd opened up to, to break her trust. He had to know better than that.

"Do you think that's smart? Even if you could get Dan to tell you everything, should you?"

She regretted her words as soon as they left her mouth. She had sworn to herself that she wouldn't interfere, and there she was harshly second guessing him. The harshness of her words was unintentional, but she had instantly reverted back to herself as a child in need of a safe space. The idea of her one confidante sharing everything brought on instant feelings of betrayal.

"You sure went from having no opinion to questioning my instincts as a parent." The change in his demeanor sent a chill through her.

"Christian, I didn't mean—"

"Save it. We're going to get going. I'm tired and have a lot on my mind."

With that, he got up and headed for the door, calling for Lily as he went. Mallory sat frozen on the couch as the realization struck her. This was the first time he'd ever been angry with her. She remained frozen in place even as Lily looked back at her with pleading eyes as she followed her father out the door. After insisting she be included in the decisions about Lily, he had quickly proven that her instincts had been correct.

CHRISTIAN

Chris felt like shit. He hadn't gotten much sleep the night before and a nap before work also wasn't happening. He had planned to take a sick day, but Lily wasn't having it. She all but begged to go to Mallory's, and since he had no desire to face her the only way Lily was going to her house was if he dropped her off on his way to work. He hadn't given Lily more than a noncommittal shrug before he went to his bedroom to lie down, but time had run out. If he wasn't going to work, he had to make the call soon.

"Well?" Lily asked from the couch as soon as he emerged from his room in search of coffee.

"Lily I—"

"Just drop me off. Whatever you guys are fighting about doesn't have anything to do with me, so I shouldn't be punished for it. I like her!"

Actually, it had everything to do with her, but he couldn't tell her that. If he was honest with himself, their fight had everything to do with him. He probably could have reacted a bit better, but she was wrong to judge him that way. As Lily's father, he had every right to know what was going on before making a major decision about her life.

"I know you like her, but—"

She cut him off again. "If she wasn't going to be around, you shouldn't have brought me to her house."

She was right. He wouldn't have introduced them if he hadn't planned on her being someone permanent in his life. He was pissed, but was it permanent? He didn't want to think about it.

Before he could respond, his phone vibrated with a text message.

Mallory: Lily is still coming over tonight, right?

He looked up at Lily, who was watching him expectantly with her arms folded. He had to make a decision, but not before coffee. Lily followed him in silence when he made his way to the kitchen.

After a few sips, he picked up his phone and sent Mallory a simple "yes" before returning his attention to his daughter. She was sitting at the small table still waiting for his response. He never had and never would mistreat her, but she knew better than to push.

"I'll drop you off over there. You still don't want to go back home?" he finally responded.

"Please don't make me. Can't you talk to Mom? She's tired of me, anyway."

"Your mother loves you." No matter his issues with the woman, he never wanted Lily to feel less than loved by either parent.

Lily didn't respond to what he said. She just stared at him with a purposely blank expression on her face. Chris wished he knew what was going on in her mind. He would definitely be stopping at Dan's after he dropped Lily off. No way was he continuing to blindly navigate the situation.

"Make sure you have everything you want to bring to Mallory's ready to go. I'll get ready for work now so we can get something to eat on the way."

A small smile spread across her face before she left him standing alone in the kitchen. The kid was too smart. She'd managed to shut him down by pointing out things he wasn't ready to hear. He wouldn't bring a fling around his daughter, and she knew it. He knew it, too, even if he wasn't ready to admit it to himself.

It took the entire drive from the restaurant for Chris to convince himself that he was capable of walking Lily all the way to Mallory's door. Even if he wasn't ready to face her, it would be rude not to walk her up. She was, after all, doing him a favor by keeping an eye on her.

He took a deep steadying breath before giving her door a light rap. Mallory opened the door and stood back to let Lily inside. She was wearing a pair of black leggings and a thin gray Henley with the first few buttons open. Her hair was piled into a messy bun, and he was instantly reminded of the lazy mornings they'd spent together, sipping coffee and enjoying each other's company. It took everything in him to keep from touching her. Instead, he reminded himself why he was there.

"Thanks," he said softly. "I have some sick days if—"

"No," she interrupted. "It's fine. Have a good night."

Before he could say anything else, he found himself staring at her door once again. He couldn't be upset after the way he left the night before. When she texted him to make sure Lily was still coming over, he told himself it was a good sign, that she understood why he'd been upset, that she'd be there when he was ready to talk to her again.

Was he ready to talk to her? He wasn't sure what he wanted. The only thing he was certain about was the need to talk to Dan. Glancing at his watch, he saw he still had quite a bit of time before he had to head to work. Just enough time to make a quick stop at the apartment downstairs.

Dan opened the door far enough to lean in the doorway with his arms folded across his chest. It was obvious he was less than happy to see him.

"Do you have a few minutes?" Chris asked.

"I have several minutes, but what makes you think they're for you?"

Chris swallowed hard. Things already weren't going well. "I was hoping I could talk to you about Lily."

Dan snorted. "Oh, *now* you want to talk about Lily. Seems to me the time to talk about her was last night."

Shit. Dan was Mallory's best friend. Of course, she'd talked to him about what happened. They had coffee together every morning. All he could do was throw honesty at the man and hope he would hear him out.

Chris glanced toward the stairs and lowered his voice. "I just need to know what's going on so I can figure this shit out."

Reluctantly, Dan opened the door the rest of the way and stepped aside. Chris walked inside and closed the door before following Dan into the kitchen.

"You look like shit," Dan said as he pressed start on the coffee maker. "Good thing I get the coffee set up after I clean the pot in the morning."

"Thanks?" Chris wasn't sure if he should acknowledge the insult or thank the man in advance for the coffee.

"So, what can I help you with?" Dan asked, finally breaking the silence, once they both had a mug of coffee in hand.

"I need to know why Lily doesn't want to go back home with her mom. This isn't something simple like trading holidays. This will end up a big thing and I need to know why."

Dan was quiet for a moment, and it was obvious he was choosing how to respond. Chris shifted his feet but kept quiet. Rambling wouldn't do him any good. Dan was going to say whatever it was he was going to say.

"You love your daughter."

It wasn't a question. He wasn't sure if or how to respond, so he nodded and waited for Dan to continue.

"Do you want her to live with you?" He really got right to the point.

"It's not about what I want. That's why I need to know."

Dan held up his hand to stop him from speaking. "If you love her and want her with you as much as she wants to be here, then why do you need to know anything else. She's had a break from whatever it is that's going on back home and still wants to be here. You are a fit parent and she's old enough to know what she wants. Fight for her."

"Do you know what's going on with her?" Chris asked plainly. He didn't have time to dance around the subject.

"That's not important."

Chris slammed his mug down on the counter. He wasn't there to play games and could feel anger getting the best of him. "If you know what's going on, you need to fucking tell me. She's my daughter."

Dan calmly set his cup down and crossed his arms. "If you came here to intimidate me into telling you anything, you might as well leave now."

"What the fuck?" Chris asked.

"Mallory has been the scared little kid before. You probably should have listened to her instead of storming off last night and making her feel like shit. If you didn't want her involved in you and Lily's lives you shouldn't have asked for her opinion on any of it."

"That's not what I came here to talk about," Chris pointed out. He picked up his mug and finished his coffee.

"Are you that dense?" Dan asked. "Pay attention, because I don't like repeating myself."

Chris took a few steps forward until they were nearly nose to nose. He opened and closed his fist several times as he fought the urge to hit him. "Who the fuck do you think you're talking to, man?"

Dan was about the same size as Chris. With more of a swimmer's build, he was obviously in shape and carried the confidence of someone who could hold his own in a fight. If Chris had any plans to fix things with Mallory, he couldn't get into an actual fight with her best friend. He reminded himself of that before taking a step back.

"Are you ready to listen to what I have to say?" Dan asked.

With a heavy sigh, Chris gave a small nod.

"As Mallory tried to explain to you last night, you don't want me to break that trust. Being a teenager is hard and she opened up to me. If she ends up here permanently, it'll be good for her to have someone safe to talk to. And if I repeat what she told me, it won't just be me that she's mad at. Is that what you want?"

"No," he choked out, feeling like a jackass.

Dan was right. He knew he was. The fact that Dan had to spell it all out like that was embarrassing. The only thing he could chalk it up to was stress. The stress of possibly making the wrong decision about things that didn't just affect him. Two people were currently depending on him to do the right thing.

"I didn't think so. You need to fix things with Mallory. She's loyal to a fault and will support you through everything. But you need to fix it. She wasn't trying to judge you, she was trying to help you. We were all children before, but Mallory's childhood was difficult, so it's never far from her mind. She'll be good for Lily to be around."

"I know. I'll talk to Mallory. It just hurts that Lily doesn't feel safe talking to me about everything. We were always close," Chris admitted.

"I know. She'll talk to you when she's ready. In the meantime, fight for her."

Chris thanked Dan before seeing himself out. He could tell Mallory hadn't been exaggerating about him saving her life. He headed to work feeling eternally grateful that both Mallory and Lily had him in their lives, even if deep down he wished he was the one they could turn to. His feelings of anger were replaced by relief. Relief that Dan was strong enough to be what his daughter needed.

Chapter 24

MALLORY

Mallory went to take a quick shower after texting Dan what she wanted from the Thai restaurant. It was date night with Dan, but she didn't feel like cooking. Avoiding Christian was exhausting. It had been an entire week since he stormed out of her apartment, and she'd managed to avoid him other than the short time it took to let Lily in or to see her off. During the week, he usually showed up to pick Lily up a little after she left for work, so that helped.

He'd asked a few times if they could talk, but she just wasn't ready. It had taken a lot for her to give her input, and his reaction reinforced her original plan to keep her distance, not from Lily, but from Christian. She enjoyed the time she spent with Lily independent of her relationship with Christian. If things got more serious between her and Christian and then they broke up, she knew that would be the end of being in her life. If she stepped back now, she could continue the way things were. That's what she told herself, anyway.

Since she never felt the need to impress Dan, she threw on a pair of sweatpants and a tank top. A low-key night of eating takeout in front of the TV was exactly what she needed. Her stomach growled as she ran the brush through her hair before putting it up in a ponytail.

When she walked out of her bedroom and into the kitchen, she was shocked to find Christian placing various takeout containers onto the kitchen island.

"Hey," he greeted, his voice barely above a whisper.

"What are you doing?" she demanded.

"Setting dinner out ..."

Unamused, she rephrased her question. "What are you doing *here*?"

"We need to talk, but you keep avoiding me," he answered simply.

"Yeah. Because I don't have anything I want to talk about." The fact she kept avoiding him should have made that painfully obvious.

"Oh no you don't," he said gently. "You aren't running. Tell me why you don't want to talk."

After selecting a container, she sat down at the island to dig in. She may have been avoiding him, but she was hungry. It was possible to ignore him while eating. The food was delicious, and when she closed her eyes and enjoyed her first bite, she nearly forgot he was there. As she let out a soft moan, she opened her eyes to find him staring at her.

"Did you come here to stare at me while I eat?"

He shook his head as if snapping himself out of a daze before chuckling to himself. "No, that's just an unexpected bonus."

"Why are you here, Christian? I'm fine with keeping an eye on Lily, regardless of what's going on with you and me. I already told you that."

Christian stilled. "That is not why I'm here, and you know it."

It was Mallory's turn to freeze. When he used that commanding voice on her, she had no choice but to pay attention to him. Trying to ignore what his voice was doing to her, she cleared her throat. "Then what is it?"

"I was wrong, and I'm sorry," he answered simply.

"About?" She knew what he was talking about, but she needed to hear it from him.

"I practically begged for your input. I'm not stupid, I know you've been careful to stay out of things that had to do with Lily. I convinced you to participate, then I stormed out when I didn't like what you had to say. So, I'm sorry," he repeated. "You already know I talked to Dan the other day. I needed to hear what he said. I should have heard it when you said it, but I was too busy waiting to hear what I wanted to."

Mallory swallowed as his words registered. The assumption had always been that she would need to explain her reaction. That he wouldn't own up to how he treated her. She should have known he was better than that, but the way he stormed out and then avoided her for a few days had her convinced he was like the others.

"Where is Lily, anyway?" Mallory asked, finally realizing what was so strange about him just showing up the way he did.

"Downstairs, with Dan."

"What do you want from me?" she came out and asked. "You can apologize for the way you reacted, but it doesn't change your feelings. I'm okay with stepping back. That's why you haven't heard from me. Just tell me what you want."

"I want you!" he shouted, surprising them both. "You don't remember everything I said before I left? I shouldn't have stormed off the way I did, and for that I'm sorry, but that doesn't cancel out what I said before. I want you to be a part of this. I want you involved. Sometimes I won't like what you say, but that's okay."

Blinking rapidly, she tried to hold back the unshed tears that pricked her eyes. There was nothing she wanted more than to be included in all of it. But it was too much too fast. No matter how bad she wanted to dive in headfirst, she had to remember it wasn't just about her. Christian wasn't ready to share every aspect with her, even though he thought he was, and that was okay.

"Christian, it's fine. I don't need to be included in everything. It's not my place. I will continue to help out with Lily, but how you choose to be a parent has nothing to do with me. If she ends up here permanently, I'll still help out."

"What are you saying?" He watched her with a stern gaze as he waited for her answer.

"I'm saying let's go back to the way things were before. Just because we have sex doesn't mean I need to be part of everything. It's not like we live together. I'm perfectly fine not playing house."

She watched as he blinked away the hurt that crossed his features. He stepped closer and placed a hand on her hip, gripping her tightly and pinning her against the kitchen island. "Just two people who are sleeping together, then? That's what we are?"

Mallory nodded. She wasn't sure if it was fear or excitement coursing through her, but she shivered when he took another step closer, further boxing her in. "Yeah. That's all we can be."

He took one more step closer, pressing his body flush against hers. His body was firm against her, and she couldn't ignore the way his arousal pressed against her stomach. This was what she'd wanted. This was what worked for them. Sex without complications.

He gripped the back of her neck and claimed her mouth with a greedy kiss. When she gasped in surprise he slipped his tongue in her mouth, sliding it along hers. Heat pooled to her center, and she eagerly kissed him back while allowing him to take control. He gripped her waist with his free hand before slipping it under her shirt and roaming up her body. She wasn't wearing anything beneath her tank top and the feel of his thumb across her nipple caused her to cry out.

"More," she moaned.

He let go of her neck and used both hands to pull her shirt off. The chill of the air hit her naked breasts, but she resisted the urge to cover herself as he stepped back to look at her. He once again pulled her close and took her mouth while running his hands over her naked flesh. When he reached the waistband of her sweats, he slipped his hands inside and pulled them down along with her panties.

As she stood before him completely bare, she was acutely aware that he was fully clothed. He put his hands over hers, stopping her when she reached for his shirt. Giving his head a quick shake, he worked to undo his belt.

"We don't have time," he breathed as he freed himself from his pants.

Before she could respond, he spun her around, so she was bent over the island, the granite cold under her skin. He ran his hands down her naked back and to her ass, cupping and massaging her before slipping a hand between her legs and to her wet slit.

"So fucking wet," he said with a groan. "Are you ready for me?"

"Yes," she breathed.

"Good. Ass up."

He pressed down on her back, so her ass was tilted up, and in one move he buried himself inside her to the hilt. She let out a loud moan as her body adjusted to the fullness. After a moment, he began to move; deep thrusts sliding her body across the island as she held on tight, attempting to keep herself steady.

"Shit," she cried out as she met each thrust.

As his movements picked up speed and became more erratic, she chased the orgasm that felt just out of reach. He snaked an arm around her waist and pulled her to him with each thrust.

"I need you to come," he gritted out, his voice strained.

"I can't," she cried. "I need more."

He let go of her, slipping his hand between her legs and pressing her clit. She spread her legs further, granting him better access, but it still wasn't enough. She needed more. She needed to feel his weight against her. She needed the closeness. Reaching a hand behind her to grab his neck, she pulled him closer. As if sensing what she needed, he leaned over her, kissing the back of her neck before moving his mouth to her ear.

"Is this what you need?" he asked.

"Yes!" She was so close.

He stroked her jaw and down her neck with his free hand, sending a shiver down her spine, as he continued thrusting into her. Giving her neck a squeeze, he growled into her ear, "Now come for me."

She did. She cried out in surprise when her orgasm ripped through her, sending shockwaves through her body as he continued the firm pressure on her neck. His movements faltered behind her as he found his release, his warmth filling her as she continued to pulse around him.

Before she had come down from the haze of her orgasm, he pulled out, leaving her bent over the island. She shivered from the cold granite beneath her torso and the cool air against the wetness between her thighs. By the time she turned around, Christian was securing his belt and moving toward the door before he turned and looked at her with a conflicted gaze.

Tears once again stung her eyes as she began gathering her clothes. She quickly stepped into her sweats and pulled her shirt over her head as he continued to watch her. Even with clothes on, she felt naked under his gaze. She blinked to keep the tears from falling.

"Mallory, I—" he began before she held out a hand and cut him off.

"Don't," she whispered. "Just go."

She turned on her heel and practically ran to the bathroom, slamming the door behind her. As soon as she was alone, the tears began making a steady trail down her face. After turning on the shower, she stripped off her clothes and stepped inside, allowing the warm current to wash over her as she slid down to sit in the bottom of the tub.

She was the one who suggested they take a step back. She was the one who insisted they were just two people who had sex. The sex wasn't much different than their other times together, but she felt cold and empty afterwards. He didn't hold her. He didn't stay … He. Didn't. Stay.

CHRISTIAN

"Just tell her you're sorry, Dad," Lily insisted as they drove back to his apartment.

If only it was that simple. No way was he going to tell his daughter why they were going home instead of spending the evening with Mallory. When he picked up the takeout and dropped Lily off with Dan, he'd hoped they would clear the air while eating dinner, and then Lily and Dan would join for dessert and maybe a movie. That did not happen, and he felt like the biggest piece of shit. It was taking all of his energy to pretend he was okay in front of Lily.

He was far from okay. Any time he blinked too long, he saw the flash of the hurt in Mallory's eyes. Treating her like one of his one-night stands was a dick move. It was one thing when he kept his distance from actual hookups. There were no expectations, and the terms were agreed upon in advance. Before Mallory, he didn't want more than that. But to treat her the way he did was not okay. Even if she said that's what she wanted.

"Dad?"

He glanced over to find his daughter watching him expectantly. "What?"

"You're still going to talk to Mom, right?"

He hadn't let himself get as far as figuring out how everything would work out, but he'd already decided to fight to keep Lily with him. If he was fighting to keep her, it had nothing to do with anyone else. It was for Lily and for him. He would figure out how to make it work once he got there. The important part was getting there.

"Yeah. I'll talk to her."

"And you'll apologize to Mallory?"

"I'll try," he answered reluctantly.

After the way he'd behaved, he wouldn't blame her for refusing to talk to him. That was another bridge to cross once he got to it. The most important thing was to make sure Lily was with him for good. Between the way she relaxed the longer she was in New Jersey, and his talk with Dan, he knew staying out of Florida was what was best for her.

"Lily, I love you and there's nothing I would like more than to have you stay here with me. It's just hard to fight when I don't know what I'm fighting against. There's nothing you can tell me that will change anything between us. You know that, right?"

Chris glanced over to find Lily fiddling with her seatbelt. As much as he wanted to press her for information, he knew she wouldn't talk to him unless she was ready. That understanding was what brought him to Florida. It was what had him booking the next available flight for them when Vivian tried to start her shit. But he wished more than anything that she would confide in him. Trust him to be her safe space.

"I like girls." Her voice was barely above a whisper as he parked on the street in front of his building.

"What?" Chris asked once he had the car parked. He'd been focused on what he was doing and wasn't sure he heard what she said.

"Great, you sound like Mom. I tried to talk to her, and she was stupid about it. Forget it."

Chris took the key from the ignition and turned to Lily before he moved to get out of the car. "Sweetheart, I didn't hear you. I was concentrating on what I was doing."

"I said I like girls!" she shouted before getting out of the car and slamming the door behind her.

Chris sat in stunned silence before scrambling out of the car behind her. She was inside the main door and waiting by the second door when he caught up to her. Her arms hugged her middle, and he could practically feel her anxiety. The lobby of his apartment building wasn't the place for a heart-to-heart, so he unlocked the door and followed her up to his apartment.

"Okay," he breathed once they were inside the privacy of his apartment. "Is that what you're so afraid to tell me?"

"It's not a phase!"

Chris held up his hands in defense. He wasn't sure why she was on the attack. "Okay, sweetheart. I would never assume it was. You love who you love. I'm not mad at it."

Her lip quivered as she looked at him, eyes wide like a deer in the headlights. "I tried to tell Mom and she said it's just a phase and that I shouldn't make a big deal about it. It's not a phase, Dad."

Chris slowly made his way over and wrapped his arms around her. "Okay. Is that why you want to stay here? Because your mom doesn't understand?"

To his horror, she completely broke down. Sobs tore through her body as she held on to him for dear life. He was reminded of how broken she was when he arrived in Florida. He'd thought she had made progress after being away from there, but she was more broken now than he'd ever seen her.

"I told my best friend Macey," she choked out between sobs. "She told people that I had a crush on her, which isn't even true. Nobody will talk to me, and Mom doesn't even care. She said it's just a phase!"

Once again, his heart shattered. No wonder she didn't want to go back. School was hard enough as it was. She could stay with him and get a fresh start without judgement and without a parent who minimized her feelings. He was by no means perfect, but if something was important to Lily, it was important to him.

"Sweetheart, I'll do everything I can to keep you here with me. Love is love and your feelings are your feelings. It's that simple."

"Promise?" she asked, looking up at him.

"Yeah. I promise."

"I love you, Dad."

Chris hugged her tightly. "I love you too, sweetheart."

Chapter 25

CHRISTIAN

It had been two weeks. Two weeks since his world changed. Two weeks since he was able to face his reflection in the mirror. Two weeks since he was able to face Mallory. He kept his word to Lily and fired the shot which he assumed would begin World War Three with his ex-wife, and that had left him so mentally exhausted that he chose the coward's way out and avoided Mallory.

He didn't want to stay away from her, but he just couldn't face her. When she suggested they take a few steps back and keep things casual, there was no reason for him to treat her the way he did. He still couldn't shake off the expression on her face when he basically left her bent over the counter and leaking his cum without much more than a goodbye. He couldn't blame her if she never spoke to him again.

"Are you going to walk up with me?" Lily asked as he parked in front of Mallory's building.

She'd continued to keep an eye on Lily even though he'd been avoiding her. He was grateful, but at the same time it made him feel like even more of an asshole. Facing her was something that he desperately needed to do, but he wasn't sure he could.

"I don't know, Lily. I need to get to work …"

"Just come up, Dad, and tell her you're sorry. It's so weird over there now. She makes a big deal of pretending like she's happy when she opens the door and it's just me. And she avoids any topic that could somehow circle back to you. It's exhausting."

With a big sigh, Chris put the car in park, and removed the key from the ignition. He couldn't go back and undo everything he'd done, but he could be a man and own up to it. Lost in thought, trying to come up with something to say, he didn't even remember the walk to her apartment. Before he knew it, she swung the door open and stared at him in surprise.

"Ch—Christian," she stuttered. "Hi."

Lily slipped around her and into the apartment, leaving Chris and Mallory staring at each other in uncomfortable silence. She wore a crop top and high-waisted leggings and had her hair in a messy bun. God, that messy bun did something to him every time he saw it. Between the bun and the tiny sliver of her exposed stomach, Chris folded his arms across his chest to keep from reaching out to her.

"Hi," he breathed. "I'm sorry."

She looked him up and down before stepping into the hall and closing the door behind herself. "For?"

He let out a nervous chuckle. "You, uh, aren't going to make this easy, are you…"

Instead of speaking, she folded her arms and looked at him, her expression impassive.

"Okay," he began, hesitating as he struggled to find the words he wanted to say. "I'm sorry for the other night. You didn't deserve that."

She raised an eyebrow and continued to watch him expectantly.

"Okay fine. I'm also sorry about the way things went when I begged you to have a real conversation only to turn into an asshole when I didn't like what you had to say," he continued, carefully gauging her reaction as he spoke. "I'm sorry for everything that put us here. I miss you."

Her face softened at that statement. He didn't say it for the reaction; he really did miss her. Constantly throughout the day he wanted to call or text her about something before he remembered they were on less than speaking terms. He couldn't sleep. His temper was even shorter than usual. Everything was fucked up.

"I lied," she admitted after a long silence.

Not wanting to guess at what she was talking about, he waited in silence for her to continue. She took a cautious step forward and placed a hand on his chest, causing him to inhale sharply at the contact.

"I don't want to take a step back. I'm not sure why I said I did, but I shouldn't have. So, I'm sorry," she said so softly he had to strain to hear her.

"I know why you said it. We both know why. I knew why you were saying it that night, and instead of talking, I acted like a complete dick," he admitted. "I really am sorry. I'll spend as long as it takes making it up to you, if you'll let me."

She surprised him by gripping his shirt and pulling him in for a kiss. Once the surprise wore off, he leaned into her, flicking his tongue along the seam of her lips until she parted them. She tasted like everything he'd been craving since he walked out of there two weeks ago.

"Does this mean you forgive me?" he asked hesitantly. He tried not to sound overly eager, but he'd be devastated if her answer was no.

"Come have dinner with my family tomorrow," she invited, completely changing the subject. "Sheila invited us, but I've been avoiding her."

"It's pretty last minute to surprise her with our presence," he pointed out, understanding why but still mentioning it. "I wish you said something sooner."

"I told you I didn't want more. This is more. And I've been avoiding her because I know I was an idiot for saying that shit, and I didn't want to have to explain anything."

Chris took a breath, trying to gather his thoughts. She lied about not wanting more. He still wasn't completely sure if she lied because she was scared, hurt, or both.

"Lily, too?" he asked after a moment.

"Of course." Her look of uncertainty was replaced with one of hope.

"I don't know," he hesitated. "It's the last minute and bringing Lily to a family dinner is a really big step."

"Think about it," she suggested. "I know you have to get to work, and I need to get back inside. Sheila always cooks enough to feed an army, and I haven't told her no yet, so don't worry about it being last minute. You can let me know when you come pick her up."

With that, she kissed him on the cheek and went back inside, leaving him staring at her closed door. He wanted to say yes, but he just didn't know what was right. Lily had enough going on, so he didn't want to add more people into her life that might not be permanent. He would think about it.

"What's the deal with your family dinners?" Chris asked Michael as he pushed the stretcher carrying their equipment into the elevator.

Michael folded his arms across his chest. "Why? Are you guys coming? Last I heard, Sheila hadn't heard back from my sister."

Chris swallowed as he tried to think of a way to explain the situation to Michael without getting himself killed. One look into his icy blue eyes and he knew he had to go with honesty ... without being completely honest.

"Well, there was a lot going on, so we haven't talked much. I just found out about it before work. I told her I'd think about it."

Michael looked as though he didn't quite believe his explanation, but fortunately he let it go. "What's there to think about? Lily's been sleeping at Mallory's when you work, and you've known me and Alyssa forever. Sheila is the kindest person on the planet, and I'm a lot like my dad."

Before Chris could respond, the elevator doors opened, and they were facing the nurses' station. Instead of someone who looked completely uninterested directing them to a room, they were all huddled around a chair behind the desk. The group made their way over to see what was going on.

"She's having chest pains," one of the nurses said as she pointed at the woman sitting in the chair.

The woman wore scrubs and had her salt and pepper hair pulled into a bun. She was sitting in the chair leaning her upper body against the desk. Her face was gray, and she was covered in a sheen of sweat. They had been expecting a resident, not a staff member.

Chris began asking questions while Michael began hooking the woman up to the monitor and taking a set of vitals. Their partners were both gathering whatever information they could from one of the nurses who stood with her.

"Hi, ma'am. What seems to be going on tonight?" Chris asked in a soothing voice.

"I just don't feel right," she said as she repositioned herself in her chair. "I wasn't feeling well when I woke up to get ready for work, but you know how it is working nights."

"Do you have any pain? Or shortness of breath?" Chris asked.

"Not really. I don't know." She repositioned herself again.

Chris's thoughts wandered back to the dinner. Michael was right, of course. There was nothing to worry about. He was certain he wanted more with Mallory, and if she was extending the invitation, she must have felt the same way.

"Mrs. Jones? Let's get you onto this stretcher, okay? We'll hold on to you while we move the chair out and put the stretcher in its place," Michael said.

Chris looked at him with an eyebrow raised wondering why they didn't just have her take two steps over to the stretcher. Michael's face was serious as he told his partner to keep the med box handy. A glance at the monitor was all the explanation he needed. Even Chris knew it didn't look right.

"Okay. My partner is going to start an IV on you. Is it okay if I lift your shirt so I can put some leads on your chest so we can send it over to the hospital before we get going?"

Chris opened his bag and took out the portable oxygen and a mask. She looked like shit, and so did her vital signs. Michael rarely got excited, but the crease in his brow and his tense jaw was enough for Chris to know he was concerned.

"Okay, be very still for me, okay?" Michael said before stepping back.

Chris watched as Michael printed a strip and looked at it. His eyes widened slightly before he handed it over to his partner. He nodded his head toward the elevator, signaling he was ready to pack up and go.

"We need to get going, but I want you to chew and swallow this aspirin, and once we get into the elevator, I'm going to put something cold on your chest, okay?"

She nodded her head in agreement, and once they were in the elevator, Michael passed the strip over for Chris to see. "Acute MI Suspected" was clearly printed across the bottom. Now he knew why the tension. It was rare for the monitor to come out and diagnose a heart attack. Typically, it would say "Abnormal" or something similar. Chris's thoughts no longer veered to the decision about dinner the next day.

Chris wasn't sure if it was his imagination, but the woman somehow looked worse by the time they reached the ambulance and loaded her inside. She wasn't as restless as she was when they found her, but her face was ridden with anxiety and she was still diaphoretic.

"You guys both staying in the back?" Chris asked, referring to Michael and his partner.

Instead of answering, Michael tossed his keys to Chris's partner as he opened up the med box and took out a few items. Taking the hint, Chris closed the doors and went around to the driver's seat. He turned the radio on to keep from paying too much attention to what was going on behind him as he drove to the hospital.

"Chris, pull over!" Michael's shout jarred his thoughts away from the radio.

He found a spot to pull over. After putting the truck in park, he went around to the back to see if they needed an additional set of hands. When he opened the door, he found Michael's partner slapping defibrillator pads onto the woman's chest. He wasn't surprised, but he was hoping they would have made it to the hospital before she crashed.

"I'll bag her while you set up to intubate," Chris offered, climbing into the back.

He grabbed the bag valve mask they kept ready to go, plugged it into the main oxygen, and began squeezing air into her lungs before pausing for Michael's partner to count out compressions. Once he reached thirty, he squeezed in two more breaths before they all backed away from the patient and waited for Chris to check the monitor.

"I'm going to shock her," he announced. "All clear?"

After ensuring no one was touching her, Michael pressed a button on the monitor, and they watched while the patient jerked lightly from the electricity. Chris bagged the patient once Michael gave the order to stop compressions but continue to ventilate.

"She's back to normal sinus rhythm, with a pulse," Michael said in surprise. "Let's get going."

It didn't take long to drive the rest of the way to the hospital. After parking in the ambulance bay, he went around to the back to open the doors. He couldn't believe it when the patient made eye-contact. The patient who was now on regular high flow oxygen. The patient who was now breathing on her own and conscious. The same patient who had basically died in the back of the ambulance mere minutes earlier.

"Welcome back, Mrs. Jones," Chris greeted as he pulled the stretcher out.

"She was breathing on her own and fighting the bag, so I didn't even attempt to tube her," Michael said as he climbed out after them.

Impressive. Everyone knew the best chance for CPR to be successful was when it was a witnessed cardiac arrest, but it still wasn't every day they went from performing CPR to having a conscious patient by the time they arrived at the hospital. That was an understatement. He could count on one hand how many times he'd seen it happen.

He was cleaning up the back of his truck while his partner was inside working on the chart when Michael stepped in. "So, I'll see you at dinner tomorrow?"

He had been thinking about it before the patient coded on the way to the hospital and he was still hesitant to meet Mallory's parents and to bring Lily to meet her parents. Even though he told her he wanted more, that felt like a huge step. But as cliché as it sounded, the patient made him realize life was short. If he dropped dead, he didn't want his last moments to be spent being afraid of what could go wrong. As often as a patient didn't make it, it took the one who did make it to wake him up.

"Yeah," he answered. "We'll be there."

MALLORY

"I'm so glad you could come!" Mallory squealed before pulling Lily into a tight hug.

With the way the last couple weeks had gone, she was expecting Christian to say no. Sure, they had a conversation and did their best to clear the air, but meeting her family was a big deal. It's a step she would never have considered when she first met Christian.

"Me too! Does this mean you and Dad aren't fighting anymore?"

Mallory nearly choked in surprise. She'd done her very best to keep Lily out of it and not let on that she was on bad terms with Christian. Hopefully he hadn't been saying anything negative about her to Lily.

"It was just obvious that all of the sudden Dad never wanted to come up when he was dropping me off or picking me up," she said as if she could read her mind. "He never said anything."

"Sweetheart," Christian said, finally moving from his spot in front of the door. "Mallory and I are fine. We had a disagreement, and we should have talked about it sooner, but everything is fine now. I'm sorry if we made things weird for you."

Lily shrugged. "It's not a big deal, I was just saying."

Before Mallory could say anything, he pulled her into a hug before placing a soft kiss on her cheek. A soothing warmth traveled down her body as that small act calmed her and made her feel more relaxed about the entire evening. She'd missed his touch, his scent.

"You look beautiful," he whispered in her ear before he stepped back.

He didn't look too bad himself, but she didn't want to embarrass him by saying just how good he looked in front of Lily. He wore dark-wash jeans and a gray button-down shirt. He wasn't over the top dressy for a family dinner, but he looked respectful. Even Lily was dressed in some of her nicer black clothing.

"You two look nice," she commented. "If you want, I can drive since I know where I'm going."

"No need. I got the address from your brother and I'm pretty sure I know where it's at. Unless you want to drive, that is."

God, things were awkward. It was obvious she wasn't the only one having trouble figuring out what to say. It probably wasn't smart to invite him when they had only barely made up.

"Can we go?" Lily asked. "I'm hungry."

She was exactly what they needed to snap out of their awkwardness and get going. Mallory grabbed what she needed and followed Christian out to his car. The drive wasn't long, but he held her hand the entire way. In front of Lily.

When they pulled up in front of her childhood home, she took one last calming breath before climbing out of the car and preparing to introduce the two most important people in her life to the family she only recently reconnected with. It was fine. Everything would be fine. What the hell was she thinking ...

"Mallory!" Sheila exclaimed as soon as she swung the front door open. "I'm so glad you guys could make it!"

She bristled slightly. "Can you let us get inside first?"

Sheila's face fell, and Mallory immediately felt a pang of regret. The anxiety of bringing Christian and Lily to meet her family was obviously wearing on her, but she had no excuse for taking it out on Sheila. The woman had been nothing but nice to her, even after Mallory had treated her so badly over the years.

"I'm sorry," she breathed. "We're all excited. I've just never ..."

"Nope. No need to apologize, I understand. I can be a bit much." Sheila chuckled and waved a hand in dismissal. "Let's get inside so you can introduce me to this beautiful girl and the handsome man who's with her."

Mallory tried once more for a cleansing breath as they stepped into the house. She had no idea why she thought this was a good idea. The smart thing would have been to wait until she was completely comfortable around her family before she brought anyone else around, let alone the man she had allowed into her heart.

"Mallory! It's so good to see you!"

She turned to see Alyssa making her way over as fast as she could considering the baby bump that seemed to have doubled in size since she'd seen her last. A genuine smile spread across her glowing face as she pulled her into a hug.

"Chris! Hey buddy," Alyssa said as she moved to give him a hug. "And Lily! You know I can't help myself from giving you a hug. I feel like you double your height each time I see you."

Mallory looked over to see Michael standing back, waiting his turn. Once Alyssa moved on to her dad and Sheila, Michael made his way over. He pulled Mallory into a hug, and it was just the comfort she needed. Having people around who already knew Christian made her feel much more at ease.

"Now," Sheila spoke up once she'd gotten her hugs from both Michael and Alyssa. "You two must be Lily and Christian. I'm so happy you could make it. Come on in and make yourselves at home."

Mallory didn't miss the shine of unshed tears sparking in Sheila's eyes. She'd been so worried about herself that she didn't stop to think about how her dad and Sheila must feel. They didn't know anything about her dating history or the abusive relationship that almost completely destroyed her. They didn't know how amazing it was that Christian was able to knock down her walls and make his way into her heart, but just the act of her bringing someone "home" to meet them must have meant the world to them. She wasn't even sure Christian quite understood the magnitude of what they were doing.

She watched as Sheila brought Lily into the kitchen while everyone else made their way to the sunroom out back. It was a nice night, and the sunroom had a large farmhouse style table that could seat everyone. Christian, surrounded mostly be people he already knew, appeared completely at ease. It made sense. Alyssa was one of his closest friends so that made Michael basically his brother-in-law.

Lily helped Sheila carry out items from the kitchen, and had the brightest smile on her face as she did. She followed behind Sheila, first carrying a basket of dinner rolls and then condiments. Once they brought everything out, Lily took the seat next to her dad, but got pulled into a conversation by Mallory's dad. The feeling of warmth she felt at the sight was completely unnecessary, and Christian's hand casually resting on her thigh wasn't helping.

"Please tell me this isn't a one-time thing," Sheila said as she stood to clear the empty plates. "Lily, honey, would you like to help me bring out dessert?"

Before Sheila finished speaking, the girl was out of her chair. Once again, Mallory couldn't keep herself from smiling at the scene in front of her.

"She likes it here," Christian said just loud enough for Mallory to hear. "Thank you."

Mallory turned in her seat to look at him. "I'm just glad this is going so well. I was freaking out on the inside."

Christian chuckled. "It wasn't just on the inside. I could tell you were panicking. I'm just glad you felt better once Michael and Alyssa showed up. Thank you for inviting us. I know this isn't easy for you. Do you mind if I come inside to talk once we get back?"

She swallowed. Needing to talk was rarely a good thing. At no time did anything good come from the phrase "we need to talk" and it took everything for Mallory to keep from spiraling into a sea of panic.

"It's nothing bad, don't worry. I just don't think we got to say all we needed to last night. Tonight, we don't have to rush," Christian explained. He was getting almost too good at reading her.

She nodded, gave his hand a squeeze, then moved her attention back to the rest of the table. Lily was back at the table and Alyssa was now holding her attention. She couldn't quite make out what was being said, but Lily was laughing and nodding her head in agreement.

"She seems to be having fun," Alyssa whispered to Christian as she nodded in Lily's direction once Lily had turned her attention elsewhere.

"Yeah. She does. She needs to know she has people. And this group surrounding the table is exactly the people she needs."

It was hard for Mallory to keep from getting overwhelmed by regret. These were the best people to be surrounded by, and she had taken them for granted. So many years wasted feeling miserable and alone, when the people at this table were right here the entire time, just waiting for her to return.

It wasn't long before they were back in the entryway saying their good-byes. Lily's face was lit up with a smile as she hugged everyone and told them what a good time she'd had. Mallory couldn't help but wear a matching smile on her own face.

"Let Christian know I would love to watch her if you're ever busy, need a break, or the two of you want a date night," Sheila said quietly as she hugged Mallory goodbye. "Thank you so much for coming over and bringing them along. My heart is so full. We've never had this opportunity with you."

All Mallory could do was nod in response. Sheila's voice cracked before she could finish speaking, and Mallory had to swallow down the lump in her throat. So many years had been lost. Years of therapy told Mallory that guilt and regret weren't useful emotions to dwell on, but damn if it didn't hurt.

"Thank you," she breathed.

"You ready?" Christian asked as he placed his hand at the small of her back.

His touch was warm and gentle, and she leaned into it before nodding in response. They walked to the car in silence. Mallory found herself once again fighting back tears, even though she wasn't sure why. She was feeling overwhelmed with emotion and wasn't sure how to handle her feelings. Christian reached over and squeezed her thigh. His firm touch helped her rein in her emotions. She would deal with her feelings once she was home. That's what she told herself anyway.

Chapter 26

CHRISTIAN

Chris sat on the couch next to Mallory. Lily had begged and pleaded to stay the night until he gave in. His plan had been to talk to Mallory as soon as they got back, but that didn't happen. Instead, Mallory made coffee and they watched a movie with Lily after which she declared she was tired and begged to just sleep over. Chris was no idiot. He knew she was trying to get him to stay over as well.

"So, can we talk?" he asked.

He had just sat down from checking on Lily, who was sound asleep and snoring loudly with one leg hanging off the bed. Her bed. The spare bedroom had basically been turned into hers without him realizing it. The comforter on the bed could only have been something she picked out. It was black with neon pink skulls all over it. There was even a shaggy black rug on the floor. The purple lava lamp was also her doing.

"Yeah, we probably should," Mallory agreed.

Christian could only lay everything out. Holding back hadn't worked out well for either of them. He'd told his daughter they just had a disagreement and were fine now, but that wasn't anywhere near the truth. They were on speaking terms, but things were not okay. They were far from okay.

"What can I do to fix this?" he asked.

Mallory let out a sigh. "I wish I knew. I know we said the things and went to dinner, but everything still feels off and I hate it."

He couldn't agree more. "When I left you—the way that I did—" He paused to gather his thoughts. "Is there any coming back from that? There are no excuses. I was angry and hurt when you said we were just two people who have sex, but I took it out on you in the worst possible way. I am so sorry."

She surprised him by taking his hand and placing it in her lap, tracing designs on his palm with her finger as she thought. The sensation almost tickled, but it was oddly soothing. He relaxed enough to sit back as he waited for her response.

"Why?" she breathed.

"Why what?" he prompted when she didn't continue.

"Why did you do it? I know you were angry and hurt, but why didn't you just yell? Or storm off again?"

The question he'd been dreading. Analyzing himself was never something he wanted to do. He never seemed to like what he found anytime he did. She was absolutely right, though. There were so many ways he could have reacted. He could have thrown something, shouted, slammed the door as he walked away ... but he went for the most personal form of attack.

"I don't know."

"Bullshit." She stopped tracing her finger over his palm so she could grab his chin and force him to look at her. "Tell me why."

"It doesn't matter," he hedged. He did know why, but he did not want to tell her his entire truth.

"Tell me." Her voice was dangerously quiet.

He knew for a fact that if he didn't cough up the truth, their conversation was over, and so was his welcome.

"Because. After I got divorced, I was done with feelings, and love, and all of that bullshit. Sex was different. I'm good at that. I made it a point to have relationships that were just about sex. Then you came along." His voice grew hoarse, and he had to clear his throat to continue. "Then you came along with your positivity and your aspirations. You made me think that maybe I could have more again. You made me crave more. To hear you say all we had was sex gutted me. It fucking gutted me. Instead of telling you that, I tried to make you feel just as hurt as I felt."

She stared at him in silence. He wouldn't have blamed her if she threw him out. She should have thrown him out. Hell, she shouldn't have let him in in the first place after how he'd behaved. But he hoped more than anything that she would give him a chance to make it up to her. If that was even possible.

"Tell me how I can fix this," he pleaded.

She stared at him in silence for a long moment before she finally spoke. "I'm so stupid," she breathed.

Chris closed his eyes and waited. He knew what was coming next—what she meant by that statement. It was over. She was done with him. She meant she was stupid for trusting him not to hurt her. For being involved with him at all. He was preparing himself to get up and leave when her voice interrupted him.

"Only someone truly stupid would have already forgiven you."

"What?" he asked, completely thrown off by what he heard.

"If I hadn't already forgiven you, I wouldn't have invited you to my dad's tonight. But I had to hear from you why you thought I deserved to be treated that way."

"You didn't deserve it!" he whisper-shouted, careful not to wake Lily.

"I know. Before you, I refused to get into anything serious. Sure, I enjoyed more than just sex, but nothing that went as far as planning futures together or any of that. My last serious relationship nearly ended me, so I never wanted to put myself in that position again. Until you. You and your stupid smile and your stupid green eyes."

Chris laughed. "Should I smile less, then?"

"Don't be a smartass," she said with a short laugh. "My point is, that's how I felt when you stormed out of here. I tried keeping at least some semblance of distance when it came to Lily. And I was so happy when you begged me to be a part of everything. Until you walked out. When you came back to talk, part of me didn't believe you really wanted those things, and part of me wanted to hurt you. That's why I said I didn't want more. So, you don't have anything to make up to me. We just have things to work through together."

"So, what's that mean?" he asked cautiously.

She grabbed his hand and returned it to her lap, resuming the finger designs. "We don't need to take a step back."

He breathed a sigh of relief.

"But," she interrupted before he could say anything. "I'm not sure we can just go back to the way things were, either."

He gripped her hand, stopping her from circling his palm and brought her hand to his mouth, placing a soft kiss on her fingertips. "We'll start from here, then."

The smile that spread across her lips was the first truly genuine and unguarded smile he'd seen in weeks. It reached her eyes, causing tiny crinkles. Without hesitation, he leaned forward and pressed his mouth against hers in a quick kiss.

"Stay the night?" she asked.

"Okay, but I'm not sleeping on the couch."

Her eyes widened in surprise. "But Lily—"

"Lily isn't stupid and she's not a baby. I'm not saying we should have wild sex, but we can sleep in the same bed. We'll leave the door open."

The smile returned to her face as she nodded in agreement. "Okay. Let's go to bed."

Chapter 27

CHRISTIAN

Chris tried to read the name of the sender on the certified mail slip. It had been nearly a month since he told Vivian he wanted to enroll Lily in school instead of bringing her back at the end of the summer. It had also been a few weeks since he started the process of having his mother's house signed over to him. After speaking to an attorney, he learned the best way would be for him to purchase it instead of her just signing it over.

Instead of going into his apartment, he turned around and got back into his car to go to the post office. There was no way he could get any sleep while wondering what was waiting for him at the post office, and it was a Saturday so they wouldn't be open much longer. He was glad he ended up leaving Lily at Mallory's after breakfast so he could read over whatever it was without an audience.

The line at the post office wasn't long, but it felt like he was in it forever. When he finally reached the counter, he passed over the notice with a shaking hand. She didn't seem to notice, smiling warmly before stepping away from the counter to retrieve his item. She returned with a large envelope and passed it over after collecting his signature. Without looking at it, he made a quick retreat to the privacy of his car.

Finally looking at the envelope, it was obvious that whatever he held inside pertained to Lily. He took a shaky breath as he tore it open and emptied the contents into the empty passenger seat. He wasn't one to show his emotions, but his eyes burned with tears as he read everything over for a second and then a third time. He was looking at everything he would need to enroll Lily into school, and a motion to move residential custody to him. Finally. After so many years being forced to be away from her for a majority of the time, it was over.

They say it isn't a good idea to count chickens before they are hatched, but dammit if things didn't appear to be falling into place. The idea of having Lily full time is the one thing that motivated him to get the process going on his mother's house. He still didn't like the idea of her giving up on returning to her home, but the woman was nothing if not stubborn. Once her mind was made up there was no changing it, and nothing was worse for a house than letting it sit empty.

His little girl had come to him a broken shell of herself. She'd been made small and fragile by the heavy weight on her shoulders. He'd watched as the spark of life returned to her eyes and she changed into, not his little girl, but a young woman who was embracing her new life. Even a blind man could see that her change had everything to do with Mallory, her family, and Dan.

Mallory may have thought she was keeping her distance and staying out of it, but she had changed Lily's entire world by just being herself. Lily's life wasn't the only one that had been changed. He couldn't wait to tell them the good news. But telling them didn't quite seem like enough.

MALLORY

Mallory pulled the cupcakes out of pan and placed them on the cooling rack so they could cool the rest of the way off while she helped Lily make the icing. Christian had text her requesting cupcakes instead of dinner, and Lily was more than excited for the opportunity to play around in the kitchen. She was planning on making a simple spaghetti dinner, but Chistian said he would bring dinner and that it was a surprise. She loved surprises more when she didn't know they were coming, and the anticipation wasn't slowly killing her. Making cupcakes was a nice distraction.

"Like this?" Lily asked as she moved the hand mixer around to blend the butter, sugar, and vanilla until smooth.

"Perfect," she encouraged. "You sure you haven't done this before?"

"Mom doesn't bake," she answered simply.

Once the icing was blended into a cream, Mallory helped her top each cupcake before placing them onto the cupcake stand. "These look almost too pretty to eat."

Lily looked at her in horror. "They aren't that pretty! I am definitely eating them. Dad needs to hurry up."

Mallory laughed as she cleaned up their mess, placing the dirty dishes into the dishwasher. If she left the bowl out much longer, she was certain Lily was going to pick it up and start licking the icing out of it. She was wiping down the counter as Christian walked through the door, holding a large white pizza box and a gift bag.

"Luigi's!" Lily shouted, completely ignoring the gift bag in his hand.

A smile tugged at Mallory's lips as she walked over to take the box from Christian so she could place it on the counter. She tried to be smooth and grab the gift bag as well, but he saw through her and pulled it out of her reach as soon as his hand was free.

"Not yet."

Chuckling, she raised to her toes and placed a chaste kiss on his lips. "I didn't know we had two surprises to look forward to. You know I hate waiting."

"Well, the pizza is just a bonus surprise," he answered smugly. "Let's eat. You'll get the other surprise with dessert."

Once again, she had to fight her body's reaction when he used that tone of voice on her. They were having a family dinner. It wasn't the time for her to melt into a puddle just because he used his stern voice on her. Things had been great between them ever since they'd talked things out and promised to move forward, but they hadn't had much alone time with Lily no further than one room away. It might be time to suggest taking Sheila up on her offer.

"Mallory?" Christian's voice snapped her out of her thoughts.

Feeling her cheeks flush, she looked up at him to find him smirking at her. "Sorry, what?"

"Well, I was going to ask if you wanted to eat here at the island or in the living room, but Lily has already plopped on floor by the couch and started a movie," Christian said with laughter in his voice. "Where did you go?"

"The living room is fine," she answered, ignoring his last question.

They joined Lily in the living room and ate in companionable silence. Lily was invested in whatever movie she'd turned on, but Mallory wasn't paying any attention. The pizza was amazing, but she just wanted to hurry up and get to dessert so she could find out what was in the bag. She was worse than a child.

She brought their empty plates to the kitchen, but refused to ask if anyone was ready for dessert. As silly as it was, she was doing her best to play it cool and pretend like she wasn't practically vibrating with excitement. When she turned around from loading the plates into the dishwasher, she found Christian leaning against the island watching her.

"These cupcakes look delicious," he said with an easy smile.

"Lily made the frosting. She's over there pretending like she hasn't been dying to eat one."

"We should end her suffering, don't you think?" Christian suggested.

"Yes!" Mallory said with an exaggerated nod. "We really need to. It's the humane thing to do."

Christian laughed and called Lily over. Before he'd finished pronouncing her name, she was up and running over to join them. She looked longingly at the cupcake stand while Mallory passed small dessert plates around. Without her realizing it, Christian had placed two small boxes onto the table. Once they took a seat around the island, he pushed the purple box toward Lily and the yellow box toward Mallory.

"Open it," Christian encouraged after Mallory took a moment to stare at the suspicious box. She'd been dying to know what was inside the gift bags, but she was having a hard time working up the courage to open it as she looked at the box in front of her. A shiver of nerves washed over her.

She spared a glance at Lily who was watching her instead of opening her own box. "Should we open them together?"

"Good idea. Okay three," Lily began the count down. "Two. One."

Mallory opened her box and looked down at a silver key with a keychain that read "Sweet home."

Lily held up a key that was attached to a keychain with "home" written in pink script across the same black background as Mallory's. Both girls looked at Christian for an explanation. He stood with his hands in his pockets, but the way he rocked back and forth on his heels told her he was anything but relaxed.

"I got some important papers in the mail today," he began to explain. "A while ago I contacted Vivian about letting Lily stay here for good. She never responded, so I figured it would be a fight and that I'd be taking her back to Florida in a few weeks."

Mallory swallowed, listening as she tried to figure out what any of this had to do with the keys.

"Well, Lily," Christian continued, turning his attention to his daughter. "I received everything I need to enroll you in school. The paperwork has already been started to have you live here, with me."

"Really?" Lily was out of her chair and in Christian's arms in no time, relief and happiness written all over her face.

"Yes, sweetheart. You can stay."

"Thank you, Dad! Can I go call Alyssa? I was telling her today that I want to babysit once she has the baby if I'm still here."

Christian chuckled at Lily while Mallory blinked back tears. She was so happy for the girl. The way her entire body slumped with relief at the words "you can stay" had her heart in an uncomfortable mixture of breaking and soaring. She watched as Lily ran to her bedroom, the key and keychain forgotten on the table.

"And the keys?" Mallory prompted once she regained her composure.

"My mom is insisting on staying in that assisted living, no matter how much I try to convince her otherwise. She asked me a while back if I would take her house. Obviously, I didn't want to. It's her house. She somehow had some sixth sense that Lily needed to stay with me. She even told me the house would be a better place to raise Lily instead of my apartment. Well, I'm in the process of buying it for nearly nothing, just to make it official. The only reason I agreed to buy it was with the hope of Lily staying."

Mallory wasn't following. Maybe she was tired, or maybe it was nerves. She stood stock-still and waited for him to explain the damn key.

"You've met my mother," he continued. "She's stubborn as hell. I need to just accept that the house is mine now, even though I'm still waiting to hear about the closing. Anyway, I'm rambling."

He stood behind where she was sitting and wrapped his arms around her. She leaned into his warm embrace and allowed him to settle her nerves as he settled his own. No matter how she was feeling, his arms were home.

"Lily came here completely broken. You saw her. But with you, and Dan, and your family, she's started to become whole again. She's trusted us enough to open up and share her needs and her feelings," he spoke quietly. "The point is, I couldn't have done any of this without you. *We* couldn't have done any of this without you. And I don't want to do anything else without you. This is the key to my house. Well, it'll be mine soon enough, and once it is I'd like to make it ours. When you're ready."

Holy shit. She hadn't expected any of this when he walked into her apartment carrying a pizza box and a gift bag that he barely managed to keep from dropping. She'd somehow sensed that whatever was in the gift bag was serious, but not this serious.

"Are you asking me to move in with you?" she asked once she found her voice.

"No," he said quickly. "I mean, yes. I want you to move *on* with me. If and when you're ready."

She continued to stare at him, not quite able to form words. Moving in with someone was the last thing she ever thought she would do. It had taken so long to pull herself out of the abyss the last time things fell apart leaving her to clean up the devastation, she swore she'd never put herself in that position again. But this was everything she wanted. The man. The house. The kid. All of it.

"You want me to move in with you," she repeated, still in disbelief.

"Yes."

He tightened his grip around her, and the firm squeeze of his body surrounding hers gave her the reassurance she needed. There was no hesitation, no pulling back. He was coming to her with honesty and strength. Closing her eyes, all she could see was the sheer joy on Lily's face when she learned she could stay in the safe bubble they had created around her. It was a bubble Mallory never wanted to be away from.

"Yes," she breathed. "Once the house is ready and we're ready, I want to do this with you. I can't imagine Lily being here and me not being part of her life. If you want me ..."

"I want you. I need you. *We* need you."

She stood from her seat and turned to face him fully. Before she could say anything, he gripped the back of her neck and pulled her close, sealing his lips to hers. The raw emotion in his kiss brought tears to her eyes and she wrapped her arms around him, trying to pull him even closer still. He broke the kiss and began placing kisses across her cheek and down her neck until he finally buried his face in her hair and hugged her tight. Slipping her hands under the back of his shirt so she could feel the warmth of his skin, she relaxed into him, thinking of nowhere she would rather be but home. And he was her home.

Epilogue

MALLORY

Mallory dropped her paint brush into the tray and climbed down the ladder. Finally. The bathroom was complete. They had finished the second coat of paint when she noticed a spot they'd missed. Christian said to leave it because no one on Earth would ever notice, but once she saw it, she couldn't unsee it. They had both taken a long weekend to get the house finished and moved into. Lily was spending the weekend with her dad and Sheila, and the truck was due to be unloaded the next morning.

"Fell better now?" Christian teased.

"No. I would feel better if you were the one up on the ladder for the hundredth time today."

His laugh vibrated through her as he pulled her into his arms. They were both a mess; all sweaty and covered in paint. If he wasn't just as disgusting as she was, she would have been self-conscious.

"The view is better when I hold the ladder for you."

"You're so dirty," Mallory said as she brushed past him toward the bathroom.

They hadn't moved any major items in yet, but the bathroom had towels and some toiletries from them staying over to work on the house. Other than that, there was an air mattress, blankets, and a laundry basket filled with clean clothes in the master bedroom.

"You've never complained before," he said, gripping her around the waist and turning her to face him.

She gasped when he pulled her against him, his arousal pressing into her. When she flicked her eyes to his, she knew he had plans for them. She grinded against him and felt a rush of heat when he let out a soft groan.

"We're all sweaty," she gently protested.

"And?" He slipped his hands up the bottom of her shirt and drew tiny circles along her bare flesh with his thumbs; the small act causing her to shiver in anticipation.

"Shower," she gritted out. "Let's take a shower."

"Mmm," he hummed. "I can take you in the shower if that's what you want."

Before she had a chance to respond, he gripped her arm and nearly dragged her into the bathroom. After turning the shower on, he kicked his shoes off as she did the same. When her shaking hands fumbled with the buttons of her flannel shirt, he moved her hands out of the way then gripped her shirt, pulling until the buttons broke free, scattering across the bathroom floor.

"No bra?" he asked in surprise.

Her nipples hardened and she couldn't be sure if it was from the chill in the air, or his hungry gaze. Closing what small distance stood between them, he slipped his fingers under the waistband of her leggings and tugged down, kneeling as he went. She stared down into his gaze as she lifted each foot to allow him to slip them the rest of the way off before tossing them over his shoulder.

"You're so beautiful," he murmured, running his hands up and down her bare legs, causing her to shiver once more. "I could look at you all day."

"Christian, stop. I'm a sweaty mess," she countered.

The look he gave her stopped her from saying anything further. "Don't argue with me. You're perfect. I like it when you're a filthy sweaty mess for me."

His words went straight to her core, and she knew he wasn't talking about working on the house. He ran his hand up her thigh and didn't stop until he reached her slit, running his finger back and forth causing her to cry out in pleasure.

"So wet, already," he said in appreciation before leaning forward and pressing his nose against her center, breathing in.

"Christian!" she gasped as she tried to pull back from embarrassment. She didn't want him that close after she'd been working and sweating all day.

"Don't. Fucking. Move." He used both hands to grip her thighs so she couldn't move away.

Fuck. There he went using that tone of voice on her. When he spoke to her like that, she would do anything he asked her to do. After a moment he pushed her thighs apart and licked down her center, flicking her clit with his tongue. Her core clenched, and she tilted her hips forward silently begging for more. The action felt so wrong, but she needed more. He licked along her slit once more and circled her clit, causing her to writhe against him.

Her breathing was already coming out in gasps and her legs shook as she struggled to stay upright while he continued licking and sucking her pussy. She gripped the back of his head and held him firmly against her, eliciting a moan from him that she felt in her core.

"Christian. Please," she cried.

He pulled back to look up at her, replacing his tongue with his fingers. "Please, what?"

She placed a firm grip on his shoulders to keep herself upright as he slipped a finger inside her. She was so wet, the sounds of her arousal echoed through the bathroom as he plunged his finger in and out, adding a second one before she could articulate her response.

"Oh, God, please!" she cried out again.

"Please, what?" he growled.

"Fuck me!"

His gaze darkened as he let her go and got to his feet. Before she could form a coherent thought, he had stripped off his clothes and was pushing her into the walk-in-shower, pausing just long enough to check the temperature. The warm water washed over her already heated body as he guided her palms to press against the shower tiles before gripping her ~~hips~~hips, so she was bent over with her ass up. One of his favorite positions.

He stroked her, teasing her clit before sliding back and plunging two fingers into her. She cried out and thrust back into his touch. He smacked her ass before removing his fingers.

"Don't move," he growled. "You're so fucking wet for me. You want to feel me? You want me to fuck you?"

"Please," she begged, doing her best not to move in search of more contact.

Once again, he gripped her hips tightly, lining himself up at her entrance. She needed to feel him. She wanted to move. Instead of burying himself inside her like she needed, he circled her entrance with his cock, teasing her. She cried out as tears of frustration pricked her eyes.

"Please," she begged once more. "I need you inside me."

He gripped her hips even tighter before finally thrusting inside her, both of them groaning in pleasure as he filled her. That single movement had her on the edge. He stilled for a moment, gripping her hips so tight she was sure she'd have bruises. She tried to thrust back into him, but he squeezed even tighter, keeping her from moving.

"Don't. I need a second," he breathed. "Just give me a minute."

"I'm so close. Please. Please let me come." She tried again to move.

He slid his hands up and around her, caressing her breasts as he pulled out and thrust back inside her achingly slowly. She tilted her breasts into his hands, and he circled and then tugged on her nipples as he continued his slow torture. She was wound so tight, one hard thrust would send her over the edge.

As if hearing her thoughts, he returned one hand to her hip, moving the other one to her center and pressed on her clit as he slammed into her. "That's it," he said as he repeated the motion. "Is this what you needed?"

"Fuck! Yes!" she shouted as she felt the thread snap and her whole body grew tense.

"Come for me," he growled as he thrust into her harder.

Her breathing hitched and currents of pleasure jolted through her body as her orgasm washed over her. Wave after wave of pleasure coursed through her as he continued to fuck her through it.

"That's my good fucking girl," he gritted out as he continued to pound into her.

As she clenched around him, she felt him pulse inside her while he continued his thrusts, following her to his own release.

"My god," he whispered in awe as he held her up with one hand, switching places so he was leaning against the tiles.

"That was ..." she trailed off as she tried to find the words to describe what that was.

"Yeah," he agreed.

He chuckled against her. "Let's get you cleaned up before we run out of hot water."

He picked up the body wash, squirted some into his hand, and began washing her. She moaned in pleasure at his gentle caress. When he'd washed every part of her body, he turned her and tipped her head under the water, but something caught her attention before he began washing her hair.

"Is that my phone ringing?" she asked.

"Ignore it," he mumbled as he began massaging the shampoo into her hair.

She groaned in pleasure as he massaged her scalp. "But it could be important," she countered weakly.

"It can wait until I'm finished with you."

There was that tone of voice again. The tone that left no room for argument and also traveled straight to her core even though she was still coming down from one of the best orgasms she'd ever had.

The phone started ringing again. Groaning, he finished rinsing her hair before moving aside so she could step out of the shower. She wrapped herself in a towel and hurried out of the bathroom, leaving wet footprints behind her. Her brother's name lit up across the screen as the phone started ringing for a third time.

"Hello?" she answered, concern outweighing her annoyance.

"Hey, sis," Michael responded. "Or I guess I should say, Aunt Mallory."

"What?!" she shouted, running back into the bathroom where Christian was finishing his shower. "Say that again. You're on speaker."

"Aunt Mallory, and I'm assuming, Uncle Chris. Samantha Rae Hunt was born at 21:37. Six pounds, twelve ounces. We would have called you to be here, but we barely made it to the hospital before she was born."

"Repeat the name?" Mallory asked, certain she hadn't heard him correctly.

"Samantha Rae. And everyone is doing great."

If that wasn't the statement that summed everything up. She had her guy. She had her family. She had her house. She had all the things she'd convinced herself she'd never have. And now she was an auntie to a little one who had been named after both her mother and her. Tears stung her eyes and began to run down her face just as Christian, still wet from the shower, wrapped his arms around her and wiped them away. Everyone *was* doing great.

Acknowledgements

Stars of Life wasn't supposed to be a series. It was a book I started writing years ago and finally, with lots of encouragement from my husband, I decided to put it out into the world. And then readers requested another book. Apparently it doesn't take much to influence me, because here we are.

But that makes it all sound easy. If it wasn't for some of the amazing people I've met in the writing community, there's no way I would be here. Stars of Life would have been a one and done. I'm so grateful for the people I've met along the way. We encourage each other when we want to quit (which can be a daily occurrence), work together in silence during writing sprints, and refuse to close our computers in solidarity when one of us is working to meet a goal.

Speaking of refusing to shut down our computers until the goals are complete ... shout out to my husband for putting up with my late nights spent on my computer with my writing crew as we work, complain, and sometimes cackle about things until all hours of the night.

Last, but not least, shout out to my readers and my amazing Street Team. Without readers this would all be for nothing. And without my Street Team getting excited and spreading the word about my books, I'd for sure give up.

THANK YOU